A DWARF KINGDOM

A DWARF KINGDOM

NICOLAS FREELING

THE MYSTERIOUS PRESS

Published by Warner Books

A Time Warner Company

First published in Great Britain in 1996 by Little, Brown and Company.

 Mysterious Press books are published by Warner Books, Inc., 1271 Avenue of the Americas, New York, NY 10020.

 A Time Warner Company

The Mysterious Press name and logo are registered trademarks of Warner Books, Inc.

Printed in the United States of America
First U.S. printing: July 1996

10 9 8 7 6 5 4 3 2 1

Library of Congress Cataloging-in-Publication Data

Freeling, Nicolas.
   A dwarf kingdom / Nicolas Freeling.
      p. cm.
   ISBN 0-89296-615-7
   1. Castang, Henri (Fictitious character)—Fiction. 2. Belgians—Travel—France—Biarritz—Fiction. 3. Police—Belgium—Brussels—Fiction. 4. Brussels (Belgium)—Fiction. 5. Biarritz (France)—Fiction. I. Title.
PR6056.R4D9   1996
823'.914—dc20   96-11954
                                             CIP

To the family—
  love unending;
  laughter unfailing;
Je maintiendrai.

A DWARF KINGDOM

One

High summer in northern Europe. Like the legendary times one's grandparents tell of in Scotland, and we don't listen, and that not politely. They went by train, pulled by a steam locomotive. Yes, but shut up, do. Go pick wild strawberries or something.

But this is the real thing. It is very very hot. We know about that; it signals a fearful thunderstorm and probably with huge freezing hailstones. No; it is still and clear and there is just a whisper of breeze from seaward. On such a day we can imagine that there are no algae on the lakes, no condoms swimming in the Baltic. No sour stink nor warning on the radio about dangerous ozone levels. On a day like this one makes an act of faith: it may be that the human race does after all have a few scraps of future left to it.

It is early July. Last weekend four million deluded French souls stormed off down the autoroutes towards the other and still hotter desert in the south. Plus four million more assorted Danes, and Swedes, and Brits; yes but do shut up. In and around the city of Bruce a great many servants of the Community have not gone on holiday: can't because on July the first the Presidency changes from one member country to another, as it does every six months; a busy and generally a ticklish moment. Here now are two relatively senior members of this bureaucracy, getting through this moment. Together with their wives, who are even more important. The day, smelly even where air-conditioned, has worn on towards evening, the long lovely evening of the northern summer, and all four are in the garden. Those millions departed have left us a bit of oxygen to breathe, and it smells here of trees and grass and old-fashioned roses. The thermometer has gone back from thirty to twenty-five. In grandfather's day there were flies, gnats, midges and mosquitoes: conveniently, he forgets this. Here there are none; yes there is something to be said for this modern world.

The garden belongs to Jerry. It is a splendid garden, initially because Gerald is grand; an important wheel in the Secretariat. 'Sherpa' is the word for people like this; 'the fellow who briefs the fellow' and they're highly paid because they're highly skilled. His name is Gutierrez but he's Scottish as well as Spanish, which helps to make him a good Belgian. He is known as Lala because of his habit of looking at bits of paper and going 'Oh la la la' at them in various keys of loathing or scepticism. He is a tall shambling man, dressed generally in rags since he doesn't like clothes until very old, shapeless and much turned and darned: his wife would need to be a good needlewoman. Which Mathilde is not, but luckily her cleaning-woman, being Portuguese, is. Grey hair stands or falls about in patches over a bumpy shiny forehead. He pushes his glasses up over all this when going 'la la', but right now he can't because he's wearing an English hat looking as though put on back to front, a Panama straw gone anything from ochre to dark brown, the ribbon marked by several high-tides of dried sweat. This academic sort of exterior is the front for a humane and civilised mind.

He is the best friend of the second man present, whose name is Henri Castang, which sounds French and is; he perhaps isn't, doesn't really know and doesn't let it bother him. There were, he says, 'a lot of Foreign soldiers' floating round Paris about that time. He's a Parisian; does that make him French? Vera, his Czech wife, says it's 'even worse than being French' to be Czech, but at least we're

all European; isn't that the point? Castang has been a
servant of the French State, and in the formal sense still
is; for thirty years an officer of the Police Judiciaire, risen
to the high grade of Divisional Commissaire. But more, it
is agreed, by luck than by judgment, since promotion came
together with being put in the cupboard. Senior police
officers aren't sacked, any more than tenured professors
at universities, and he has only been guilty of irritating
his superiors. The Director of the PJ, who has his own
interpretations of the word justice, posted him to a job
in the Communauté; in French eyes much the same as
being sent to Pointe-à-Pitre. But kinder.

He is an Advisor in the legal-affairs branch. It had
been felt that a broad empirical experience of criminal
procedure would stir up the paperbound theoreticians.
Useful in committees. How many grammes of alcohol
in the blood constitute an offence of drunken driving?
Castang will tell you: 'Lots it is and none at all.' Everybody
blames the bureaucrats-in-Bruce for the obstructions of
their own national administrations.

He's smallish for a cop, a lightweight, and has generally
been called wiry. The abdominal muscles are getting a
bit slack with age and (says Vera) overeating. He is
clean-shaved; the face is leathery, with a look of patches
sewn together. Some truth in that, for he has been kicked
in the face a few times and has some gold teeth too. His
hair is dark, of a stiffish sort which shows silver threads.

Whereas Vera's is fair and limp, politely called ash-
blonde, meaning you hardly notice it going grey. She's
indifferent to the colour but curses the texture. Light and
thin, in her late forties she could be called stringy because
it begins to show in the throat and arms. She is wearing
a cotton print frock, close in the bodice and ample in
the skirt. Plain, expensive, good-looking; this can also be
said of the woman inside it. The day may be very hot,
the humidity very high: she looks cool and comfortable
because she is self-disciplined.

The fourth person present is Gerald's wife Mathilde. These descriptions are boring but necessary; in this case especially so. A tsunami, an earthquake wave, is about to hit Belgium. One has to look at Mathilde. To remember, afterwards.

Jerry calls her Tillie. 'Oh Tilda, I do so palpitate' and so one does because she's a great beauty. Because of her looks, and her man's name, it is assumed that she's Spanish. Perhaps she is, but she comes out of Hamburg. Blue-black hair, a wonderful olive skin of a colour that is never sallow but warmed by the ripe blood within. This ripeness is that of the roses, the peaches, on the garden wall. One must ask Jerry to describe her – before the tsunami. And Castang too, for he has that happiest of relations with her, an *amitié amoureuse*. One could ask Vera also because there is no shadow of jealousy there. It 'is not one to sleep with other women's men.' Jerry? 'She doesn't go back on her word.'

Castang, who has desired her intensely and is physically very conscious of her, would speak in terms of police observation – crude, but with detachment. 'Incredible, that hair. She has no moustache. You don't see under her arms because she has more sense than to wear sleeveless frocks. And you do not speculate about her pubic hair because she is simply not that kind of woman. Her ears – policemen are trained to look at ears.

Vera has drawn her; pencil sketches. Would not attempt to paint her; bluntly, 'I'm not good enough.' But look at those temples – the forehead, the line of the eyebrow, the modelling of the orbits: what a colossal beauty she'll be at seventy. But her beauty is more than this, and she is more than her beauty.

She sings. A lyric soprano and a good one. She does not sing professionally, and one wonders why; she has been well trained. But without 'going on the stage' any sort of *lied*, anytime and anywhere. Perhaps they can get her to sing this evening, for in the open air it is still better.

Here in the garden she might do Susanna's '*Deh vieni*'. Or Schubert. Jerry might say 'Mechtild' which he does when being formal. "Do 'Fain would I change that note.'" Or Jacques Brel, if without the local accent.

The house is nothing extraordinary; a cottage built on to over a century or more, and which the Lalas have made comfortable with up-to-date plumbing. But the garden is amazing; as old as the house, large, and the feature is that it's walled. No one knows why. 'Perhaps the chap was a bricklayer,' says Jerry who is very proud of it and works hard at it. He has an old man to help, who potters about, fount of antique plant lore, chews tobacco, 'probably spits on the roses' since no greenfly dare show its nose, here. They are old-fashioned roses, grow hugely up the wall, flower profusely and smell wonderful; 'fed with blood and bones' in a ghoulish voice. There are fruit trees, of varieties and flavours thought extinct: down at the end are vegetables cherished by the old boy; and in a dreadful corner behind the toolshed and the compost is 'Jerry's collection' which Mathilde, ashamed, complains of.

This is an appalling assembly of garden gnomes, facetious and obscene; 'unspeakable vulgarity'. Jerry shouts with laughter saying the garden would not be itself without tutelary spirits. Every right-minded garden has them – 'Priapus, Faunus, attendant satyrs.' There's a flasher, a wanker, several well-known politicians. When first shown these, Castang put on a straight face enquiring,

'Do they come alive at night?'

'I wouldn't be a bit surprised,' says Gerald. Vera like Mathilde sees nothing funny about them. At least they're not on view.

There is though a fountain, with a naked nymph, lead and very beautiful, dragged back at vast expense from Sicily. People make jokes about all this, and Jerry always laughs, and Castang doesn't. It's too much like the jokes always made in his direction at parties. 'If we find someone assassinated in the library – a Commissioner,

for preference – the Kripo's here already.' He has long
run out of witty comments. Somebody will always remark
that half the people present are certainly criminals, and
the other half designated victims 'whom no one will be
sorry to lose'. What are you all being funny about? But
then he'd get told he was French and has no sense of
humour. He shouldn't have been facetious about these
dwarfs either: they aren't in the least funny.

The garden is long, and only looks narrow. Gerald
has had it for many years and has looked it up in
antique cadastral maps. There used to be a near-village of
crooked little houses, and narrow ways between gardens:
all swept away long ago bar this one, kept intact by a
very-old-granny. 'Used to talk about Wicked-King-Leopold
as though she'd emptied the pots at the palace.' And
halfway down is a lawn, and a tree for sitting under.
'Like Alfred Austin, who said his idea of heaven was the
servants bringing tea and messengers with news of British
Victories by land and by sea . . . come to think of it, one
knows quite a few who are still exactly like this.'

They are sitting under the tree now. The cherries are
over (of a sort unobtainable in any shop and the Lalas have
a picking-party) but there are lots of agile spiders. Jerry is
opening some wine, found in a village near Strasbourg,
where business takes him now and again.

"This was quite old, and forgotten, miraculously, in a
corner of the cellar. Extraordinary taste of green herbs
– mint, predominantly – you know, as though crushed
underfoot?" And while he chats thus happily something
is happening.

Down by the far end, where a box hedge announces
the vegetables, a figure has appeared, stands quietly,
looking. This apparition is not in itself sinister. But in
the gathering twilight which goes on forever, changing
the colour of stone and brick, giving a sharp outline to
leaf and water, putting a brilliant unearthly glow upon
every flower, one is no longer sure. It advances slowly,

casual and altogether at ease; pleasurably. Nobody has seen it but Castang, facing that way, thinking, 'Odd.' And his reaction odder. He is sprawled in a deckchair with his feet up, and it didn't occur to him to move. Why not? For with a jolt he has instant recall of a Brel poem and one that Mathilde sings; many are disturbing but this one chilling.

> Look well out, child, look well out.
> At the height of the reeds
> A man is coming
> Whom I do not know.
> Look well, child.

That man is riding a horse,

> Too proud a horse
> To be that of a neighbour

and this man walks, slow and loose. Castang knows there is a door in the wall, down there. There is a solid lock to it, but for Jerry's old man it's a short cut. Must have had a few beers and forgotten.

Watching, supine, as it got closer, the face should have jolted him into reacting, for it was itself without reaction; a face completely blank, a face neither good nor bad and showing nothing but a perfect indifference. Young; hardly more than a boy; early twenties. Given any animation at all, be that either insolence or shyness, apology or aggression, the face would have been good-looking. The figure of this young man was ordinary, and neat; jeans and T-shirt and basketball shoes. Looked like everyone and no one; all the features were there, regular and ordinary, and afterwards he could remember nothing of them worth the mention. There was nobody there.

Busy with the cork and with talking to himself – "So it ought to be a tough one, after all this time spent waiting for us" – Jerry had noticed nothing. The footsteps were silent on grass. Bits of training had stuck with Castang: his peripheral vision is good. The 'sixth sense' cliché would have been more to the point, because he remained gripped by that paralysis. He would look for excuses; heat, age, laziness. It is a sound principle to retire police officers at fifty. Even his famous sense of smell isn't what it was.

Well of course, this is Jerry's house, and social observance is that he should take the lead; so that when he did look up –

"Hallo; come to join us, have you? That's nice. But it isn't a party, I'm afraid." The young man didn't move, didn't utter, did not stop smiling. Try again.

"Door open, was it? I have to apologise; shouldn't have been. I'm sorry but it's private ground." A satisfaction is that the lovely wall is three metres high, discouraging to intruders since if you can't see in you are thereby the less tempted to break in. The front gate has an electronic lock and the house is masked by shrubbery, and is also alarmed since the insurance company insists on that.

Now when you do have an intruder it's like the Tar Baby; says nothing. Jerry has to start afresh.

"Is there perhaps anything I can do for you?" It is difficult to talk to this younger generation. To be over-familiar will be as unwelcome as to be pompous. Recall the French General who asked his son, 'Are you hungry? Are you cold?' "You're not lost? Don't need help?" And the smile just gets broader.

Gerald acquired a slight frown; was this going to be tiresome? One is dealing with the simple-minded; there are a number of variations. Mentally deficient, that's quite common. Stoned out of sight on some dangerous drug, still more so.

"Not been too long in the sun, have you?" Which is quite reasonable on a day like this. Third possibility occurs. Poles, Finns!! – been at the vodka like nobody's business, now speechless and shortly to be footless. One can call the police but it might be kinder not to. "Damn, we know no Norwegian." Jerry is becoming flustered; the smile keeps getting broader and Castang, belatedly, is getting on his feet. If you find an unknown animal in the garden and shoo at it, it might rush up a tree. You don't go up the tree after it since it might be dangerous. Animals which behave unpredictably might have rabies and you had better call the fire brigade.

It does look rather like a Finn; pale skin and hair; pale eyes. Whatever it is, between the two of them, one should be able to handle this quietly.

The two women hadn't got up. Women are better at these situations than men; they aren't embarrassed. But there is a social convention of 'Leave this to me.'

The young man wasn't listening to Gerald. He didn't care about being social; wasn't worried about Jerry making contact, not being aggressive or not appearing over-conciliatory. He gave a flat, low whistle and from behind the bushes another figure appeared. This one approached with plodding, heavy steps. Something about the walk, which was shuffling and clumsy. Castang is trying now to register details. A description might be needed later; a witness. Unless it occurred to these characters to suppress the witness.

Older, but was perhaps younger than he looked. Gingery hair. Low intelligence. Some neurological damage, from a car accident or something of the sort, since polio is now pretty well eradicated. That in-toed, dance-step walk – like John Wayne. Similar clothes to the other; just dirtier.

When the young man spoke at last it was in ordinary French. One couldn't tell an accent from this little. An amused tone.

"Come on then Georgie-Porgie. Business."

Gerald 'drew himself up'.

"This won't do, I'm afraid." The young man seemed to see him for the first time.

"That's right. 'I'm afraid.' Now you've got it. You – are – afraid." And this was a good joke.

"I see," said Gerald. He had now a new voice, deprecating, nearly the oh-lah of his business tones: here's another stupidity. "You are gangsters. That's bad luck for you really, since we have nothing that would interest you. We are not violent people and you have no need to be violent. We shan't stop you because we can't. We know better than to run around or yell. Try not to break more than you have to." The young man paid no attention to this good advice; scanned around him as though curious, but not very.

Georgie, the thick-muscled one, had a bag under his arm; the sort of cylindrical carry-all that people insist upon dragging on to planes, to the discomfort of the next-in-line and a stewardess's irritation. As though it contained all he had, in the way of personal possessions. They'll probably ask for a carrier to hold the loot, thought Castang, amused in a way.

Georgie put this on the ground, unzipped it. Out came a radio, which was also put on the ground; loud tinny rock came from this. But next came something much nastier; a panga, or machete, with a plastic handle. As though to clear a path with in the jungle, and Castang abandoned any ideas of intervention.

Georgie handed this across to the young man, who tucked it under his arm, as a downy young second-lieutenant tucks a swagger cane. The comparison is made a little sharper (as one turns the focusing screw of binoculars) by the negligent, supercilious air; that of having to oversee an unreliable non-com in charge of a fatigue party. Who puts on a display of zeal, saying, "Shut up, Fatso," and giving Gerald, who is not fat and hasn't spoken, a hard push to dump him in the deckchair: turns to Castang, who prudently sits before getting shoved. Spencer Tracy in similar circumstances (much of his left arm was also synthetic) gave a fat villain a fearful karate chop in the neck. One would then launch oneself in a flying leap boots first to demolish the other pig. Aged twenty-five, on the police gymnastics team and proud of street abilities – who knows?

"Look for a bit of string or something." And Georgie lollops off with that odd gait, like a rabbit feeding. In the house there will be a garage, perhaps a workshop. Or there's the toolshed: gardeners use bits of string.

There was a strange interlude. Resembling a moment of humour, or even good-humour. The young man stood surveying the group with an empty, uncaring face. They did not interest him; they were an unimportant problem of disposal and that was all. Neither of the two women was a screamer: both of the men were trying to rationalise. His eye fell on the opened, unpoured bottle, and he took two steps and picked it up, looked at it incuriously, poured the four glasses – carefully, without spilling – and handed them around. How would one interpret this? The Russian soldier, who will kill you if he feels like it, has also moments of simple kindness. Castang, grateful to moisten his throat, thought it more likely to be 'Make do while you can'. Not 'A pity to waste this good juice'. Perhaps neither of the two concepts would occur to him; he took none himself. Whatever he was addicted to it wasn't alcohol, or tasting a pleasure slowly, nor even sadism. All four drank in silence and he watched, like a supervisor at a written examination. A broken glass is a weapon, thought Castang. But a machete has a much longer reach. I'm not just slow but sitting down. And he's well aware of these facts.

Georgie had not far to search. His eye was caught by a length of black cable on the ground: Gerald has been using the electric trimmer, unplugged it but left it lying about. He felt around pockets, produced a clasp-knife and opened it with teeth because his nails were bitten; topped and tailed the cable, looped it up in a skein, counting the loops; twenty-five metres. Brought it back – "How's this?"

"Cut it in half." To the two men – "Lie on the grass. Face down." It is difficult to make knots in rubber-sheathed cable, but not when one has great strength in the hands. Georgie roped them; the hands tied behind, the cord looped around the neck and going back to tie the feet together, the knees bent. This is quite deadly; struggle and you strangle. He did not bother to tie the women. What would be the point? They don't count.

The young man handed the machete to Georgie, who put it on the grass, sat down, listened to the music with what perhaps was ecstasy. The four of them kept quiet because they could do nothing else. Vera is not fleet of foot: if she tries to run her leg might give way suddenly. Mathilde doubtless told herself that she would be less fleet of foot from here to the gate than even lumpish Georgie sitting there with a toothpick from some café in his mouth. The young man strolled into the house, to look about him at leisure.

Castang thinks only of being professional. It won't do him much good, but the mind is not fertile in useful suggestions.

He has met these people before. Not for some time, nor often; they seem to be getting more numerous. The word psychopath gets thrown about over-lavishly, but for want of a more exact term, it will do.

They are indifferent to life, to society, to anything much but their immediate satisfaction. They aren't amenable to normal human feelings. They feel superior to everyone, enjoy this and like to indulge the enjoyment; show contempt; inflict humiliations. Money appeals since it smooths paths, but elaborate schemes take up time, are too much trouble. Ordinary desires; food, or sex, or a nice sleep; these are not very strong in them. They are likely to eat pills in large quantities.

He hoped the fellow would find money quickly since it was likeliest that then he'd go away. He'd probably think of locking the women in the cellar, to delay police interference; one hoped it might be nothing worse. That oafish acolyte does not know that he'll get ditched too. Such people only draw attention to one. Errand-runners of this low calibre can be picked up anywhere, and given to the police afterwards to provide a distraction. The type itself is chameleon, knows how to appear harmless, is cunning, resourceful, difficult to catch. Colourless; even now I could not give a good description.

Jerry is not likely to have a lot of money. One hopes there's some in his wallet and Mathilde's handbag. He travels a good deal and is likely to have some foreign currency in his desk: a few Swiss francs would be a good idea.

There are other considerations, and urgent. In this position cramp arrives quickly and painfully. One is losing circulation. Attempts to relieve this constrict the throat. And don't lose consciousness or shortly you'll be dead.

Detach, er, loosen. The mind, for instance. Concentrate upon something; it doesn't have to be pleasant, it'll still be ... Nothing comes but police reports, which cross his desk unendingly because somebody supposed to filter them thought that these would interest the criminology studies unit: of, uh, social significance. This one concerned gipsies. Yes, the Communauté worries about gipsies. They don't fit into the slots provided, marked 'Housing', 'Education', and, er, so forth.

Some old men spent their sunset days fishing; kept expensive equipment in a shack (well padlocked) by the bank of the Loire. Two gipsy boys, teen-aged, thought also of going fishing, a pleasant pastime. Having no equipment at all they found it perfectly normal to break into the shack so conveniently provided and help themselves to goodies. This happened two-three times. Vexed (I'm giving you the basic outline, Monsieur le Juge) by repetitions, by depredations, by complaints made without result – we must notice that this is B&E and not mere pilfering – the old boys laid in wait and caught these youngsters red-handed, slapped the children about quite roughly (their definition of a clip over the ear) and proposed to turn them over to the police. Since such brats are as agile as eels, they tied them up. As I am now, Monsieur le Juge, as you see me. And unfortunately for all concerned, being frightened boys, they would not stop struggling and strangled themselves. Since the concept of legitimate defence has been raised we would like a judicial opinion.

Homicide in defence of the life or safety of the person has often been deemed justifiable; quite so. In defence of property such a claim is bound to fail. Thank you, Mr States Attorney.

Vera was thinking that she had quite strong fingers. If she could just reach that little bit further she might try to undo Gerald's feet. She'd have to wiggle the chair a bit closer and doesn't quite dare try. That lout appears wrapped up in his radio, but . . .

And even with his feet loose what could Jerry do? He'd have ado to stand, let alone to run.

If Mathilde thought anything it is not known.

When the young man came back he appeared relaxed, but then so he had at the start. Castang didn't think he belonged to the regiment which busts things simply because they are pretty. It was likely that he'd found money because the Lump asked "Okay then?" and he shrugged, but not as though effort were fruitless. He sat down then inside Castang's sightline and it could be seen that he was carrying a jewellery box. Mathilde likes such things, and Jerry enjoys giving them to her. He turned it out in a heap on the grass and began picking through, holding things up to the light and smiling at them. It was a horrible sight but Castang was glad that he could see no further.

"That's all right then, but you said I could have a woman."

"Take one then. Both for all I care. Don't be too long about it; I'm getting bored."

"I don't want the skinny one; that's no good. The other's all right." The young man made no answer, wasn't interested. He was trying rings on, a necklace. In the lid of the box was a mirror, and he held this up to admire the different effects he was getting.

Castang could not obliterate the scuffle, the low sad cries of outrage and of pain. He tried to obliterate, but he must not lose consciousness.

"God she's dryer than a nun, she's no fun."

Some weeks ago Castang had come to this house, in anguish, in misery and lassitude. Everything had conspired to his desolation, and he'd had a furious fight with his wife. He picked up the phone.

"Is Jerry there?"

"No, but if you want to, come on across." He had.

"Hallo. D'you want a drink?"

"No. I want to howl."

"Sit. Put your feet up and lie." She didn't ask what was amiss. He felt her coming to sit beside him, felt her hand on his forehead and closed his eyes. She began to sing very softly.

Now, with his eyes shut again and trying to breathe he is trying to distance himself, to hear her voice, once again.

"'*Raste, Krieger! Krieg ist aus . . .*'" A long-swinging, slow and supple melody.

"Is that Schubert?"

"Yes, and Sir Walter Scott – 'Ellen's Song' but I only know it in German."

He was trying for it now. 'Soldier, rest; the warfare over . . .'

It must have been close to this moment that Gerald gave up.

The pain in Castang's legs had grown acute. The lapse into unconsciousness would be a delivery. From a long way off he heard her voice now defeated; that of a little girl holding up her hand.

"May I go to the bathroom, please?" And there was

some kind of mumbled reply, no doubt a jeer. Time must have passed, one had no idea how much. The last thing he could remember was a loud hoarse shout or scream of fear and pain and rage; the falsetto scream of a man.

Here now was something he has known and lived through already; before. The two occasions had telescoped: he thought he was again drowning, in the Lake of Lugano. The Carabinieri pulled him out. There was a red sweaty face staring into his; there was something over his mouth. He was being pulled about in several unpleasant ways and all he could find to gasp out was "Don't." Then no, this was another occasion. Less exciting, and perhaps still nastier. It was only the fire brigade, giving him oxygen but there was no fire; he felt a bit confused about that.

They had a lot on their hands. Once fairly sure he was safe they left him lying somewhere to rest; this was nice; Raste, Krieger. He drifted in and out of fragments of real life, a lot of shouting and trampling and mumbling.

Then there was a doctor. She seemed a kindly enough female; she had hard hands. His throat was painful.

"No wonder. You were strangled with cable."

"Vera . . ."

"Is that your wife? She's all right; some shock but no injuries. We've taken the others to hospital. You're all right too, that's to say clinically. Badly bruised, your feet will be painful with the circulation returning. Feels worse than it is. There's a police officer here, anxious for you to say a few words. I've given you a shot, for the heart; I don't think bringing you in will serve much useful purpose: rest is what you need."

"Raste, Krieger."

"Just so. Here's this damn cop. Keep it short."

"Mr Castang."

"No. Bugger off."

"We've been asking your wife, uh, her statement's a bit confused, a bit fragmentary, uh, we'd like if you

could confirm a few points, this is a grave business.
One of them got away. If you could add anything to the
description—"

"Get my wife." There was a lot of argument; he heaved
himself up. He had been intending to bellow; didn't; it
would hurt his throat. Policemen . . . He closed his eyes
instead: he was tired, he'd have a little rest.

"History does repeat itself, doesn't it?" Vera's voice,
close to his ear. She gave a high, nervous giggle. Unlike
her. Due to shock. "No, I didn't get raped." Yes, he
remembered that occasion too. She hadn't been too sure
whether she had or not.

"Have we got a car?"

"I don't think I could drive."

"No. Get one of these bloody policemen. Where's
Mathilde?"

"They've taken her to hospital. I'll tell you at home."

"Jerry?"

"I think he's dead." Four monosyllables. "They say they
think there's a chance of reanimating him."

"Do you feel all right?"

"I suppose more or less."

"Let's get home somehow."

The English are quite right. There's nothing like a nice
cup of tea.

Castang realised with a start that he hadn't said this, or
even thought it. Mertens' words, out of Mertens' mouth.
An old friend.

"Policemen's tea. What they call 'A good sergeant-
major's brew.'" Central Commissaire Mertens is the head
of Serious Crimes. Well for him, he was drinking Castang's
best cognac. He was at home, they were sitting in his
living-room. He made a shot at gathering his wits. They'd
got around then, to calling a senior officer. Now speaking
in a quiet voice, suitable for children.

"Those idiots who take statements from people in shock,

and then they tell you you're contradicting yourself. However ... that chap is still loose but we'll pick him up easily; got'm by now probably.

"I've sent your wife to bed. She got pushed about a bit but nothing to mention. Physically, that is. Told me she'd once been raped herself and seeing it done is worse: I can understand this ...

"I've got your story, up to the time you passed out. Now I'll fill you in. These two men – we've got the clever one with the jewellery hung all over him."

"How did you do that?"

"Shut up and I'll tell you. Rape women and they might go catatonic. The Spanish woman went mataglap." The word has survived in Holland from old colonial times; the Javanese peasant 'running amok', a homicidal madness; a happening to be dreaded.

"She's not Spanish, she's German."

"She exacted her vengeance," heavily. "There's no question of pegging her. She went to the bathroom to clean herself up. They let her, she seemed passive. Bathroom's full of the usual rubbish. She hunted about for a weapon – razor-blade or whatever but there weren't any. What she found was a tiny phial of acid. You get warts or something on your skin you can burn them off, little touch, go carefully. It's very small, she hid it in her fist, came out and threw it in his face."

"Oh Jesus."

"Right, he'll need his eyes to weep with and he won't find them. The other, the lumping one, he took that cutlass thing and cut her down. We're not even sure she'll survive it. And her mind ... it's marginal. He threw away the sabre, ran.

"Your wife rang the fire brigade, best thing she could have done. Oxygen for you, for the other man. That's said to be too late. Call that an accident, a suicide, a homicide – the judge will have to make up his own mind about that.

"First aid for the other two, but a terrible head wound, acid in the eyes, they aren't equipped for that. Asphyxia yes, strangulation yes, good, they got a move on, ambulance – criminal brigade. A lot of good they'll do," said their head.

"For you, my son, I've a sleeping pill, the doctor gave me two of them."

They did not manage to reanimate Gerald.

Mathilde died during the night.

The young intruder, it was said, might recover partial sight in one eye. The other would not get beyond a blur. Even with quite rapid treatment, they told the police, that's not the sort of stuff you want to get, and then blundering about in a strange house looking for water . . .

The oaf was picked up stealing a car, and held overnight pending more serious charges.

Castang slept for twelve hours. An over-heavy sleep, with broken interludes.

On that July day, further south, it had been blisteringly hot, all across Europe. The Tour de France riders had to climb the Mont Ventoux, in central Provence; the windy mountain also called the Bald One. It is of the sort the French call 'peeled' because nothing grows. The sun ricochets off the bare stone. A pitiless place of legend and tragedy. It is less than two thousand metres and many of the classic Tour passages are much higher; none more severe. The climb is twenty-two kilometres of asphyxiating effort. Castang had watched on television, when he should have been working, but so did all of Europe. By night the Bald Mountain is full of gibbering ghosts, but the noon-day terror is enough for anyone.

Many years ago here, Kubler, the magnificent Swiss, launched his attack.

'Attention, Ferdi,' warned Raphael Geminiani, 'the Ventoux is not like other mountains,' to get the legendary answer—

'Ferdi not like other riders.' One sees no reason to doubt the legend that Kubler that night, delirious, kept shouting 'Ferdi is dead. Ferdi has killed himself in the Ventoux.' It has also held the literal meaning. A stone by the roadside marks the spot where Tommy Simpson fell off his bike and died: his body had been fired by speed-pill, but the heart and lungs could not keep up.

Castang woke also through the moment when the Belgian Cannibal, Monsieur Merkcx, had to be given oxygen at the summit.

You can also get killed going down. The riders here are clocked at a hundred and twenty to the hour. The road is now a smooth asphalt ribbon with safety-bars on the bends. In the days of Geminiani, the Big Rifle (no great climber, but made up, downhill) it was a rough track in the eroded rock, the margins full of loose stones, and this, also, Castang found himself riding. The word 'reckless' is now worn down into glib cliché. One hopes to die in a clean bed, rather than under the sun in a cholera epidemic.

Vera made coffee; as pale as himself but she said nothing about the shouting, the thrashing about. She put the pot down with a bigger bump than she intended.

"Could perhaps something funny happen, please? To make us laugh?" He cut some bread, and then shied away from it.

"Lydia rang," she said, for want of anything better.

"What, from New York?"

"She's coming home. She'll be here this evening."

"Oh, that will be nice." Yes, his eldest daughter – and also the funny one.

A pause here, to think, also, of how troublesome and irritating a girl. The people one loves; invariable.

"This is the end. Of work here. You know that." It was said in the voice she uses to talk about potatoes, could not be more undramatic, but not to be mistaken. She's not going to go back on this. But he agrees, doesn't he.

Finished with climbing mountains. There is no opposition. She's his wife, she 'plays on his side'. But if one of her principles is at stake, then she's not on anybody's side.

He made an effort at a joke.

"Every time I see a friend of mine, he's dead." All too true: Harold Claverhouse and his wife Iris. Eamonn Hickey laughing at calamities. Now Jerry. Now Mathilde. What abominable curse do I carry for those that I love?

"No, I've come too close to the edge, too many times." He hasn't spoken about 'the mountain' but even if he hadn't talked in his sleep women have uncanny accuracy in their instincts. He pushed his coffee cup across for more.

"I'll go into the office this afternoon."

"Nobody, for an instant, would expect it."

"It's a duty. No, you're quite right. But to Suarez, to let him know, personally – I owe him that."

"I don't want you taking the bicycle." How does she know, about the bicycle?

"No," smiling. "I'm taking the car. Unless you want it and then I'll walk to the tram stop."

"I'm not going," unsmiling, "any further than the edge of my ironing board."

Mr Suarez isn't funny; doesn't – thank heaven – try to be. Nor is he like Harold, who delegated everything and spent his afternoons with dictionaries. A conventionally austere Spanish gentleman, meticulous, and fussy about detail. He can be a niggler but he doesn't haver. Castang has found him a good chief, betimes a peppery taskmaster.

He looked up, said kindly, "There was no need."

"No, but I wanted to tell you as soon as might be. That's only fair. Give you time to think around it." A favourite piece of Suarez-vocabulary; he does not think 'about' a matter.

Finding it difficult to say Castang was facetious.

"Cops say in the States 'End of Watch'."

"I see. I'm sure, am I, that I see aright?"

"You do." Harold would have recognised police car-radio jargon. Known also that the phrase is a metaphor for death. Might well have answered 'Ten-Four' the way elderly English gentlemen will still say 'Roger'. But this too is in his way a good man.

"I don't feel I can go on. Of course they were close friends of mine. And in the past too . . . But I've given it thought. I thought, too, that you'd agree."

"Well now," still kindly, "whether I do or don't is of little consequence. We must think of you. Police Commissaires retire at fifty. There's a considerable file on the subject."

A glimmer of humour there. How often has Suarez cursed at Castang and his Pension. Paris has been going on about it, arguing . . . "We can view that as settled. What your further entitlement may be remains to establish; I'll go into it." Doesn't haver. "I should have liked to keep you awhile, but your decision is eminently respectable. I'll put it through. You'd be entitled to some terminal leave; you could take that now if you wished."

"Wouldn't be very fair, would it? Leaving everyone disorganised. And I've a desk full of loose ends." And now he could see that round face, with the hair cut in a short fringe, looking pleased.

"There's that man with his nervous breakdown," medi-tating, "and I've three pregnant secretaries, they always come in groups. We have flexibilities, but never enough margins. Come in, in a day or so, and I'll have seen what I find."

"Yes," said Castang. Mr Suarez raised his eyes, which are always mournful though the rest of him shines with health. He is an exercise maniac, and this terrible fitness makes everyone feel tired. But he is overburdened and that he says is his job. Harold would feel sometimes put-upon, and sulk.

"Our misfortunes have clung to you. You haven't com-plained about them. You have earned much; the gratitude of the living and the affection – which is undying – of the dead."

He said this in Spanish. The kindness – really very unexpected – touched Castang, much.

Late that afternoon the Judge of Instruction's office telephoned.

"She'd like very much to see you tomorrow morning but was worried you might not be up to it."

"I'd be up to it," said Castang, "but I have to go to a funeral."

"Oh dear," as though it were his own.

"I might manage around this time tomorrow."

"I'm looking at her book, to see if I can fix that. Yes, there's somebody who has to be extracted from prison, but I dare say he can be switched around."

"He'll enjoy it. It helps pass the time."

"Yes," not quite sure he was joking. "I'll tell her then."

Then there was that boring argument who should go to the airport to pick up Lydia.

"I'll go. I've left the car outside."

"I will go," said Vera. "I need some air." He didn't feel enthusiastic about having to do the dinner.

"I've done the dinner. It needs only to be put in the oven. And I've done her room. And the ironing. Now I want to drive to the airport with all the windows open. And the roof." It's unanswerable.

He pottered about unhappily, to end in 'the music room' which would sound grand if either of them could play a note on any instrument, which they can't. So that here is to be found only recorded music, which is better than nothing and there's a lot of it: a big room, but then it's a big house, much too big now for them.

This is 'her's' really but he has treasures of his own, scratchy old things dating back to the seventy-eights of his boyhood; the swing era. He is feeling so horribly old. Ah . . . the Bobcats.

The funeral had been hideous. Castang was accustomed to saying that one learns from funerals. They can even be richly funny. One would prefer it to be a moment for showing solidarity and slipping discreetly away: not possible; all eyes are upon them and some with a sort of indignation, that they aren't dead, too. Because one must make conventional replies to conventional expressions of grief, they were maintained in their formal role. Dignity was thrust upon them.

Dignity . . . and Vera was thinking of a stupid joke doing the rounds; a supermarket chain making publicity of the Three Musketeers, so that there had been sniggering over d'Artagnan's daughter getting raped in the Safeway: yes and I also giggled. Are the girls lighthearted? Are they now anaesthetised? – the little needle slipped into the spine, the epidural to give us painless childbirth?

Are they now quite indifferent to the display of their sex for the vulgar delectation? It is the pivot of her physical and psychological being. The naked girl by Velazquez – in London – a wonder of controlled plasticity, holds a looking-glass: it is thought that she is studying her own cunt, and if so is it vanity or perplexity at the male obsession with this ludicrous vulva? She is both aesthetically perfect and gynaecologically absurd; an astonishing painting.

And this place of menstruation and parturition was the start of the family, the source of security and equilibrium, of tenderness and generosity, the long apprenticeship in giving and taking. I had to learn it too, hard and painful, and it lasts a lifetime. But also of 'Family I hate you'. It can be an asphyxia of pain and hatred and life-long frustration; a space occupied by a humiliated man in fear of castration.

Isn't there too, in America, a picture of the famous

'1940 Dodge'? Today's teenagers would hardly understand the couple in the back; the sweaty struggle with the bra clip, that awkward overheated penis and the painful fiasco. But wasn't it a lot less boring than the drearily mechanical upsydownsy? Each generation envies the other, and one can't help feeling sorry for both.

Castang took a sidelong look at his wife's face and learned nothing from it but perhaps he took some comfort. His own funeral thoughts were of the utmost banality. Millions untold and every second die and are born, fornicate, defecate, etcetera, etcetera. Quite so. It cannot be termed memorable or edifying. Still, he must be given a bit of credit. He too is thinking of pain, and of a young man suffering. Not only of this older woman who had been to him the dearest of friends.

Both were too stunned, still, to feel much grief. Grief is in everything: joy too is grief, or are both an expression of the same illusion? Castang is a professional, much like the minister conducting the service. Vera, proud, secret, intensely controlled, does not shed tears. Many people there thought her cold.

"Thank god, Lydia's coming tonight." And yes, that will be a comfort. Their eldest daughter, the bright and the silly, the amusing and dismaying, the intensely annoying; she is joy and grief permanently intertwined, and what's the difference?

Castang had taken precautions; the car parked in accessible and intelligent fashion; one will make one's escape in a direction opposite to that taken by the mob. The Communauté is present in force, and recollection has been effected with grace and style. But let's get moving: there's a business lunch, and the Ministers of Agriculture – and (yet again) the dispute about fisheries.

"Why are we going this way?" asked Vera.

"Because we're going to have a good lunch, and a great deal to drink. Along here there is a restaurant. It has two stars. The thing about the ones with three stars is they aren't only a lot dearer but you can't get in, without three months' advance notice."

"Excellent initiative. I'm feeling awful and perhaps it's because I'm very hungry."

"Funeral baked meats are always supposed to be hilarious. So they will."

"Yes indeed. Mr Polly. ''Am do get in my teeth so, nowadays.' So no ham, all right?"

And after two glasses of wine, "Now I can talk about it. But what about the Judge of instruction?"

"She'll just have to wait. I told her not before three, with my dark suit still on, and the white shirt to show the blood. Allow me to fill your glass." As always in Belgium one tends to overeat before even reaching the main course. Remedied by experience. Remediable, at least, but what is not is Vera's need to spit out what is on her mind.

"What I find especially horrible is never getting away from vile happenings. I had thought we were finished with that. This sense of *déjà vu.* You found Iris dead. You had to be rescued from drowning. These boys. Does it all go on and on? Is this still simply our normal condition?"

"Probably," said Castang finishing the bottle. "Doubtless. Make it yes, and be done with it. In life or in letters, the crime theme predominates. Take it away and the human condition is merely gossip."

Vera had been raped too, once upon a time. She had killed the man in the struggle. The gendarmerie, the judge of instruction, the local Procureur had all agreed without hesitating upon a decision to take no further steps in the matter. There are times, one might claim, when there's something to be said for marriage to a senior police officer. He doesn't want her mind travelling upon these paths. "You know what Thomas Bernhard said? To write of a man drinking a glass of milk is boring. But to write of the same man thinking of how to blow up the Prado Museum while drinking the same glass of milk – that becomes interesting." He was pleased with her laugh.

"This is a nice place," she decided. "The waitresses are pretty." Theirs is a simple, friendly girl; an ample bosom, a fine Belgian bottom. Even the headwaiter is lacking in pretention. A hypocrite he surely is, but not over-servile: he laughs at Castang's bad jokes and his own are less bad.

"One must arrange, you see, that Goya blows up first, and then Velazquez. But not the director, since we need him for the guilty party."

Expensive restaurants have nothing to do with reality. But when they are any good they do fortify one against this wretched business of living.

As Vera says, "I come here to be treated like a princess. As a beautiful and valuable object, to be cherished. Not as though one were merely vile." When it is time to get back to the human condition, eating and drinking and laughing have helped heal. The bill is of less importance than who is going to drive. Vera, in these circumstances; she's the less reckless.

Lydia came bursting in, just the way she always had. Black and white suit, mini-skirt to show her long legs, wild of hair; as loving and as noisy as ever.

"Darling Pa. Oh god – Bobcats! This lovely house, I've never been away. I swear, I'll never go away again. Oh god, that's Nappy Lamarr."

"You know him?" stupidly.

"I had a boyfriend in New York. Terribly sweet but god he was dull. One never got away from his heroes. Bunny Berigan and Tommy Ladnier. Miff Mole and his Molers! It became ex-cru-ciating."

"Man said 'Nappy, you getting pretty old,' and he said '*Qué*, Old? Just because I was a waiter at the Last Supper?'" Lydia's laugh was no longer a schoolgirl giggle. His daughter had grown up. Two years she had been away: the green young thing was a ripe, poised young woman. But still direct.

"Ma told me – the horrible happenings – coming back from the airport. One says, of course, that belongs in Billings, Montana. All around one every day and one protects oneself with jokes. Until – but never mind. I'm here, I'll look after you." Castang was touched.

"What happened to the boyfriend?"

"Faded away, one has found better since. We were at a party, somebody put on an old Ellington number, he stood there in the middle of the room, saying 'Good old Sonny Greer' in this voice simply crawling with abject sentimentalism. Think they're so tough and the marshmallow topping is all the way through. Let's go in the kitchen, I mustn't leave Ma by herself." Bursting back, shouting, "Can I help?" And promptly sat down; that much hadn't changed. "Marvellous Smell . . . oh god, shepherds pie, all these years I've been dreaming of it."

"Make the salad," said Vera.

"You never did any cooking?" enquired Castang.

"Well, no, there's so many kinds of takeaway. Unless for boys, big deal, rush to Zabels and do the shopping. Being French they all think one will be this great cook, just as being French one is sure to screw in exciting new ways."

"One doesn't?" amused, pouring drinks.

"Certainly not, and this for them is the great fascination. Happy with food. Their mouth, you know, is bigger than their dick." Vera, a little taken-aback. And with her own mouth full of the salad she was supposed to be tasting, "Come on Ma, I haven't taken any nun's vows." Unwilling to be taken-aback Castang said,

"Work?"

"Darling Philippa," in a gooey voice which might have been the salad. "This huge mouth from ear to ear and all covered in jangly jewellery. Heaven to me. You know I cannot spell. My English was ropey. I said Pronto on the phone, and they all went about saying pronto for three days, that's as long as anything lasts. What they think today they won't tomorrow. Except for talking about Cunt, but Philippa was kind, she protected me."

"You were grossly incompetent."

"I no longer am. They are, mostly."

"But they were interesting."

"They seem so at first. Come on very bright. Using street talk out of snobbery, it sounds terrific when you hear it. Write it down it's out of date before you hit the printer. They stamp about shouting for something new. Anything that really is new frightens them. Long faces then, and muttering that it won't sell. Buy something they don't want, out of fear someone else will get it." Lydia cast about, searching for an example the poor dears would understand. "There was a movie a few years back. The painter and his model. So she has an excuse to walk about naked the whole time; they liked that. Made another one, only this time there are three naked girls And a priest. Too much of it is like this. So I got bored and I pissed off," taking a third helping of shepherds pie.

Castang who had then been greatly astonished, and never dared ask how it came about, was now delighted. Lydia, a timid child under that brash exterior, had walked in, fresh off the boat, and simply asked for a job. A woman of character had taken the ghastly girl on out of sheer kindness; had put up patiently with this notorious incompetent and fashioned her into what one now saw; Able.

"You shared an apartment with some girls." Lydia who had never been known to share anything.

"Terrific sweeties, huge, all two metres tall. Terrifying. But so nice. They all are so nice, you know. We did have fights sometimes, three hours locked in the bathroom."

Wasn't it all exactly what he needed, wanted? A laugh and a success story.

She went to change, after supper. Why? asked Castang, puzzled; to dodge the washing-up? And you think you understand girls, said Vera. Showing us, that's all.

Lydia reappeared in something see-through, so that

Castang said, "Mom, lookit that lady, she forgot to put her dress on," and even Vera, mildly taken aback, said, "What's that, your petticoat?"

"What's a Petticoat?" vexed; she'd never liked being teased.

"Your tits are showing," amused.

"What tits? I haven't got any." True that she was thinner than she used to be.

"The judge of instruction this afternoon was also showing a good deal," said Castang peacefully, and Vera had the tact to keep silence, for once.

The Palace of Justice, in Bruce, is of gigantic size and great ugliness. Like that restaurant, thought Castang, it has nothing to do with realities. But the judge was a young and pretty woman. That was real. Judges have too often been old men living in the stuffy, dim-lit world of lace-curtained bourgeoisdom; heavy old houses dust–, sound– and burglar-proofed. Even a vivid, a virulent imagination cannot see them pushing trolleys in the supermarket. They are divorced from our world: they do not scan small-ads for jobs. But instructing judges often are young, because these are generally the first posts on offer to the newly formed magistrate. Not all that many will make a career here; in judicial circles it's a lousy job, drowned in paperwork and always blamed for the never-catching-up: a daily contact with the unwashed, such as prisoners, press, or police. A plebeian activity, and after a year or so of probation many seek a switch to the Bench or the Prosecutor's Office. One is sorry to alliterate, but these are more patrician. There are some though who find it interesting and like it being exacting.

For instruction means examination; the inquisitorial style of European justice as opposed to the accusatorial of a British court-room. An endless parade of witnesses, all liars; of lawyers, all bent upon obstruction and chicanery; of black hearts prevaricating, whitewashing their grime before the prospect of it made public. These judges are filters, in which much filth comes to stick.

They are supposedly impartial, here to decide whether there is substance to imputations; enough to put before a tribunal. The basic rule is neither to charge nor to discharge: it is nearly always broken. For what is the chap doing here, if the presumptions against him are not already strong? To defend him? – a pile of lawyers are already taking up an aggressive stance. Unless, of course, he be poor; alone; bewildered. Sometimes, then, he can be glad of his judge.

In consequence, the instructing judge gets a bad name; loathed by the press for suspected leaking to a competitor; by the police for hindering the cruder aspects of their zeal; by the public, for just being there. For a magistrate, again, to be young is to be vulnerable. They are inexperienced in the wily ways; they are bullied by prosecutors, and depend for their advancement upon the good opinion of tribunals. They are marked, and upon the marks given depends their promotion.

And worst of all are the political pressures. Ministries are ever ready to protect a relation or an influential friend or someone's son-in-law. Ever anxious to avoid incriminating gossip and smells of juicy scandal. That saddening fact; the elected think only of being re-elected. It is all present to a mind like Castang's. Over the years he has had a great deal to do with examining magistrates.

This isn't 'the famous one'. She (also a young and pretty woman) signed the order bringing three Ministers to trial, before such ideas became fashionable. So doing she became Joan of Arc for the public. This is one of her colleagues. Castang has an acquaintance with her. She also is called fair, clear-headed, and not very timid.

On this hot an afternoon these offices are not cool. Of course they aren't air-conditioned; the State couldn't afford it. There is a door which shuts and a chair to sit on, and what more could one want? Madame was in a cotton frock low in front. One noticed, but Desire is in the Palais an infrequent emotion. Her skin is freckled but her manner cool.

"Here is your statement, as transcribed by policemen; we won't hold it against you. I'd like your recollections now to be clearer, more exact. Feel up to that, do you?

"Very well, you missed the exciting bit. Temporary loss of consciousness due to strangulation, I've a medical certificate and the report from the fire brigade; we aren't questioning that. Your wife is the only available witness to the core of the matter. We'll have her tomorrow, if possible. I want your opinion first on the preliminary scene and the states of mind.

"The woman who was raped; there'd be a charge against her, of grave bodily harm. Flinging acid in someone's face. There's a premeditation there. I'd call it graver than an attempted or even successful homicide when improvised. A plea of temporary insanity might succeed in front of a jury. But I'm not a jury."

Vera hit the man trying to rape her with a heavy piece of wood. The French instructing judge took the self-defence for granted.

"You'd have to know the woman concerned."

"Yes. Right now I'm asking you. How violent was this rape? I wish you to describe it."

"I didn't see it."

"Are you claiming you were unconscious at the time?"

"No."

"Because that's not what you told the investigating officer."

"I probably couldn't have seen much because of the noose round my neck."

"What is this probably?"

"You may conclude that I didn't try hard."

"You are a police officer of rank and experience."

"I was in love with the woman." Castang could feel sweat running down his ribs and wished he had not drunk so much at lunch.

"As you are – professionally – aware, judicial action against the woman is extinguished by her death. We'll go back – with your permission – a little earlier."

"Yes Madame."

"These two men are in jail, held at my disposal. They'll stay there, obviously. The one is in the prison hospital, being treated for injuries to his eyesight: I won't get to see him for a few days. The list of charges imputable is as long as your arm and it's not my job to be sorry for him; I'd like to get your emotions untangled.

"The other is a lout, with a homicide charge on his neck. A diminished responsibility? – I've ordered a psychiatric report, which will be contested. I need you. The intelligence is plainly low; I want opinions of influencibility by the stronger character.

"I incline at present to let the second homicide charge fall, since this is unclear. You survived the noosing and the strangulation. Accident or even suicide could be – will be – pleaded and knowing doctors as I do they'll refuse to pronounce.

"I'll probably be pressing rape and incitement to rape; that seems clearly established. It may depend upon your wife whether I remain reserved on the homicide. The Procureur du Roi wants to push for the double murder, to keep the press happy. I'm not sure I agree; I'm not convinced the Assize Court will like it either.

"I'm going to question you now, as a professional observer; we can even call you a professional witness. That carries weight. And as a civilised – disciplined – human being.

"So let's begin, shall we?"

Searchingly, for an hour and a half. In the old days the clerk took it all down word by word, a laborious process. Judges still take notes; the pen a formidable instrument of concentration and coercion. Like a conductor's baton. When she put it down—

"This really got to you; hit you very hard, didn't it?"

"I've noticed it progressively these last three years. A time in Italy, I found the body of a woman I'd just had breakfast with, blown away by a rifle bullet. I kneeled down and sicked up like a greeny."

She nodded: the law states that where possible the Procureur and the Judge of Instruction shall visit a scene-of-crime *in situ* and shall there observe the physical evidence. No bad rule. Apply it to writers and much bad fiction would not be written.

"No bad idea to retire cops early. Over thirty one is no longer fit for war ... At what age, one wonders, should one apply this to judges?" Nice white teeth the woman has.

The police are like doctors in the need to block emotion. But they need to use force too often. It translates into brutality.

"Balance," he said. "Old judges are like old cops, meaning old bastards. Or are they the less likely to be bent? If cynical," he added, "you'd say they've been bent these thirty years already."

She took off her glasses to smile.

"We have too much power. We are feared; it breeds hatred. A moment's pettishness, irritability, inattention even, one will pay for dearly. Never to show fatigue or boredom, never to show either sympathy or antipathy. To conquer nausea – worse, to conquer indifference. In their eye, their little affair is so very urgent, so supremely important. To be alert for that tiny whisper promising advantage or influence. To handle a journalist as though it were a snake – over-timid, they loathe that and get itchy, but squeeze them roughly, they'll bite. Lawyers; if anything, worse still. The men seek to intimidate and the women to humiliate ... You'd like this fucking job?"

It came at the right moment and he laughed.

Outside her door, in handcuffs, a cop on the bench alongside, was 'the lout'. Looking as dense as ever but the sight sent a shudder. Electric currents ran through legs and arms and a gripe settled in Castang's gut. This . . . one must say man has been 'extracted'. Madame le Juge spoke of nausea and of indifference. She will have a number of simple techniques in between witnesses – I have used them myself. To clasp the hands behind the neck; stretch and turn, matching your breathing. You go for a pee and you wash your hands. Vera used to say, 'Read a page of a poem'. He had only to stop and stand for a moment, to refuse to run away.

The man looked up hopefully.

"Not got a fag about you, mate?" The horrifying thing was that he was looking at Castang without the slightest sign of recognition.

He fished in his pocket, took one and settled it in the corner of his own mouth, threw the pack to where it was caught, unhandily, since attached to the cop by a length of chain.

"Thanks chief." Castang found a lighter in his trouser pocket.

"'Whatever's the matter with Mary Jane? She isn't ill and she hasn't a pain'," asked Lydia.

"Something simple," her mother answered. "But being French he makes it complicated."

"He always says he isn't really French."

"That's just it; he doesn't know. Simpler for me. Czech – Stalinist."

"So being simple what do you say?"

"I think I say three close friends in a row come to a bad end and he'd somehow made matters worse."

"But that's ridiculous."

"It's tied up with being a cop for too long and wanting to get out of it and he thinks making a poor job."

"What utter balls." At her age everything seems clear-cut, but Vera was still glad to hear her say so.

"At your age I was very silly. I caused a great deal of trouble, and my parents a lot of unnecessary pain. He's been paying for this ever since. He took the responsibility for my foolishness and it was a big handicap in his career. He doesn't complain, saddled all these years with the stupid Czech cow."

"This also is utter balls."

"Utter ovaries you mean," Vera is always supposed to have 'no sense of humour'; one is never quite sure about this.

"You had some corners knocked off you in France. I lost a few in New York. Are you doing the supper?" Face-savingly, since Vera has her apron on. "I'm going to talk to him, where is he?"

"Sulking in the music room. *Kindertotenlieder* or whatever, he does wallow rather. Fetch him a drink, show him your new frock."

Not Mahler. Lenny Goodman Quartet.

"I hate Gene Krupa," said Lydia. "Self-advertiser."

"Hey," showing a willingness to be interrupted, "that was my present." A single malt 'off the plane'. "You're supposed to be addicted to the salty dogs and the silver bullets."

"Wouldn't have brought it if I didn't like it."

"You're oddly like me. Odd's not the right word."

"I'd find it odder if I wasn't. Listen, you worry me. I was prepared to find Ma badly dented by this experience, and she's being resilient about it. Whereas you've been handling things like this since forever."

"The woman meant a lot to me."

"I know."

"Your mother . . ."

"She knows. We aren't being angelical. If there's a road accident I close my eyes and hurry past. Other things one looks at when one has to."

"I wasn't sleeping with her."

"She knows that too. She can tell, you know. Damn, I'm conjugating this verb. *Conocer, saber.*"

"I didn't know you knew any Spanish – now I've slipped on the same banana."

"Don't tell me about her. Tell me about you."

Castang topped up the drinks. Their shared northern blood – Vera doesn't like the flavour. An Islay, tasting of seaweed and iodine . . .

"I've got abraded, I suppose. One thinks oneself hard stone. Rubbed down, over the years, by the grinding. Polished. Whereas suddenly, one is badly eroded. I had a thing once with rare stamps. Man showed me. Screened, if they've been restored patches show. Thins, they're called. Under a strong light, bits of me have worn thin."

Lydia sat staring at nothing. Her imagination, too, is like mine.

"You've become nice. You're no longer sarcastic towards me." She took a good pull at her Scotch. "Odd language, American. They freshen their drinks and then they sip them. Munching meanwhile on a sandwich."

"What d'you want, them to talk Sioux? Don't be so Europeanly snobbish." She came suddenly and gave him a big kiss. "We'll fix you up. Like in the Brel song, take you to the bordel, *la mère Françoise* has some new girls in."

"Your mother . . ." laughing.

Vera put her head in and said, "Supper's ready. God, stinks in here, somebody open a few windows."

A month or so passed. This seemed to be necessary, to clear up sticky bits left in the office. There was also the long discussion about the house, with people who deal in property. Palavers; it could be sold, and still leave a lot of money after the mortgage was paid off. Yes, erm, and no, and maybe: 'Norman answers'. He went on feeling Mary-Jane, refusing to eat her pudding. Bored. Couldn't get interested. Needed a holiday and didn't want it.

"I have an idea," said Vera. "The tourist season's over and I'd like to go to the seaside."

"Uh."

"I want to go to the Golfe de Gascogne."

"And get shot at by Spanish fishermen."

"You've always liked Biarritz – old haunt of yours."

"And with too many nasty memories."

"It's time you settled your ghosts. It's a very good idea. You can be massaged under water by delicious girls. Thalassotherapy."

"Oh god" and in the same moment he thought how nice this would be.

No question, one was eroded. Lydia, who had disappeared – 'gone after a job' – had been right. "Once I went to the desert. They have balancing rocks. A pillar, and sometimes the stone below is softer, erodes faster. The one on top sits there, balanced on a point. But sooner or later, it topples." Not only in Arizona.

There were bad omens, driving across France. At the frontier, already, Vera shivered. Why?

"I no longer like it. I no longer feel safe. No rule of law, here. A government which does as it pleases." After all these years, with a husband a police officer ... Castang fell into a subdued silence. For a lifetime he has laughed at the euphemisms. These are far worse than any American puritanism of calling the lavatory the bathroom. The French world, in which the greatest thieves are 'indiscreet', the oldest whore is 'charming company' and a violent child-rapist 'an indelicate individual'. These people can no longer see realities. They stopped for the night in Beaune, where one eats and drinks so well. The television was showing the weather forecast, and the girl was talking about an abundant nebulosity. What the fuck does she mean – is that mist? Once he had been off duty with pneumonia. A service note handed to his superior stated that 'This officer is suffering from an infectious state of bronchial origin'. Richard had been sarcastic for a week. Does the whole world then talk like this now? He cheered up only next day when an autoroute exit near Sète pointed directions towards Poussan, Gigean and Bouzigues: this was so plainly a firm of Funeral Directors. Or conceivably, thought Vera, crooked notaries.

"Indelicate notaries," corrected Castang. "Just as the Cannes Film Festival always reminds one of Eskimo Nell. 'Forty whores tore down their drawers at Deadeye Dick's command.'" But even a French autoroute will reach an end and one will think of strolling by the seaside. Panama hat, parasol; it's an Edwardian little town.

Strolling forsooth! Castang aghast. What has happened to this place? Cars parked end to end and nowhere to put his own and will you kindly look at these building sites. Drinking tea on a terrace; formerly placid; fuming. Vera if anything amused by this nostalgia peculiar to those in middle age, imprudent enough to revisit the scenes of youthful enjoyment. Still much vexed – "But what is it, a mere ten years since I was here last!"

A simple enough fact: over the last ten years the number of cars in Europe has doubled. This is a very small town and couldn't be anything else because there's no room: seaward you are stuck between two rocky promontories and landward you climb a steep hill. If the municipal authority of a hundred such seaside resorts has not had the courage to ban cars altogether, this is the result: vile, noisy, and smelly turmoil, putting everyone in a bad temper. Courage, rather than forethought, since shopkeepers are both influential voters and the last to realise the benefits of making people walk.

Vera returning unperturbed from fact-finding, says she'll drive if he'll steer, and in the car, all unstressed calm, begins to sing, goddammit. Her choice of lyric on these occasions is always instructive.

Have I seen her since then?
Only now and agen,
As together they ride
Side by side
Down the Old Spanish Trail!

But probably this was dictated by obscure subliminal instincts, and nowise done on purpose.

Next morning was the loveliest sort of late-summer day. They were having breakfast on a terrace with sea in sight, on the uncrowded, unfashionable and inexpensive southern side of the town which Vera is already calling 'the dorp'. The old Spanish trail is just outside the door and Thalassotherapy across the road.

"You see? You had only to have faith."

She has addresses of several flats to be hired because the tourists have all gone home. Her suggestion is that he should go and get Thalassa organised while she does the logistics of supply. He would like to pick quarrels but cannot think of any convincing objection.

"And then we'll go and eat fish. How far is Saint-Jean-de-Luz?"

"From here? Twenty minutes down the road."

"Hendaye?"

"Say thirty."

"And Spain? San Sebastian?"

"Make it forty-five."

"So who has to stay here hotly cursing?"

"I must give a phone-call to old Richard."

"I was wondering when you'd think of that."

Richard, ex- (several years more ex- than himself) had been for many years his Divisional Commissaire in the Police Judiciaire. The younger, energetic Castang (it had been a dozen years and more) had learned much. The older man – he had known Vichy come and go – had taught him more; more unusually taken a liking to and even a fondness for his over-hasty and accident-prone subordinate; a fondness extending to the timid, worried young Czech woman. He'd had a Spanish wife: Judith had also been friends with Vera. She was dead now, and Richard was an old man who, when retired, went to live in Biarritz and play golf. They had no news of him – never been one for Christmas cards . . .

By lunchtime (over the fish) they had both quite encouraging matters to report. Vera, a furnished flat, to be sure a dog like all such: as with hired cars, you look with some care at everything likely to be broken for which you might get blamed later; the place is filthy and this peculiar smell . . . Agent with a fixed, pained and patient expression, exasperated by the foibles of this ghastly woman but in need of the business. "All right once I had the windows open for ten minutes and on condition of a gallon of disinfectant. So I bargained rather shrewdly over the price. How about you?"

"I saw a doctor; young, rather pretty, some good Victorian jewellery. This was quite pleasurable, nothing wrong with the heart, blood pressure a bit high. These treatments are altogether apposite and the tired businessmen come down in flocks. No naked girls alas, one-piece black bathing-suits of austere East German design and any elderly satyrs would get karate-chopped pronto. I will be taken to pieces and reassembled, a fortnight will be right, she says any longer is self-defeating."

Monsieur Richard appeared to have changed both address and phone number. Castang looked in the book; there wouldn't be that many of them. 'Richard A.' seemed to be some way out, towards Ciboure; the voice when he got it was right. Expressed pleasure. Come up for a drink. Can you find the way or will I give you directions?

This was a change. 'Way's impossible to find but you're supposed to be a cop, or so I have been led to believe,' would have been more like it. But we are all getting older.

"You go," said Vera coming out of the bathroom. "I've

been washing my hair." Well, yes. It is possible that old friends have become a bore. Worse, they might decide that you have become a bore.

Even with the map this was by no means clear. A wooded, canyony part of the world. The coast goes up and down as well as in and out. Where it is flat there will be a bit of beach, a village now sprawling out in housing allotments, straggling as far as the main road. Where it climbs into headlands, pines and gorse bushes. Very suitable, these contours, to the design and construction of yet another golf club. In former times the successful butcher, enterprise de Pompes Funèbres (Poussan, Gigean and Bouzigues) had built himself a Hatter's Castle on these heights; an Estate around a rambling ramshackle *palazzo* in the Spanish-gothic-renaissance manner of the Third Republic: Eugénie by then mourning her only son lost in Zululand, the black-draped widow much sympathised with by the other Widow at Windsor. Some of these incredible castles still survive, in and around Biarritz. Others have passed into the claws of the Speculators.

Deals were done on these pieces of barren land. One could carve out a patch, build oneself a bungalow, arrange oneself with the relevant Authority. Electricity cable. Phone line. Services would eventually follow. A few people established in the enclave – and most of them rich – and a dirt road would get exchanged for asphalt, street lights would appear, and the wagon would come out to empty dustbins.

Richard had been an admired specialist of much delicacy and expertise in the world of the power structures. Office chums; he was on *tu* and *toi* terms with the chef-de-cabinet in any municipal, ministerial or prefectorial grouping. A divisional commissaire in the Police Judiciaire is no big wheel in the departmental or regional world. He has not been to one of the grand schools whose mere membership will put you on terms of equality with anyone, and all over France. His circle of influence is limited and his social standing low. Police! people think. Brutish, unintelligent and quicker with the gun than the sensitive finger; further coarsened by the rubbing-up against the Unwashed. Even if you want your daughter taken off a drugs charge, a dangerous driving ticket lifted for your son-in-law, there are better addresses. The people Richard had been to school with were all in secondary, anonymous, grey functions, but they all knew how to retard or accelerate a piece of paper; get it to the top of the pile or lose it altogether. As for the Rich, they were all cronies of his at the golf club, and if he wanted something for peppercorns like a good discount from the builder he'd know where to look.

Corrupt? It was a question Castang would not have been able to answer since he had never put it. In any conventional sense, then no. Richard neither gave nor took bribes, and no money of obscure provenance or uncertain attribution had ever stuck to his fingers which were long, well-shaped. Called by colleagues 'Athos' for the elegance and languor, refusal of chaffering and hatred of any hard work. Gun? – he hadn't touched one since the Liberation. The cigars were cheap Brazilians but you'd take them for Havanas; the suits were off the peg but looked thousand-dollar.

But traffic of influence? One would have to say yes. He knew too many secrets. He would never need to threaten blackmail.

Under the polished and long-toughened exterior was a generosity and a kindliness Castang could call very readily to mind. To Vera he had said, 'You make me wish I had a daughter.'

It took some searching for; a narrow road newly laid. A lot of trees; the enclosures of large gardens and glimpses of some lavish houses; luxuriant shrubberies sheltered by the cliff from fierce sea winds. At a crossing he got out to ask, of a girl walking a dog. The last bit of road was still dirt: at the end was a house, new but looking neglected. The gate was harsh with fresh rust; the garden had a forlorn, overgrown look. This wasn't like Richard at all. Nor was the tottery old man who appeared on the steps.

"Heard the car. Not many come up this far." The voice was authentic and there were traces of a formidable personality. "Good to see you," putting both his hands on Castang's shoulders. "Place is a shithouse. Not going to apologise. Judith's dead, you know. Here by myself. Do nothing much. People come and clean, tidy up, make a meal, not that I care. Sit if you don't mind where you're sitting. Where's Vera?"

"Washed her hair and felt tired. Tomorrow maybe – we're here for a couple of weeks."

"I've some wine left. They won't let me drink it, piddling on about hepatitis, a cancer's what it is but it doesn't interest me. 'Hound, d'you want to live forever?'" and timed the pop of the cork for emphasis, with the old exactitude. "Here, find a good home for this then." A Bordeaux of an excellent year, a name that snapped like a banner in the wind, we mustn't let the Brits get away with it all.

"Pain?"

"Not to speak of. I think about the heroin trade, and of the poor buggers too who say they could do with a shot of morphia, please. Don't get it, given the hide-my-eyes mentality of this our fine country." Correct; '*la nébulosité abondante.*' Castang isn't asking how long have you got; that's always a silly question. Not very long by the look. It does cross his mind that 'Every time I see a friend of mine he's dead.' "So have you come to straighten out the fishing industry? The Baja de Viscaja out here, I look forth" – he has a fine view! – "and listen for the sounds of cannon."

"I've no business at all, I'm retired. I've swallowed a lot of dust lately, Vera thought the sea water cure would help. I liked the idea – here's where I got into trouble with the Ministry, and the sack on that account. Place holds a meaning for me."

Richard's laugh was now a dry cackle.

"I had something to do with that, getting you sent to Bruce. Your *sous-chef* there in Paris, we were at school together."

"It was a good idea. I've enjoyed it there, with the Communauté. Nice job and well paid. But in the long run, too many gnomes."

"Gnomes." The drawn yellowed face was relishing the word.

"Little men in red caps sitting on mushrooms, don't believe it. Digging tunnels, yes. Hi-ho, hi-ho, 'tis off to Frankfurt we go. Tunnel, under the stock exchange. Wheelbarrow yes, for bringing home the poppy."

"Syndicate in Lloyds," said Richard. "Dwarf there with the fishing-rod, used to be my fag at school."

"Syndicate in Biarritz," corrected Castang. "Dwarf with the lantern, old mate, the good old days in Indochina. Smoking opium with Graham Greene." At last, a real, full-hearted laugh.

Castang finished the bottle.

"Not got any Bourgogne, up to this class?"

"I have."

"I'll be back tomorrow."

"I see," said Vera.

"Obstinacy? A lonely dignity. Won't let them take him off to hospitals. Quite right, can you see him sitting there with the other deadies, allowed to look at football, teenage soap operas at the happy hour, jolly nurses saying eat up your nice yoghurt?"

"No. I won't let it happen to you either. When are you going for your session?"

"It's less busy in the afternoons. He takes a siesta then."

"I really have very little to do," looking round the hard impersonal little living-room. There were already what he called her pieces of paper – cheap stuff bought in rolls

for economy, cut off with kitchen scissors and pinned to a
piece of plywood, a dozen at a time; torn off and pushed in
the shoulder bag, when not torn up on the spot. She sits in
sheltered corners, 'looks at clouds'. When the boys come
out to practise on their surfboards she draws them.

At the end of Richard's plot of ground was the cliff; a
patch of rough grass and gorse. He had brought out a
deckchair to enjoy a lovely evening of late September;
the stars coming out, the lighthouses beginning to wink.
A windbreak had been planted, 'shitty tamarisks', but the
sightlines were uninterrupted.

"Wow," said Vera, coming up behind, bending to kiss.
"Spain!"

"Yes, past Fontarrabia. Down there on the left is Saint-
Jean. Then the point, that's Hendaye harbour. Can't see
the estuary from here. Mercifully, bloody Biarritz neither.
So no dwarfs. You see? – not a bad buy, this house."

"And I thought of doing some housekeeping."

"Don't bother," said Richard comfortably. "A path from
my bed to the door I keep clear and the rest I don't even
look at. I stay out here, all I can. Send messages in code,
to the fish-boats. The Spaniards will slit, gut and backbone
you while you're screaming to Brussels for help."

"Terrible goings-on too in the Gulf of Finland," agreed
Vera.

She fell into the habit of an hour with the broom and
the duster, then sitting with him. He liked to talk, but tired
easily. When Castang bought some roof slats, constructed
a makeshift easel, she stretched a canvas and began to
paint; one of her 'better efforts'.

One day she managed to buttonhole the doctor on his
round, outside in his car. ('Big BMW – what else?')

"He won't say, of course, meaning he doesn't know.
Some dwarf mutter, about if-we-had-him-in-the-clinic. It
could be six months, but he admits it could be tomorrow."

Thalassotherapy had finished, and Castang a new man.
But Vera refused to go home.

"This flat's not costing much. Out of season, and I can get a good discount if I prolong. I'm not leaving him to die alone." Judith had been childless. One can adopt children, beset though this is in France with legal difficulties, but 'one hadn't'. A mistake? 'One's life was full of irrecoverable mistakes,' said Richard. 'From the police standpoint, nothing but one judicial error after another. It wasn't so much the making mistakes that was the worry; it was the covering them up after and pretending they hadn't happened.' Castang, forever reproached with the great-mistake of marrying that little Czech girl, agreed.

What would happen anyhow, thus, happened both soon and casually, quite as though Richard had decided to save everyone trouble while keeping to the end in character. He was on the kitchen floor, holding a potato-peeler. The gas turned out; trust him to see to it that there should be no dramas. Vera was much more taken aback by what was to follow.

Castang saw to things. As a police officer he had 'seen to' a few hundred deaths, and in every imaginable circumstance. Municipal bureaucrats have simple wants; that everything should be tidy. Richard would have agreed with Julien Sorel, who made sure that his own death, guillotined, should be 'without affectation'. With the municipal police he saw to the Protection of Property, the locking and shuttering. On the chimney-piece was an envelope addressed to himself in that small and squiggly but oddly readable handwriting.

"Been ill for some time?" asked the cop. "Knew it was mortal? Not a suicide note? Took some pills maybe, huh?"

"It's conceivable. Liked to stay in charge. It has no importance to you, right?"

"Doctor said natural and that's good enough for me."

"I knew him well, and I'd quite expect him to see it coming."

"I'd better look." A short note, and an envelope addressed to Vera.

Dear Henri,
In the bottom drawer of the bureau is some paperwork, a quantity of information about gnomes which will probably be of no interest but may serve an eventual purpose. The notary, aptly named Dieudonné, may be of help. I should recommend prudence, which has never been your outstanding characteristic.

Yours
Adrien R.

In the desk was a folder sealed with tape and his name written on it. The police officer shrugged, and he took it with him.

The other note was of the same succinct but faintly mystifying nature.

Dear Vera,
What is the reward of virtue? My own experience has been that both concepts are ambiguous. However, I feel confidence in your judgment. If there are unforeseen consequences, or should Henri make an ass of himself, which is probable, there is in Pau an advocate named Bastien, may be relied upon.

Most affectionately yours
Adrien R.

"What does this mean?"

"I have no idea. One of his obscure jokes. I was rather looking forward to going home. Not heartless to suggest that cremation is quite a rapid business. Or is that making an ass of myself?" A bit plaintive, and just a little ruffled. Prudence being a virtue; virtue being its own reward. Or so they say.

"I don't say stay. But surely long enough to see this notary, who 'may be of help'."

"Who rarely are, but who always cost a lot of money. There – don't cry."

"He made an end," wiping the trickle, "because he didn't want to keep us hanging about."

"Look – I'll go and ring him up, the aptly-named." Impatience is explainable: the agent had rung up from Bruce to say he had a good buyer for the house. More notaries ... Castang acidulous; air-tickets are expensive. In short, a quarrel, and what is now this further nonsense?

There was an obstructive secretary, vague about appointments in anything under six weeks. He had to make rather a thing of his urgent business affairs in Brussels. Some throat-clearing, before it was decided that they could be fitted in. At some inconvenience to Maître. Castang didn't think him much of a God-Sent. Forced to contain himself, because of a silent and tearful Vera.

A large beautiful house, subsuming a large and beautiful garden. Both were redolent of that very quiet prosperity which likes to be in good taste when this will help underline the message: that not all the wealth is Ill Gotten. One could feel certain that the car when visible would be a twelve-cylinder Jaguar. The secretary, a tall pale blonde upright behind much grey office machinery as silent as the house, nodded curtly. The waiting-room pictures were reproductions of well-known impressionists, in expensive frames – 'Inondation de la Seine à Marly' – an impression here that somebody had done rather well out of it; like a notary.

The private cabinet was confidential; oak panelling and that buttoned leather padding on the doors which distinguishes the higher *échelon* in France, of the legal and medical professions. As is said of Jaguars, the loudest noise is the clock; a fine English grandfather. As for Maître

– rolypoly, overshaved, jovial; gold-rimmed glasses and a manner so polished you skated off it.

"These instructions are quite recent. I was in fact able to have the necessary papers drawn for his signature only a few days ago. I have no comment to make. His death was foreseen and I've had a word with his medical advisor: there will be no doubt upon clarity of mind or firmness of intention.

"There are a number of legal requirements – the State, erm; various taxes and penalties, succession rights and erm, diverse deductions. To make it brief, yourself, Madame, are named as sole heir and assign of Monsieur Richard's properties mobile and immobile. Roughly speaking the house and contents, I'll have to examine and draw up in proper form, mm. The bank, erm, if you'll permit I'll abbreviate the detail of the fiscal authority's demands – we manage as a rule to reach amicable agreement – in a nutshell, Madame, there are no outstanding debts, mortgages, encumbrances; you could feel quite comfortable. Hardly substantial but if you chose to sell it might be called appreciable."

"Can I refuse?" Vera in a perplexity. He gave her the indulgent smile with which one encourages a backward child at its sums.

"You can. If I might ask, dear Madame, what would be the point? There is no contestant; it will not be disputed; Monsieur Richard was without family. We have only the State to satisfy. Penalties attach but erm, we'll manage. Regarding this deed of gift there's erm, an unpaid account which I must render to you, of stamp duties, my own honorarium, trivial, trivial.

"No doubt it all comes as a surprise, you'll wish to think matters over, I shall be happy to give such guidance erm, effect such instructions as you may see fit," accompanying them with every courtesy to the door, the front door, the step . . . "Your servant Madame; a pleasure, Monsieur . . ."

"Then they take two per cent of the gross," muttered Castang, "telling you you're bloody lucky the State's only taken thirty, and it's all trivial-erm-trivial, we might just avoid getting sold up by the bailiff."

"Shut up; I'm thinking."

One did see about prudence, and making-an-ass-of-myself. Richard's humour had not been of the exploding-cigar school (though if dim-witted subordinates were thereby to be jolted out of lethargy ...) – still, as a surprise it was efficient, and if kindness, gratitude played their part, one had to admit, entirely in character.

"I think I'd like to keep this house," after wheels had gone round in silence.

"Cars in Spain are thirty per cent cheaper," in an attempt at frivolity. "It's certainly a nice house."

"And it's mine. I've never had anything before." This was true.

"And when you come to see how the law works, a woman finds she's a non-existent nobody." And this, also, was true. Castang wondered whether he should suggest a bottle of champagne even if there's nothing for lunch but a tuna sandwich.

"Well," getting glasses, "one sits down and thinks about it. Draw up a list, pro and contra. First thing which occurs, this is Plouc-Land here. We're accustomed to a metropolitan area, a cosmopolitan world. Think of theatres, concerts. This is a backwoods village, the other end of nowhere, seven golf-courses; we retire, yes, and How Far? As against that, right, yes, the seaside. Sunny, wonderful climate, pretty view, nice gardens. Pay the colossal death-duties and the rest is free; maybe."

"It's mine," said Vera.

Looking round the horrible little tourist flat, Castang thought yes it Was a nice house. They'd made up their minds to sell, in Bruce, and they had a buyer. One could bank all they would get and not have to worry. This house was the right size. He could see, all right. Vera was only forty-seven; a life in front of her. But what am I to do? Garden, and play golf?

"I'm not going to try and influence you either way," he said.

"What I think," said Vera putting sweet peppers under the grill, "is invest in it, a bit. We clean it right out and repaint, say. Live in it a while, say a year. One will have seen by then the for and against. Can't see us losing if we decide to sell, then, or rent, even. Where do we want to live? Paris? – no! Berlin? Prague?" She's being 'rhetorical' but he gets the point.

Lydia, complaining at the vast expense but asqueak with excitement, flew down for the weekend and was contagious with enthusiasm.

"If I come and read aloud to kindly-disposed old gentlemen do I get a lollipop too? Have to gratify their senile lusts first, no doubt. I say, you could be really snug by Christmas. I'll come down for a holiday next year, seeing it's all free."

Castang would remember it as a time of youth rediscovered, innocence made fresh – the cottage, when he had been a young and underpaid police inspector, and the serious-crimes squad had remade all the plumbing with materials most of which had been stolen, rewired the electricity, retiled the roof: a time when Vera still walked with difficulty and the two little girls got under everyone's feet. Housepainters' colours are of an alarming chemical crudity and Vera blended, while telling Castang to get out from under her feet; he spent refreshing hours in the garden, and intoxicated himself with plant catalogues. A fortnight of the most extraordinary domesticity. If this were retirement it was something lapped in peace and placidity he should have known to be false; unreal and treacherous.

In Biarritz a whole row of balconies fell off a desirable residence with a loud noise and a great cloud of dust.

Mercifully nobody was hurt, for even in the street it was too early on a Sunday morning for anyone to be about, so that he thought this merely funny. The management issued a flustered press statement; there might have been a slight miscalculation somewhere but nothing Structural; no no no no. One laughed heartily but this, too, was not seen as a warning. These blocks, of gross concept and grotesque prices, looking like monstrous vanilla ice-creams, have everywhere been run up in the place of houses mostly ugly, but at worst human in scale. Nobody has been deterred from pressing on with the 'remodelling' of the little town. Between the lighthouse and the Virgin, rocky point where the old fishing village stood, the central beachfront has been ripped out. A great many dwarfs have made a great deal of money out of this despoliation.

To be sure, Castang was used to it. It has happened to the whole of the immense coastline of France. There are 'towns' made out of nothing, where concrete has been squeezed like toothpaste along five miles of sandy beach, where in winter a few hundred souls live in dispirited dolour, but in July and August a hundred thousand naked bodies can be smelt frying. On the south coast it has gone on since his childhood. Quite recently it has been thought that a stop should be set. One or two Mayors have even been jailed; Stalin-size concrete dwarfs prevented just in time from erecting statues of themselves on the seafront.

But Biarritz . . . he had been sentimentally fond of the ridiculous Edwardian toytown, bastard child of the Empress Eugénie and the railway age. Odds and ends of police enquiry had brought him here three or four times, and he had exaggerated existing pretexts, invented imaginary ones. He had eaten extravagantly in the Café de Paris, drunk beer in phony English pubs, enjoyed the tweedy tailors and bogus Georgian antiques which kept still the flavour of the twenties, of Noël Coward in a Sulka dressing-gown and Westminster in yachting gear; Lalique glass and Asprey cocktail-shakers and the art-déco casino and 'I once had an aunt who went to Tasmania'. And the real too; the golfing colonels and the pederast beachboys, and above all the people, the Basques who scratched a living on a stormy coast. To the official eye shockingly, he felt indulgence – not much for terrorists, who assassinate, but for the little people who gave them shelter. Now that he found himself embedded in the villages – Bidart and Ciboure, perfect hotbeds of disaffection towards the Republic – he also found himself delightfully recalcitrant towards officialdom; his erstwhile masters . . .

One would shop in the dignified old town of Bayonne; one would go for fish to the market of Saint-Jean. One doesn't have to bother – he said – with the vileness of the new, the dwarf Biarritz. From their clifftop, it isn't even visible.

On a morning in early winter, mild and sunny with a little sea-fret of pearl and opal haze now lifting off, Castang was in the garden with a beer. Judith had been serious, nigh-professional in her gardening, but this had not been her house. Richard had made barely a dabble, not even very interested. One had to start afresh and practically from scratch. It was nicer thinking about this with a beer than getting one's shirt off and digging. There was a ring at the gate and he walked slowly down towards it. Richard had got that much right; the nosy-parkers didn't get past it. A car was parked on the sandy weedy verge of the dirt road; expensive V-6 model. Looking at that first was one of those old ingrown cop patterns. The man would have been taken aback to learn he'd got a bad mark before he'd even got his mouth open. Cars in France are still expressions of the macho personality.

"Is it Monsieur Castang?" Castaing they all say in the south.

"It is."

"Bonjour, it's Leclerc, Estate Agents. Didn't bother to phone since I was around anyhow. Thinking of a business deal which would be up your street. Thought we'd talk."

"Up my street. Well. Say on." He hasn't opened the gate.

"Is there somewhere we could converse?"

"Je vous écoute." In French it has a more formal sound than 'I'm listening'.

"Private matter."

"But nobody's listening."

"You act as though I were selling insurance or something."

Castang used the weeding fork to scrape some mud off his boots.

"Perhaps you'd prefer to come down to the office – here's my card – and I could lay it out for you," with some merry laughter.

"Put it in writing," mildly.

The French hang notices on the gate saying 'Fierce Dog' and there are moments when he feels French. They live behind a great many bars, and keep guns there. They've been known to put up notices saying 'Boobytraps' and 'Warning – Explosives'! Since Jerry and Mathilde, has he become frightened? Police experience had long ago told him that housebreakers can get in anywhere. One can still dislike the importunate and the intrusive. The French bristle, like their dogs.

No, plain wariness rather than paranoia; followed by curiosity. A letter appeared; long envelope, good quality, pale green. Within, a letterhead, pictures of desirable residences – dark green. Laying it on thick; the French will always prefer a ladleful of polished verbiage to a spoonful of fact, but this was more than fishing. Who was the fisherman? Why? Smelling all this tasty bait, an ex-cop looks for a hook, so that he went to see. Hm, a nice office in a courtyard containing Leclerc's nice big car and a nice Japanese four-four and the secretary's nice little car

... Her voice was warm with the certainty of Monsieur's inexpressible delight at seeing him. Monsieur had on a creamy suit, linen-finish like his writing paper, and dear god a double-breasted waistcoat, and the office had a padded door to rival notaries. This was the flossy end of the house agency business. Terribly pally, and highly confidential.

Well you see, there was a client, and he'd been looking for a clifftop house, which y'know has become a rarity, and he'd taken such a fancy to Monsieur Castang's nice little property there, and the offer was really one that nobody could refuse because whatever the market would bear he'd ackshally slap another ten per cent over and above.

Castang said no, of course. As would any businessman, but the cop was thinking that the gaudier the bait the more barbed the hook.

No but listen, ssshh, the client had been wishful of doing business with Monsieur Richard recently so sadly deceased, and now that Monsieur Castang had come into this property, look, about capital-gains-tax, this can you know be arranged *sub rosa*, bank in Luxembourg, what, even Swiss francs if he'd prefer.

No need to drag Vera into this, and never mind the hook even, for if they offer this big a bribe the deal has to be fraudulent since they're confident of one swallowing it on sheer greed ...

No.

But what could possibly cause you to hesitate? Don't think now of holding out for more since while an extremely generous man the client ... while ready to pay for a caprice ...

"I dare say," said Castang, "that we have all our own kinds of caprice. Mine is that this house belonged to an old friend and I'm keeping it."

"A word for your ear – it would be a mistake, you know. I don't say that for myself ... just give me one moment – do you mind my asking your former profession?"

"Administration," smiling a little. They'd linked him with Richard!

"I have this impression, forgive me, you're telling me that the finance aspect isn't the only ... I wonder if I should say this. The client might be obstinate too. Used to getting their own way, y'know. Come – a small adjustment shan't part us."

"I don't want the matter pursued. You'd be wasting your time."

"Obstinacy, cher Monsieur" being sorrowful about it.

Outside, he couldn't help wondering whether one shouldn't ... Two good property windfalls, never again would one have worries. Richard had known about this before his death. He used to say, 'I only know one thing. Once bent, a cop stays bent. And I can smell them out.' The old boy was himself a past master at keeping people guessing. Corruption is mm, a state of mind. No cop could ever say he's never done favours, nor had them done him. But you don't cross the line.

Himself, he had been undone by politics. Who had ever given corruption a moment's thought? The '*bustarella*' as the Italians called the little-envelope; the '*tangenti*' – ourselves we call them the pot-of-wine. Little joke-words, nursery-words. Throughout Europe, the domino-effect had been identical. We were and are rotted, every last one of us. Oh, 'technically' I stayed straight, and who have I to thank for that? A woman of unusually strong character and nakedly simplistic morals. If I were to say to Vera that her little house turns out to be a juicy deal she'll stare at me with her eyes gone blank, and she'll simply say 'No'.

Castang had not pitied himself much at seeing his career cut short by a petty piece of political infighting. One couldn't begin to count colleagues pushed sideways by a word dropped in the corridors of the Ministry.

Simply, one thanked the Almighty for the unbent. Not

only Vera! The scrupulous Monsieur Suarez in Brussels. Or Mathilde.

Vera was happy with her new house. What workman had ever dreamed of expecting a bribe? She made jokes and coffee, she brought them a beer and asked about their children. They ate out of her hand. It would never have occurred to her that a workman would need bribing to do his job as he should.

Now she wanted to give a party; the only small snag being that most of one's friends, remarked Castang, seem to live in Bruce. Not that sort of party (patiently): she'd only meant the family, for Christmas.

Laudable, but Lydia has disappeared again, 'said to have found' a new job in Paris 'with some Germans'. The Bertelsmann finger is in every imaginable pie and don't get into a fuss because that girl always falls on her feet. And Emma is in Berlin; that's rather a long way off.

Is this a problem? Not of communication; she writes letters, readable, even grammatical, which Lydia (illiterate And innumerate) never did. There's a phone, even if it does seem to be off the hook most of the time. But she's sounding oddly evasive, which isn't the girl we know. Vera wailing ever so slightly.

But what are the facts; let's be sensible. Emma has a Berliner boyfriend, name of Johannes and very nice; Castang has met him, if briefly.

"That's just the point; I haven't. Still haven't. So I wanted to ask them both for the end of the year, I wish to Know him."

"Are his parents a difficulty? Germans are strong on family parties at Christmas. Maybe she has to be Tactful."

"I asked about that. They aren't on good terms, and that's their choosing rather than his."

"Well, apart from anything else that plane is damned

expensive and they are poor." Jobs in the music world . . . especially in the former East-Bloc. Communist governments subsidised much cultural activity, and Bonn is very penny-pinching.

"We are rich. I said I'd pay. Emma had an idiotic tale of wanting to come by car if they came at all. John apparently saying he wanted to see something of France. As though one saw anything but desert."

"You're being obtuse; just send them a cheque. That's only John saying he refuses to tap us for handouts."

"I may be dim but I remember very well being poor. Didn't have any rich in-laws neither."

All that Castang had to do was pick the phone up. Vera doesn't use the thing properly. Her intense frugality means putting it down, feeling guilty about the bill ticking up. It is true that he belonged also to this generation. Richard used to say 'Stop that bloody gossiping' even when it was only with Toulouse. Monsieur Suarez tended to launch disciplinary economy drives. 'Every damned secretary coffee-housing with girlfriends in Geneva . . .' One had never really got accustomed to the phone being Singapore-next-door.

"Hallo Em. Your mother is in a slight stew. I can't grasp what's going on. The Volkswagen will take an eternity and work out as expensive as Lufthansa. Tell them it's my credit card and they can phone to confirm."

"Of course." Cool voice, sensible. "That isn't the problem at all."

"Is it John?"

"Not in the slightest. The problem's biological, I was keeping it as a surprise, but now that you ask, I've a small baby which creates a vast heap of junk, and the Volkswagen copes with this better than Lufthansa, that's all." Castang has burst out laughing.

"Won't Granny be pleased!" Vera both pleased and furious doesn't know whether to laugh or cry and is doing both. It will be a family party after all. If that's what they'll enjoy, let them come by bicycle. "I'm passing you Ma, before she explodes." Vera merely vexed with herself, on account of tears.

Two

John was pushing the pram, through the old streets of Biarritz; enjoying the job, fascinated by the scene. Wind blew his hair about and he pushed it back without thinking. This is a nuisance he is accustomed to but it bothers Emma. He would like a Basque beret, but hasn't quite dared yet.

Johannes Weber was called John by everyone because he was like that; direct, uncomplicated. Even physically the name suits him; nordically fair and straightforward handsome features: he is tall and well-muscled. As for 'Weber' it is a famous name in music, but in or around Germany it's very ordinary and even in France it arouses no comment. A straight nose that sticks out and burrows into a book or a score, and this hair which Emma complains about, which is straight, fair and won't obey rules. Whatever way you comb or part it a moment later it has flopped limply back, ragged and ungainly. Short or long it makes no difference, and he won't put stickum on it. Now suppose, says Emma, that one's ambitions were realised and John were to become a Dirigent. Conducting, he would look splendid in tails and a white tie, but that awful hair will tempt people to laugh. Since, he says peaceably, he has no occasion for getting up in public and waving a stick, what's the fuss about?

The streets go up and down steeply; all the more fun for him and the child both. One gives the pram (ramshackle thing) a shove. Count the beats until it pauses, runs back, and you catch it. Going down is trickier; he keeps his fingertips lightly on the bar, practises precise steering. These French pavements are narrow, awkward; horrible gutters, sharp dips and drops. One has already learned that dogshit is a universal hazard. It takes care and concentration. He is meticulous, in domestic detail as in music, and Emma likes him taking the baby out. He looks: it is peaceably asleep (likes all the bumping up and down), is well wrapped up but not too hot, isn't sucking its thumb. From Castang ('Henri') he has already learned a French cradle song, nice little melody—

> *Une chanson-ne douce-e*
> *Que m'a chanté ma maman,*
> *En suçant ma pouce-e . . .*

La la la la – descending thirds; a good *berceuse.*

Good place this, too: people, as one learns, a bit Spanish, more than a bit Basque, still extremely French. Amusing too; Henri grumbles, grousing about it being ruined; looks fine to him. Lot of wind today, draughty, be raining by this afternoon: who cares, we're on holiday. Hell of a long way from Berlin, never mind that, it's worth it. He had never – really – been outside Germany before. A childhood spent in the DDR – there weren't many places to go! Poland or Czechoslovakia, both looking exactly like East Germany and well, thanks a lot. Since being with Emma – poor – a four-day bus trip to Paris; far too much to see and no time to take anything in properly.

Emma had been very dubious about this enormous trip right across France but he'd over-persuaded her. Plenty of mileage left in the old Vau-way; quite a few marks went a long way in France (and Henri kept slipping him more: generous.) And now the Sea – the Atlantic Ocean, dammit – he'd never seen anything but the Baltic. Germans called any piddling piece of water a '*See*'. Vera (he likes her very much) made jokes about the Lipno lake, calling it the

Seacoast of Bohemia – he'd been there on a camping holiday as a nipper; DDR fresh-air-scheme.

For John thought in German, compound-words . . . He was learning some English and was glad of this opportunity to pick up some French words. Not easy to get his tongue around. Languages are important if one wants a career in music. He envied Emma, brought up in Bruxelles (easier to say Brussel) and who spoke English as easily as she did French.

There were worries about work but this was not the place for them. Once back home would be time enough to get one's teeth into that bone: there was just-that-little chance of the *répétiteur* job in Leipzig, but we have far too many people chasing too few jobs. Emma – her parents too, so unlike his own – understood, didn't go nagging-on-about-it. John crossed the road, easing the pram up and off the gutter. The child was dead-oh, all this fresh sea air.

He had seen a little shop; he was in a back street. He'd left the car on the seafront, up on the point, easy to find again. A bookshop, with some second-hand tat, some sheet music which had caught his eye; he peered, trying to make out the unfamiliar French titles. There was a board too, with small-ads written on cards. He can make some of it out – abbreviations – 'Mattress'. '*Poêle*', he knows this word, it means a frying-pan; what the hell is a *poêle-à-mazout?* He stood staring with his nose to the window, holding the bar of the pram against his back, jiggling it absently to give the child the impression of movement if it woke.

The word 'Piano' caught his eye – same in any language – but it was the Thing that interested him.

Not this – for sale in a back street would be some battered old Yam, sounding like a barrel-organ. Having one at all; John's dream; how can one live without? But sad news for the aspirant musician: getting one is hard enough and how did you live with it? As essential tools went this must be about the worst. Fitting it into a small room ... but first, through the streets, awkward, fragile, hideously heavy. In Berlin they lived up several flights of narrow stairs – but even if one had a lift ...

He had seen photographs of houses, tall, narrow, gabled; Hanseatic houses; beautiful things, seventeenth century. They were warehouses, they overlooked canals, their builders had thought of this problem; up in the gable is a sturdy support masoned in to the brickwork, with an arm, and a pulley ... John's imagination has whisked him into a golden fantasy of living in a house like that; in Amsterdam, Bremen ... do any of those houses survive in Rostock, in Stralsund?

Everyone understood that he passed out of this world, standing rigid, mesmerised; practically in a coma. This goes far beyond any notion of how much is that doggy-in-the-window. Metaphysically it is further than the distance between Biarritz and Bremen. The idea-piano had swallowed the central, the essential realities of professional and domestic existence. Who could possibly guess at how long this lasted? Sometimes it is only a fraction of a second. Putting a girdle round the earth in forty minutes would appear extremely striking to an audience in Shakespeare's time but we can bounce our voice off a satellite from here to Hawaii in less than a second, which is much more than it takes to be sitting on the beach eating the crackling off the roast pork.

The police, who lack imagination, said a minute or more, surely: people in the street; a car – there must have been a car. Castang remembered a smash-and-grab raid, when such were fashionable; they used to ram jewellers' windows with an old truck. All over in a flash, the eye-witnesses invariably said. Stuff and rubbish; they took their time, and now we're wasting our own.

Because John turned round, and the baby wasn't there.

Disbelief and disorientation are the early symptoms, appearing before panic. Textbook definitions of trauma are in any case arid; their authors have never been shot.

Castang – who has – knew more about that massive jolt to the nerve centres.

John thought, 'I'm in the wrong street.' This was 'the wrong pram'. The distrust of eye or touch was so great that he felt the nest of wrappings; it was warm and smelled of baby. Since he could trust nothing, not even gravity, he looked at the pavement: the child must have fallen out. One was hallucinating. True enough, and many a gothic tale suggested that one had heard the dreadful voice, felt the vampire breath, been brushed by the flying dagger – but there is no mark upon the snow.

Laboured breathing returned, and with it the pain of the bullet wound. Buildings and lamp posts had again their accustomed verticality. John thought he had been dreaming and it must be that he still was. This could not be real. A German monosyllable came heavily blonking into consciousness. '*Doch*!' There was no bullet wound, if still the sensation of a heavy flowerpot having fallen on one's head.

A page of prose and all of it meaningless. One can be reminded of the clerihew about the critic Jacques Derrida.

> There ain't no readah.
> There ain't no writer
> Eidah.

Start again, from where he saw the small-ad about the piano.

The baby is back in its pram.

No. It is not.

John accosted passers-by, in German. Nobody understood German. They looked at him withdrawingly. Drunk. Acid trip.

He could speak no French or Spanish. But he could not trust his own voice; there was an enormous roaring in his ear. Still, he could walk, to his own surprise. What was he to do?

'The *Polizei*' ... John scarcely gave them a thought. 'They don't speak German.' He knew perfectly well that they'd find someone who did, and pretty quick. But it would be quite difficult to find anyone of John's generation who has any confidence at all in the police, and this would hold good all over the world. He had himself a confused sentimental notion that the French police, while a brutal crowd and probably drunk, would still be a great deal to be preferred to the laddies in green with white hats. Emma has disabused him.

He did make a firm effort at collecting fragments of rationality. Take the pram, walk – stop breaking into a run, and stop talking to yourself. Take the car, drive carefully. Time is of no great consequence here; the thing is to be collected. This is the work of someone quite deranged. Be methodical in approaching the absurd. Memorise with exactitude: be factual, simple.

Castang – now there is a Professional.

But god, what was one to say to Emma? Everyone has already said it. That they are very young; that they are penniless and virtually jobless; that this baby is a great mistake; that an *Abtreibung* is virtually effortless, nigh painless. And Emma had set her teeth. No I won't. He'd said that too. What now?

'Darling I've managed to lose it. Doesn't matter; we can always start another.'

'Oh come on, darling, that's really foolish. Come On – aborting is nothing at all.' Odd – the word means something altogether different in German.

Castang had not said anything like this. Neither had Vera. John had been struck by that. He talked to his own parents as little as might be. Oh they hadn't Said. But a distinct impression that the baby should have been put out with the dustbins.

'Henri' – a name difficult to pronounce in the un-French mouth. Castang had grinned; would Enrique perhaps be easier? Bruxelles had been full of people saying Heinrich to tease him.

He was sitting peaceably reading the paper over a fourth cup of coffee.

"Quite right. Don't worry, I'm still a professional." The boy was shaking. For Monsieur le Commissaire Divisionnaire, it's exactly the same heavy flowerpot off a third-floor balcony, and one doesn't say it and one doesn't show it. One has to ask a few brief questions. This is the starting-point of an enquiry. The only difference is that one no longer has a Criminal Brigade.

"The girls are next door, having an extremely late breakfast. Tell them in just the same words; that you had a moment of inattention and Claire's been stolen; I should think the usual deranged female. That we're going straight away; I'm putting my shoes on." They'll know how to cope – women do it differently, that's all. A half-hour, was it? – that won't make any odds.

"Ready? I'll drive, shall I?" John had hold of himself. It was a comfort – yes, to them both – that Castang can speak some German. Sure, sloppy as to grammar, guesswork as to gender. But one isn't frozen.

In these last few – lovely – days he has thought that John, who lacks self-confidence, has been coming to feel trust in them. Certainly he feels trust in John. 'Our Em' – she's found a good man.'

"There are three sorts of police here. It's much the same as with you at home." Third gear and second even for a slow turn to be neat. The coast road; third-fourth-fifth. "The gendarmerie, everywhere outside town limits. You were in the town, so Municipal Police first. In our book, that's a half-trained bunch of slobs good for nothing but to run *clochards* off the beach, but out of tact we go there first. It's their territory you know; one must be polite. And they've a network after all. This will be some sad deprived unbalanced woman – hungry." And with all his heart he hoped that it might be so.

"Immediately upon that, the PJ – the Kripo. They'll make faces but you let me handle them. I still know a few passwords; it might even be someone I was at school with.

"That's in Bayonne, the Regional Service. Professional network there, not just hospitals and taxis, but the legal machinery. This is a very formal country, where one has to do things by the Book. The Procureur – that's the *Staatsanwalt.* We must mobilise this machine. Depositions – don't worry, I'll interpret for you. We need a judge – the *Untersuchungsrichter.*

"There are in fact four sorts, because there's also the political police." That is said – and thought – a little wryly. RG – the usual French euphemism and meaningless because it is supposed to be, and very suitable too, a secret service, had put an end to his own police career. "You have to know that anything and everything is political round here. Basque Liberation Front, some of their leading spirits have been picked off in recent months. Triumphant press release says they're decapitated, which encourages them to plant a bomb or two." This line in bright chat does help in lessening the stunned feeling. Castang was anxious to take out the drama.

He parked where it said Police Cars Only. The desk man was in no hurry to attend to public grievances. Castang said, "Come along son, wake up," in a friendly tone which was poorly received. "Who am I? I'm the Ost-See-Naked-Bathers-Verein. Not got all day," conversationally. He had an identity card with a tricolour stripe across it, which changed their tune, and when a cop bounced in shouting, "Whose car is that?" he was shushed. A superior was produced, a statement was made. John saw that getting-it-on-the-computer is the same as in German. He felt less helpless.

"I don't believe in the bullying tone," said Castang getting back into the car, "but they use it themselves and understand it. If they think it possible one might put in a word with Monsieur the Mayor, I don't know him but they don't know that, one will get things done that much quicker. That's crude. But they are crude. Vera doesn't agree. Believes in being polite and humble whatever the circumstances. The one is as good as the other, I suppose. Next port of call things will be different."

In Bayonne a quiet office, and glass partitions showing other quiet offices in which people got on with their affairs, all involving piles of paper. One of these quiet men got up to find out their business, looking them up and down with a shrewdish eye. It might have been a fiscal administration; he was in shirt-sleeves but wasn't wearing any guns. He and Castang conversed in low tones. It was not like a television series.

John would have to say that he took in nothing. It was not so much the language as being dazed, hurt, in pain. He had only known pain in a commonplace physical shape. Like – like the circulation coming back into one's hands, after they have been frozen. This was a new kind, a heartache. One is hearing this in all the major moments of music; oh you know, the funeral march in the third symphony, Otello saying '*Un bacio*' but one had never understood before. Right, one's experience was getting enlarged.

When, later, he came to look at the pleasant city of Bayonne he could have sworn he'd never been there. No recollection of where the PJ offices were. Vague idea of somewhere like an insurance company – that nobody wore any shoulder holsters did strike him. Of somebody listening to Castang with a closed, blank face but still attentive; of having his elbow jogged – "We're going upstairs to see Le Patron," and of another, pleasantly furnished office, another still man in early middle age; and of an armchair, comfortable, where he kept falling asleep and waking up with a start.

"Ach," said Castang, "bit of delayed shock, we'll pay no attention." The other agreed with a smile. "He's first class and I set a lot of store by him." Nod, the message received. This was work, but of a different sort. They had to size one another up.

The man's name was Martre: he did look a bit like a marten, a slim reddish-brown man with small penetrating eyes. Young for a Div; quite a bit younger than Castang. They didn't know each other; there was a moment of wondering whether they had met, and where. Hadn't been here long, and his first big post; would be keen to keep his hands clear of complications. And his arse likewise. Antennae were waving in a small breeze. He had a probable ghost of an idea that this might mean trouble. He knew his job, his office downstairs showed that. But was he just adroit, and a good technician? Both men were at work on finding out a little bit more.

"Bruxelles, that's interesting." He had Castang's old visiting card on his desk, the one that said '*Conseiller auprès de la Communauté*'. "Union they call it nowadays."

"Disunion more like. We got – get – some useful work under way. Slow job. I was detached on mission, remained on strength in Paris. Took retirement just a couple of months back." Nod. It would not have been good form to wonder aloud how much banishment had been involved.

"I hear about this Europol: one wonders what it amounts to."

"Won't amount to very much, not if Charley Pasqua has anything to say about it." No harm in that, since it is no secret that the Minister, at the head of all French police establishments, gets very heated about his national sovereignty.

"Intelligent man," suggested Martre. "Able."

"Oh yes, decidedly." Silence for a bar, a narrow little smile and – "Even a bit too much so for his own good?" So this wasn't one of the unquestioning faithful, and Castang could take a risk.

"Hasn't read enough history. Ought to remember what happened to Fouché, after Waterloo."

"Yes, perhaps, a bit too fond of manipulating anything and everybody."

"You feel interference?"

"Didn't you, there in Bruxelles?"

"Obliquely, yes. Understand me, I was only a technical advisor on stuff like Schengen or the Europol, but I was expected to sing the official song and there were long faces when I didn't. Little memos going back to Charley, all right. It was time I left. Fact; you can't be both French and European. Fundamental divergence."

"I understand. I get something of the same, in my dealings with the Spanish."

"Get up at six, and chant the '*Marseillaise*' while shaving. Make sure they can hear you."

"That's it," with another of those minute smiles. "Well, colleague, this little trouble of yours – give me a ring perhaps, in twenty-four hours."

"It's my grandchild," said Castang simply. It pleased him that Martre stood up, and that he got a good honest handshake.

Apart from sinking into a doze, or not speaking French, John wouldn't have grasped much of all that. Castang did a recap, brief, on the way home.

"That's all we need. You've signed an official complaint. A note goes to the Procureur but they don't wait, to move. Important to get on the right terms. Formal French kind of social manners. No display of haste. Left- or right-wing groups exist everywhere, police or lawyers. The Commissaires are like Mayors, the great majority far out right-wing, a fact that's often caused me trouble.

"There can sometimes be local politics. Much like the local rugby teams, Bayonne is the Aviron and Biarritz the Olympique, and the rivalry between them is insane. Both unite in their horror of the brutish-and-beastly Catalans, down in Perpignan. So if this turns out to be gendarmerie business . . ." This was all Chinese to John, but he has decided on Faith.

"Like Dortmund and Schalke? – only ten kilometres apart but one has to belong to one or the other."

"Exactly. Or being French means hating Germans; if friendly towards Arabs you have to hate Jews. Look, the overwhelming probability is that we have a dotty woman who acted on a sudden impulse and they may well have got her by now. But I have to look further," said Castang, but this to himself.

"Martre, that's a hammer?"

"No, that's a *marteau*, this is a marten, let's be glad it's not a polecat."

Emma whitefaced, and the air electric with tension. Like crossing a field beneath the path of the power lines, drooping from their tall metal towers: one will feel it, before looking up and seeing it. Vera, white only around the lips. She puts it out of sight and one has to know her well to gauge how much isn't, and won't be, brought to the surface.

"Tea, please," said Castang. "I don't suppose anyone wants to eat." Blank looks, as though he said something incomprehensible. Patient, since this was a very stupid suggestion, and revolted too, since he was also being perfectly disgusting.

It was only a day or so since Vera, turning the pages of the daily paper in this very room, had looked up from whatever scene of famine, flood or massacre. 'All very neatly packaged and encapsulated and predigested. One could be reading all this off the back of some cornflakes box. Oh dear, and Well . . ., and Champ-Champ.'

"Ought to eat, though," went on Castang boringly, brightly. "Essential to keep our behaviour normal." It was in the trenches of 1914 that boys started getting all this helpful advice about regular meals, changing your socks and be sure to keep your bowels open. This must have been the first war to have well-ordered post deliveries. He met his daughter's eye and dropped his own.

It is good for us to remember Sir George Sitwell telling

his son Osbert, 'In case of a bombardment, retire at once to the undercroft. You will not, of course, have to face anything like the weight of gunfire your mother and I had to endure in Scarborough.' Aware that his daughter felt contempt for his great silliness, Castang knew also that Emma put it down to lovingness. He strangled a few more cheery clichés; he had better keep to himself the one about good news arriving within about half-an-hour.

He wasn't too certain what to think: one is sure only that no thought at all is better than any. The frustrated female does, it's true, steal babies out of prams. The more, perhaps, since there've been several recently. Is it because they've read about it in the paper – which sets them off? Or is it like airline crashes, which always come in bunches, and one does have to presume that airliners have not been sitting around reading about one another's misadventures.

Now the fashion for taking hostages, widespread in Italy a year or two back ... Martre didn't think so: the Basque separatist movement had never gone in much for ... one never knows though, a technique which might perhaps appeal. As, uh, a tactical reply to some recent arrests in France, greatly gloated over. To, say, Monsieur Pasqua being triumphalist on television, in that Ricard accent: 'Terrorism has been de-Cap-i-Tated.'

"Do you see? – this might be somebody saying 'We've got news for you, Charley.' Your being an ex-cop and all." Castang made an unshaved jaw rasp under his palm. "I haven't been publicising the ex-cop stuff." And Why Me? This kind of horror-story is supposed only to happen to Someone Else.

That afternoon Castang with some faint notion that this would be tactful, something about the children might prefer being on their own a while, told Vera it would do them both a lot of good to have a brisk walk along the seafront; known as going out for a blow. John's ear for music means that he is good at the nuances of intonations, even in other languages. Not 'mimicry' since he isn't at all thinking of being funny. Monsieur Martre's way of saying 'Yes . . . yes' apropos of nothing at all, absent-minded. But it came out sounding like yerss-yerss.

"Looking over my head, your father's, not talking to anyone and going *Ouais, ouais,* like that. And at one moment, I woke up suddenly, and this eye swivelling about crossed mine so that he remembered my existence, and this cold-blooded bastard gave me the most unexpected smile; gentle, so surprisingly sweet, as though I'd been a little girl brought in barefoot off the street."

"Cuddle me," said Emma. "Make me forget everything. Take all my clothes off."

Castang, that night, had already got into bed, complaining rather about a gammy leg – rheumatism? – smoking too much? – probably just psychosomatic. Working cops tend to sleep in their underclothes which they say saves trouble with all that dressing and undressing. Vera had put up with this for a good few years while exerting leverage towards Marks-and-Spencer-pyjamas 'which get wound tighter and tighter round one as one turns – feel like Tutankhamen . . .' Nowadays beautiful (and expensive) boxer shorts adorn the twister.

Vera was standing by the bed, bare-legged in a cotton nightie.

"What are our chances?"

This silly a question she would never normally ask. Never had; knowing better. So that Castang made his voice colourless.

"As of now, good. As of tomorrow – good to moderate. As of any further off – becoming poorer. Why d'you ask?" irritably. "I don't know any better than you do." The eyes, normally so expressive, were like empty holes. Not even the two barrels of a double twelve-bore; just two blank dark-blue steel tubes. "What are you doing fidgeting about? Do you want to put the light out? Then open the window."

Vera took the nightie off and climbed in on top of him muttering something incoherent and probably in Czech anyhow. One would say though that the bottom looked better than the eyes.

"Is it possible, do you think," said Vera in the dark, "that this could have anything to do with Richard?"

To be sure, one does fall asleep from time to time. There is no value in it: it hasn't done one any good. The finding oneself awake, again, is that much more torment. One will say, afterwards, 'I haven't slept', 'I couldn't sleep'. It was not an exact truth but the reality was worse.

Not sleeping, Castang reached out to grasp realities and they turned to nothing in his hands. You are going down stairs, carrying something that must not be broken or spilled; you meet the phenomenon of the extra step, which you thought was there and wasn't. You reach for the banister; it is there to support you, to steady your balance. It is a solid object, perceived with perfect clarity, and you grip it, and as you fall quite slowly down the stairs you ask yourself what mirage has perplexed your eyesight, your hand, your built in apprehension of distance and direction.

He had talked so much nonsense. A lot of wiseacre chat with a man (a man real enough, a PJ man like himself) – about what? About the Minister, a man who made the remark that truth in politics does not exist, and foolish would be the man to believe that it did.

The Minister was real enough – or was he? No, because he was in a position of great power, of an authority nigh absolute over objects like policemen. But in politics, Monsieur, a Minister is a nobody. Tomorrow, he isn't even there. Castang had spread these great clouds of nonsense around himself, like a cuttlefish making itself invisible – does it imagine? – in its own ink. What for?

There is only one reality. That in police statistics a stolen baby does not offer very good odds on recovery – alive. For himself he is a father; yes and a grandfather. That is not a role to play, to be assumed as though by an actor. This too is a reality. But foremost, I am a police officer. Still. Neither is this a role. It also is a reality.

Vera felt herself sticky all over. Sweat, secretions of fear, distillations as of an infection that had entered her body. She was naked too, which she disliked, in bed anyhow. She got out. There was her nightdress, a limp rag and evil-smelling. It didn't do to stand by an open window. It was among the French an article of faith, that the air of the night is filled with noxious influences and evil spirits. She left the room, in search of a safer place. She turned the shower on to rather hot, stood under it. Turned it to cold; her circulation was not good. Gasped, didn't scream – she never screamed. Uttered perhaps some animal noises, but she was afraid she'd been doing so in bed and this would anyhow be less hideously audible. Rubbed vigorously and went in search of a clean, cool and proper-smelling nightdress.

Her imagination is of a literary sort. Strindberg said that dream and reality are one. A Swedish remark whose truth had now to be acknowledged. That everything can happen. The dream is the truth. This is at all times perceptible to children. To adults also, from time to time. As Bergman learned. As Fanny and Alexander are busy learning.

Emma lay still, forcing herself to be still. A lot of tumbling about would only make John the more restless. His misery was the more cruelly intense; the imagined guilt clawing him. Claws of a leopard, ripping and tearing. Picturing that; a dreadful vision. Would it for even one second lessen her own; could there be any alleviation in trying to think of another's? She had woken up. She was again little; eight, ten? She lived in a village, in an Amazonian jungle. Many dreadful beasts live here; there are snakes, scorpions, immense spiders but these she does not greatly fear. One has lived with them always. One's father, one's mother have taught her how protections exist. They are there: as long as this is so one is safe. Only one unconquerable dread has never left her; that of going to the riverside to fetch water. And there, while knee-deep in a pool, waiting for the disturbed sand and mud to settle, that the water will be again clear.

Now it has happened. The crocodile has seized her in its blunt but unbreakable grip. It carries her down, down into unimaginable murky depths. She will not be eaten, not at once. She will asphyxiate first. It is happening now.

Emma was not like her sister. She was her mother's child. Highly disciplined. One does not throw oneself about or yell. This close strong tie, this umbilical cord, this family thing strangles some children. Lydia had fought against it with passion, with hatred. Herself, no. So that when she had known John, to whom 'family' was a filth, an obscenity, she had given herself utterly; clear-sighted, in full knowledge. That did not mean a casting out, a forgetting or a neglecting, an effacement. Her mother, her father, were needed still, loved, wanted. Now. John is her family now, but she has not lost, she has here two more human beings, she relies upon them, they rely upon her. We are going to survive. I am not alone on this riverbank. My father knows how to deal with crocodiles. He can break that terribly powerful spinal column. Idiot Pa too, on and on about behaving normally; *eating* normally. I love you, and you make me shit, you know that?

John was thinking – or was it dreaming? – about the word he was setting to music; was it for a song? The word 'marvellous': Emma had used it, in another life. 'The most marvellous view'. Had she been talking English? A good word, a dactyl with a strong tonic on the first syllable, so that a soprano singing in low notes will make a leap here into the top of her register and neither 'wunderbar' nor 'mer-veil-leux' will be quite the same, because in English the two short syllables fall away attractively; light and easy. That was in another world: it is strange that music should still be going on.

An extraordinary joke – yes, Joke – that this should have happened here. The place is real enough; I have learned that now. He had seen it as a toy town, setting for a ballet, perhaps satirical? Chorus of policemen, in capes and képis? Soldiers in 1860 uniforms. Chorus of nursemaids pushing prams along the seafront. One would have a baby, and the baby would disappear, and keep reappearing in disturbing, embarrassing comic circumstances.

Don't forget the chorus of garden gnomes, Castang's voice growled in his ear. Oh yes, highly satirical!

A joke: isn't this the only way to handle it?

John was not a Berliner. Provincial plodder, he told himself; from a small, unfunny, extremely unhumorous Saxon town. But has lived in Berlin long enough, beginning to get the drift. This is the city for humour.

He remembers a picture which had gone the rounds, making as it did an apt, a good sharp illustration of a Berliner joke. One sees the vista of the Alexanderplatz on a bad day; chilly, misty, hideously draughty. In the foreground the statue of Karl Marx, looking deeply depressed, as well he might. But on the plinth of the statue a Berliner has written 'Next time round it will all be better'.

Decidedly, that is the way to handle this occasion.

It hasn't happened. There never was a Hitler (invention of comic-strip artists). And even if there were, we'd know how to obliterate him. And even if we failed at that – well, next time round it'll be altogether different. There's the slogan for me, thought John. *Beim nächsten mal wird alles besser.*

It had been in another world, one without urgencies, in which jobs get put off because really one cannot be bothered: who the hell is this man Bastian anyhow and what is he doing in Pau? And why, and . . . this was all weeks ago. After that chap came sneaking round with ridiculous stories about an eager customer; Castang feeling some vague curiosity and telling himself that this was being prudent, really. Nothing wrong, surely, with this house. The cliff is not about to fall into the sea. House was sound, indeed unusually well built. Title was sound, the notary had said so and this is what notaries are for. All that was left was Richard being-enigmatic in that tiresome way he affected: if there seems to be anything funny see this chap Bastian.

This autoroute from Biarritz to Pau is a funny one too. No doubt it is a perfectly sound piece of engineering, but a foothill road, with a lot of up and down in it and fast shooting curves where one does well to keep an eye out for the tricky side winds. You do want to stay awake, not drink too much at lunch. Perhaps some of these tenets would also apply to Pau itself: it is no longer altogether the sleepy little town of Henri IV when King of Navarre (remaining unchanged for another three hundred years). It's now quite large, determinedly modern, while still very French, backward and provincial; a French combination, one would almost be tempted to say a Castang combination.

For today, and the temptation here is to say now as ever-shall-be there are Parisians who won't cross the river to the Left Bank; go only to places they already know and would ask, 'Where Is Pau?' A constipated lot, moving rigidly along mental tramlines, hating nothing so much as change. When meeting them – perhaps in business – one has to remember that they are never wrong, never have been, and must never, never be contradicted.

So that Pau is now a place of enterprise and discovery, and has a flourishing university. They make things hereabouts, and think about things; not just about making more *foie-gras* out of bigger and better ducks. But Castang's never been there, and to him it's still all Henri IV, about whom he knows nothing; he'd read Dumas as a child. Dumas makes an entertaining figure of Henri, witty and full of jokes; a great one too for the girls and the local vino. These always pretty and delightful, and invariably ever-ready girls do sound a bit James-Bond, and so does Henri. Elsewhere, he is said to have had bad teeth. Stank something awful. Unpatriotic sentiments these. Everyone did stink then; Queen Elizabeth's teeth were also notorious, and one would have tried to stay upwind of Sir Walter Raleigh; but the girls don't seem to have minded much.

Henri's Château overlooks a pretty old town; also the famous magnolia trees; also the marvellous panoramic view of the Pyrenees. Where there is a Castle there will be a Palais de Justice not far away, and where there is an old quarter one will find lawyers. They like old buildings, of great historic charm and flavour, this last further sophisticated by narrow cobbled alleyways and splendid concentrated perfumes of dust, damp stonework, drains, and cabbage. This goes to the head of tourists, who think that France smells of garlic and Chanel Number Five and Gauloise cigarettes. It doesn't. It's dirt and urine, at pretty violent odds with the disinfectant called Eau-de-Javel.

Nothing in France could be more historic (flavourful) than justice. This profession becomes modernised with the greatest possible reluctance, and there are French judges to whom the Dreyfus case was yestereve. There are women too, thank heaven, with high heels and long black-stockinged legs, and who manage to give a sexy tilt to their robe. The white stock sets off a white neck, and Castang when in court feels a warm, a profound gratitude.

Elated might be the right word; the cocktail of lipstick, perfume, earrings and a nice arch to a pretty eyebrow: banal anywhere else, may be, but in court intoxicating. The day will come when the musty old men with robes like the inside of a vacuum-cleaner are outnumbered. One will never get rid of them; they are a formidable clan. No nest of intermarriage will be quite so tortuously incestful as this one, just as in England your attorney, Commissioner for Oaths and all the rest, should really have polished the bench with his behind at Winchester or Westminster if he's ever to get his woolsacks operational.

Certainly Maître Bastian is like this; of dubious cleanliness in a cabinet full of leatherbound jurisprudence and classical pornography; related to every Procureur's brother-in-law from Narbonne to Gap. Facile characterisations but sometimes there is not a lot more to say of people.

"Richard made a sort of deathbed donation."

"Heard he'd died," agreed Maître.

"Gave his house to my wife, that was quite a surprise."

"Hadn't any heirs."

"No difficulty about this, as the notary tells me. I've retired this year. Been looking around for something suitable. My wife would quite like to keep this house."

"Quite so. Must have put on a bit of value, around there."

"Richard was a former colleague. My chief in fact for some few years. Nothing much among his papers – a reference to yourself, slightly obscure. Along the lines of you might be of help if ever one was to meet with any trouble." Maître looked as though any such suggestion should not be in the least obscure, but

"Want me to act for you, is that it?" was all he said.

"Hard to say. Notary says the title is sound and the deed of gift regular. What would there be to dispute? However, perhaps it's just a coincidence, somebody working through an agent has made me a pressing offer for this bit of property; ready they say to pay a stiff price. I've turned this down. One would maybe wonder whether there weren't more to this than meets the eye. That possibly, is to imagine troubles where none exist, or it could be elementary prudence."

"Not clear what you want of me." Dwarf in a Disguise, thought Castang crossly.

"I don't want anybody's secrets spilling over into my existence. If I get an impression I've inherited something more complex than it seems, I'd better find out about it, hadn't I?"

Maître produced a pipe, put it in his mouth, lit it, puffed at it. Took it out to look at a couple of times before putting it back again; all this gives one time for thinking about whatever one might change one's mind about saying.

"Richard stayed cop, right up to the end of his life. Now the impression I have of you is of a man who draws a line under it, added up his totals and that's the end of that.

"Richard liked to keep his finger on a few things. Professional habit, might come in handy, even if mostly only golfclub gossip. A few notes taken, hardly more than that – I've never looked – of an indiscreet phrase dropped, a few words exchanged, it might be. Not a dossier in any sense. Nothing evidential, I feel sure; he'd have told me if it were. No more than a few pointers. No way would this be pressure material. But knowing something about favours given – or received – that's useful if you want a favour done, or maybe if you've a position to protect."

"Look," said Castang, "do you know anything I don't, and maybe I should?"

"Richard left some papers with me. This was on a confidential basis. There was a murmur that this material might be defamatory. I've never read them, don't know what's in them. But understand me. If he decided to put papers where they would not be seen or found, he had doubtless good reasons for doing so, and they had better stay that way. Wouldn't you agree? Suppose a hypothesis, that this in some hands might be thought damaging."

"I'm asking no favours," said Castang, finding himself in a false position and vexed by it. "Richard left me a word, suggesting that I consult you in case of any difficulty. Here is this word, which authenticates my approach. I don't know that there is any difficulty. I'm seeking to be prudent."

"Puts a different complexion on matters," puffing at the pipe. It smelt disagreeable, thought Castang. "I'm here to advise you. You've had an approach, seeking to buy this property, formerly Richard's. The approach is anonymous, through an agent. It seems to you a little over-insistent, a little pressing. You'd rather like to know whether there's something behind this, and if so who. That it?

"Well, perhaps I can find that out for you, and perhaps I can't but I can make a few enquiries. There's been a good deal of speculation in that part of the world. Some of these land deals have not always been straightforward. It may be that this particular piece of property could acquire an importance out of proportion to its size or nominal value, on account of its position. Is this what you're thinking of?"

"It did occur to me."

"Very well," said Maître. "If you so instruct me, I'll see what I can do."

Fox, thought Castang, driving back – too fast – along the autoroute. There's not much traffic. Let's see what this old car can do, for once. Vexed. Perplexed. Irritated.

It was this, too, conceivably, that made him stop in Biarritz for a beer, and an inchoate, colourful – but soothing – idea of buying something for his wife. A bunch of flowers is never a bad idea. Something bigger is perhaps a silly idea, the result of driving too fast and feeling stimulated. Not unwelcome, and if ludicrously extravagant can be held back until Christmas, which is shortly. He stopped and gawked, outside a dress shop.

In the city he would make jokes, indulge fantasies. Shop girls would giggle and bring outrageous things to encourage him. Here in what Vera calls 'the dorp' were two serious middle-aged ladies; blouses, pullovers interminable and boring. No no no; this was all the new outfit for the Mayor's wife, appearing in public on Armistice Day. Boredom would blunt his eye. He'd end up with something as ugly as it was unsuitable. The girl would say Thank-you-Darling, while feeling hopeful it could be changed, without his noticing.

There was no one in the shop but a woman pottering, looking at price-tickets and making faces at them. The two harpies had seen at once that she was a waste of their time; leaving them free to sink their claws deeper into Castang. Who was looking for a face-saving formula to get him safely out of the door. This woman had been eavesdropping, hiding smiles at his comments upon provincial finery. Good-looking woman too; slim, fair-haired. One must say in Castang's defence that Parisian though he still was, he was not given to casual pickups in public places. Never has been, come to that. She looked up on her way out, smiled; and in an unexpectedly deep voice said, "Why not a nightie?" This impressed Castang as good advice, neither 'The head wardress on her day off' nor 'One of Madame Claude's girls picking me up at the bar' but she was on her way down the street before he could thank her. It was still amazingly difficult to make these provincial ladies understand that one did not want the things they thought were pulsatingly sexy: a man, they were persuaded, really only liking the objects to be found in mail-order catalogues (exists also in black, peach and champagne).

One could tease Vera. This can be a temptation because of her great innocence, and a capacity to believe the most unlikely things when told her in a sincere voice. 'Found something really nice, for you. Come right back into fashion these, slinky you know, a bit clinging. Wonderful, crêpe de chine, didn't think it still existed, cut on the bias, frock by Madeleine Vionnet. Need that thirties hair style, shingle is it, string of pearls and the cocktail shaker, must get you these marvellous knickers with legs, down to the tops of your stockings—' She would be nigh crying with rage by now and the effort not to let it show. One would go that scrap too far – 'long cigarette holder' – before she would twig and show signs of becoming cross. Easy enough to please her in reality; as long as it covered her top adequately, chilly and goosebumpy like all women, even these two silly old cows will understand that much. She is interested in her appearance only in fits and starts, walks about in rags because she can't be bothered, but is grateful for goodies at Christmas-time.

A Christmas party, it was something to look forward to. The house had lost that lugubrious look, of belonging to someone else, and who has had the bad taste to die there a few weeks ago. It is true that Vera is 'good with houses', and that she has been working hard. The house looks now as though they themselves have lived in it for long enough that everything fits smoothly. Like a car, thought Castang; past ten thousand you can feel it loosening up.

She says, 'it will be nice to have again a baby in the house.' Normal, reasonable sort of sentiments; maybe he isn't totally convinced that this is his idea of heaven, but being grandfather isn't disagreeable either. This is not a Big house, but well enough designed, solidly enough built, that when the child yells the whole place isn't ringing with the monstrous din. He has a quiet corner still for old men to sit in and grumble.

However morose the Christmas spirit (Popes, Queens and Presidents too, uttering rubbish about the happy fireside), the thing is not to sit around amidst the jinglebells, but see the happy fireside is well stocked up. Logs – er, whatever. Isn't it nice being rich! Want a grandfather clock, do we, chiming away there? 'No, quite, but I wouldn't mind a gold hunter watch, I suppose probably English, even if it is reproduction. Put in the waistcoat pocket, and they don't just chime but press the thingy it chimes again the last hour you see, so that in the dark you can say ha – three.' But suppose, said Vera, it were five to four? He didn't know either. Like most policemen his is the kind where the strap was dearer than the watch. Need to be a perfect idiot to have anything but a mickeymouse in this trade. One knows straight off when they've gone bent, they can't resist the gold rolex.

'House warming'? – ridiculous expression but Vera has bought a lot of house-warming things, got the girl to wrap them all up in the pretty paper, so much scotch tape a man breaks his wrist getting it all open, and I don't believe that glitter-string is bio-degradable, neither.

The phone had rung, and he had answered. He'd told Emma to call from a little way out; he'd come and do the guide bit over the twisty part. Party started with enthusiastic waving from the verge at a distinctly grimy Volkswagen with German plates; John unflustered, even stolid, Em both tired and dirty. Yes it Was a long way. No, the child's asleep, they like the movement. Is that Biarritz down there? "Looks horrible, have I ever been here?"

"Yes, when you were still small."

"Was that the drama, Lyddy getting drowned? It'll come back to me. Let's get on, I need a shower very badly indeed." Emma flopped on the sofa, had her feet up in the same breath; John much too polite to say, 'Need a beer badly' but she said it for him; he leapt to his feet as Vera came in: top marks for good manners.

His daughter 'flung herself under the shower', came back with wet hair but much refreshed, was attracted towards a powerful stink surrounding the baby in its basket, Vera insisting that this is a delicious smell, fountain in fact of eternal youth. Lounging with their hands in their pockets the men looked (she said) hideously pleased with themselves.

"What's her name?"

"Claire."

"Nothing else?"

"Hasn't needed anything else. One can add more names as it goes along. Did you buy these?" unpopping the bottom half and surveying complicated French inventions. "What bin do they go in?"

"All on the compost heap," said Castang proudly.

"Come on then greedy-guts, here's a nice clean tit," and yes, said John, wouldn't say no at all to a second beer; good, these. Belgian, said Castang.

The two men were brought together the way things

fall out, naturally and without there being reasons. At Christmas-time women enjoy themselves in female ways. They don't have to be mother-and-daughter. In an unknown house; her own home the meagre flat up five flights of stairs and Berlin two thousand kilometres away and it feels like double that – Emma still feels 'home'. Enjoying her mother, with whom she had always got on well, enjoying her own fresh-made maturity as a mother herself; liking this mix of motherhood and childhood and there being now three generations of girls, here together. Nice to slop about if you feel that way, not washing or doing your hair, just as it's nice to dress up and make a fuss of going out shopping together. She enjoyed wrapping up fidgety little parcels, decorating things in silly trashy ways, baking biscuits that nobody would eat, dumping the child on the floor and lying on the floor oneself. Along their own lines, the men are just the same.

Castang in these few months had 'attached himself' – like a shell-fish (you must take them by surprise for once they seize fast almost impossible to pry loose) – to this Atlantic corner. The house feels right. It had gone right from the start, so that Vera too says that she has 'become encrusted'. They had both come to love the soft September rain for which one doesn't bother putting on a coat. The native weather forecasts: here ('teaching John French') was one he had himself learned in Trouville – a faraway Norman coastline, but the phrase is the same from Portugal to the Hebrides. 'If you can see Le Havre it's going to rain. If you can't it's raining already' . . . One is just half-way-along this extraordinary Celtic fringe, the mythical maritime edge of the Abendland. Castang's German, fluent and vivid while quite illiterate in grammar and spelling, is just right for talking to John. Slipping too into English, the pidgin or '*sabir*' of northern Europe.

"Think of growing up in Stralsund or Hamburg. Just as one would need to have been a barefoot little raggedy-arse in Alexandria and talk that Levantine patois of Greek and Arab and Provençal. James Joyce in Trieste, I don't understand it but ask Vera, she does; South-Serbs or whatever, she can follow.

> Here we lay
> All the Day
> In the Bay of Biscay-O.

Baja de Viscaya is the Golfe de Gascogne; the vowels seem to have got a bit arbitrary but the Scots can all talk Danish."

"Winter storms," said John. They were lying-up on the edge of the cliff under the scud – salt on the binocular lenses.

"Summer too, and e-qui-noc-tial – is that a German word? – all the year round: lightning, the place is famous for it."

They rolled around to look at the house, crouching there below the hump of the promontory; low and straggling, protected all along the seaward side by the verandah running the whole length; good red cedar, Richard made a good job, thought Castang, lies there on the swell like a ship. Not really pretty, no elegant Levantine felucca bringing wine and oranges (what would we give them? – tar and timber, candles and whale-oil). Vera in fact says this is a dirty British coaster with a salt-caked smokestack, and that this was Richard's golf-playing anglophile style.

The New Year was not going to pass without music. A German Silvester-Abend please, said Castang. We've no piano because nobody could play it; so Stu-pido of us not to have anticipated John who brings a bit of civilisation to the barbarians. Vera sings but god, if you heard her on the street would You give her a penny? Emma sings but not enough: we have to fall back on records; we've plenty to eat and there's lots of booze.

Midnight strikes. Boats will sound sirens. They hear the wind.

"*Die Zeit*," sings Emma in her uneven untrained contralto, "*das ist ein wunderbar Ding.*" For earlier, they had been eating oysters and listening to Lotte Lehmann: she is the Marschallin . . .

"Nobody is so good," agreed John judicially, "but fishblood Heger, what a lousy conductor."

"So who else is good?" asked Castang in a police voice (drunken – ignorant.)

"If I may say so, Henri, that's a silly remark." And yes, so it was. "Thousands are good now and then. Who was good yesterday and will still be good tomorrow? Besides Lotte, and Doctor Strauss?

"Doctor Klemperer," said Vera, "all it takes is the opening chords of *Fidelio* and I start to cry dreadfully."

"Vera," said John, a bit drunk but dignified, "I don't suppose you'd consider marrying me would you?"

Who are the free musicians? The French critic, Alain Lompech, said he only knew three. Two pianists; Sviatoslav Richter and Martha Argerich (one of Castang's Great Loves); one conductor – Carlos Kleiber.

"So now we'll go in," they were standing in a group at the cliff, "and we'll have *Fidelio.*"

"And that," said Emma, "sorts out the men from the boys. The utter horrors. The ingrained horizontal vulgarian crowd-pleasers."

"Bernstein!" said John heartfelt.

"That bad?"

"Oh yes, the worst ever."

"But Doctor Klemperer it will be."

"Yes, that's the real thing." They came out again to breathe at four in the morning, and "This is perfect happiness," said Castang.

The police, when drunk, will often utter some slick sentiment, some utter banality. '*Plaisir d'amour ne dure qu'un moment*' – a sententious cracker-motto. Castang knows that happiness is an egg. A piece of art until some hooligan throws it at you.

The New Year had still been a perfect moment. Every-thing, from fireworks brought by John as a surprise, to Doctor Klemperer.

They had enjoyed themselves; a day, two, three. Why, even this morning ... Castang had said that perfect happiness could also be breakfast.

"Perfect greed," said Vera, a Jansenist.

But you see, Emma had made bread, of flour brought with her; the children had much talent for these treats. Not quite Russian, but if you put sour cream on it, and smoked salmon on that, you get a Russian effect. The coffee was good too. However much pains you take you can never be certain of this beforehand.

"Why is it only good when it's scotch?"

"I don't know but the French never get it right." One of the things learned in Brussels; a thing learned from Jerry, and there was a momentary flash of pain; sharp but it did not last.

This pain lasted.

John had come home, distraught. Trying hard to keep control of himself. Castang, trying to be professional.

'*Chagrin d'amour*.' 'Night or Blücher, Mister.' One of Jerry's phrases. The pain which he was trying to live with shot again to a sharp peak. So try to remember Jerry, who had no great admiration for the Duke of Wellington. 'Don't be impressed by this profound military genius working his painful way from Portugal to the Pyrenees – more to the point is to ask why the hell it took him so long.'

"Look, this is an accident. Most likely just an incident.

"We've reported it, to the police, the Gendarmerie, and we must give them a few hours."

"Get my child back," said Emma.

"Yes." Speaking painfully; speaking with pain; noticing the 'semantic difference'.

In his police career he has had things like this. Not a kidnap that he could recall. Such things used to be rarities.

More recent – more frequent. Not so often 'criminal', done for a ransom, but things like divorced fathers stealing a child away, with some confused notion of 'I've got rights too': sour little vengeances; ideas that giving others pain will somehow alleviate one's own. But he has had children who went out to play and did not come back. There is no consolation. He has given calming-advice. Now he has to give it to himself.

"We're likely to be bothered by the press. These things get out, however discreet one tries to be. Do you agree? – leave all this to me. A place like this – anything for a bit of excitement. So don't answer the telephone, nor the door. I stay here; I hold the fort.

"Might it be a good idea, John, if you took Emma, went out for a walk?

"Look, I have some experience of this sort of thing. We've done what we can, let the pros work. I've been PJ myself. They'll work for us. But journalists – maybe even the local television studio. One mustn't be surprised. To them it's an excitement. It won't last."

"Get my child back," said Emma.

"Yes. It's only that this is not police work like the time when you were small, and I was the chief, like the man in the Bible, saying Do this, and it got done. I'm a nobody, now. You must give me time."

Time, he said to himself now. *Die Zeit.* Talking to himself, sitting in the same place; what was there to do now, but wait? The children had gone out together, to temper their misery in the wind; rain now; this weather here turned around quicker than you could change your socks. Where was Vera? Working somewhere; the household chores, these do not alter and 'Work is the only remedy'. He agreed, and what could he do? He'd said it; police work had to be left to the real policemen and he was now an old man with a few rusted memories of procedures now largely out of date. No, not old but feeling bloody old. *Zeit?* There are two sorts of time (said the poet, sagely.)

Y a le temps qui attend
Et le temps qui espère.

The one which waits and the one which hopes. He opened
the window, to feel the rain, to listen to the sea.

Y a deux sortes de gens.
Il y a les vivants
Et ceux qui sont en mer.

We, the living. And those who are at sea. Take your time.
Like the Duke of Thing, really only a defensive general,
but at that job, a good one. This is no moment for
Attacking. This sort of general waits the other bugger out.
And yes, there's the phone ringing. No; not the police.

"Monsieur Castang? Press, Sud-West." Or that was what
it sounded like. Had he been talking in German to
himself then?

"This is a bit odd, or is it? They're giving out this story
about some dotty girl feeling she has to steal a baby
somewhere. That what you think? . . . Yes, of course I
want a story for my paper. Doing my job, okay? As I
hear it, you're an ex-PJ Commissaire, yourself. Bit of a
coincidence, aint it? Got any clues? I was just wondering,
were you a bit on the political side? What was it now
exactly, your assignation, RG was it? Ever have anything
to do with the politics hereabouts? . . . No no, I've been
doing my homework. Few years ago was a story; it's in
the files. Fellow – like you people say you were anxious
to interview – and slipped off, it was suggested, with the
complicity or call it indulgence of some . . . Same name
as you. Just wondered."

A bit damp under the arms there, Castang. He hadn't
thought they'd be likely to remember that. Not that it
matters much; it's an old story and there's no evidence. He
didn't know any of the local revolutionaries, and maybe he
wished he did. He'd ask them! 'D'you know anybody who

goes about stealing babies out of prams? Or why?' It wasn't their kind of operation; he agreed with Martre. They'd feel contempt, very probably, for that kind of mentality.

Another buttonholed John, outside the door; stone-walled by his not talking French, but quite prepared to form a theory that an anti-German grievance had played a role here. 'Know what I mean? Someone been in a camp, say, deported for forced labour?' There is the kind of journalist who doesn't bother with anything as boring as facts, and whose concept of the job is to plant rumours which encourage the public into dirty-minded imaginings.

He knew it wasn't a big enough story to carry any weight. It's just that nothing happens in a seaside town in the month of January. A road accident will knock it off the page. Fisticuffs in a rugby match. By tomorrow it'll be forgotten. Telling John and Emma this did not make them happier. An ex-police Commissaire with a German son-in-law; baby stolen bold-as-brass right there in the street – a tasty little item, but cobweb-thin. Damnation, there was a station-wagon outside with the insignia of the local television. "Stay inside, but don't close shutters; don't appear hostile."

"We'd like to do you in the living-room, warmer you know, more human interest."

"Sorry, boys, I'll walk along the street for you but no further than the gate." They feigned astonishment. Surely everybody wants to be on the camera. "But we'll be no trouble to you at all."

"Son, your editor won't even want it: much too boring."

It was quite outside their experience that anyone would ever use this word about his own self.

But the police, the gendarmerie, did not ring, did not call. No kindly firemen, with a bundle wrapped in a blanket. The four of them spent a wretched night.

Castang had been very happy with his daughter. Rested after the journey she had looked splendid; as tall as himself (which was nothing extravagant; he was small as cops went) and quite a bit taller than her mother, and less skinny than Skinny-Lyd. Child-bearing had ripened her and she was plainly a good mother (give Lydia a baby and she'd drop it, or stick pins in it) – those shapely hands were full of security and comfort. Pretty? The face is now a fine oval; the eyes are large and lovely; there's just a hint of the Slav looks that had made Vera so striking as a young girl.

"Has Emma any talent, d'you think?" he'd asked John. She'd always been a nice bright competent girl and had never shown any particular sign.

"Talent, what's talent?" By now John was quite at ease with both of them. "Who's got talent, have I, have you? All I know is Berlin's full of bums playing the fiddle in the street and they should be married to her. They should be so lucky."

And John, what does one know about Herr Weber? One was finding out fast and one liked what one saw and heard. Grace, as well as patience and tranquillity (and, undoubtedly, talent . . .). Vera agreed.

"I feel proud of him. We know nothing about music but he'll be a good one. Sensitivity there is and to spare, and nothing sickly about it. Sachsen – the Wessies sniggered, and of course the Brandenburgers all sneer, and by all accounts his parents do sound pretty awful, but they made him."

And now look how well he shows up. Look now at this load of guilt he's carrying for losing the child, and he stands up to it. Readiness; *Bereitsein.* The alarm rings in the morning and his feet are clear of the bed. It's a good man that she has there.

Castang is even muttering that tedious old cliché: when the leaves fall you can tell which are evergreens.

He slept badly. They all did and none of them said so. There was a lot of wind and the woodwork made noises. One would easily imagine footsteps and breakers and prowlers, sneaking about outside to pin nasty messages to shutters. He even got out of bed a couple of times to feel his feet bare on a floor, to flex his toes and insteps; to feel himself alert. Readiness. He walked through the house, the second time. Went downstairs, sat at his desk in the 'study' – and then he did something he hadn't done in years: he looked for the key, which was on the profile of a picture frame, he unlocked a drawer of the bureau. Here was his old gunbelt, the leather gone rather greasy. At the back, wrapped in a piece of flannel, his service pistol which he'd never turned in. Even on duty he'd seldom carried it. A plain and unpretentious object; no fancy glocks or expensive berettas, a simple and now old S&W. Thirty-eight, a four-incher. Oily, and of course unloaded. He cleaned it, and even thought of loading it. No no, that goes too far. Castang's age and experience has induced a healthy attitude towards guns; that you will get further with it unloaded, ninety-nine times. True, the hundredth had happened to him too. There was some ammunition around, some place; it might be as well to remember where.

His attitude towards ghosts is likewise sensible. Irish; to say, 'I don't believe in them but they're there.' If there were a ghost around here it would be Richard, as one had seen him last in this room, wearing beautiful white silk pyjamas, rather baggy, much like an elderly Chinese war-lord in a rare moment of domestic benevolence. He looked up and 'got a jump' – the ghost was Vera, in the smart nightie he had given her (pretext for demoting two to ragbag status). She said nothing at all and walked out again.

A family united; yes, just barely. The determination, to hold on whatever may happen; this resolution, solidarity, is found among ordinary people, it exists, whatever one may think of the world; it is even frequent. A night has passed and they have had the opportunity to show three-in-the-morning courage. All four are cursed with imagination. A quality sometimes useful to police officers, though on the whole one very often wished one hadn't, and as often thought one could very well do without it.

Divided, torn, hideously churned, pulled apart by conflicting loyalties, Emma was having a bad time. The mother of a child only a few months old, and she feels it there in the profundities of female guts as much as in the heart and head. Do something, she wants to shout, do anything, no matter what. Go out and arrest people, shut them up in jail, Torture them. As a small child, one wondered what one's father Did. One heard, already, vividly horrible stories from other children about the villainies of the police. One was robust, in resisting these; one hit other children and did things utterly forbidden; pulling their hair viciously, twisting their arm or spitting at them. Did the police do things like this? As one grew up, one came to know that they did, and also much worse. The People, said Lydia (aged what, about ten?) deserved all they got. Look at the way they thieve, out of every shop; look how they cheat and lie, look what traitors and cowards they all are. General de Gaulle (a huge, ungainly but formidable presence in the imagination of every French child) said '*C'était des Veaux*'. This word, insulting enough since it means Calf, also contains '*veule*', and if your father said that of you it was really bad. Not just shirking your piano practice but really lacking in all courage and self-command, and being a snivelling hypocrite into the bargain.

Emma wants to scream at her father. You know every filthy trick, you have done disgusting things that as a child I shuddered to think of and I put them out of my mind because you are my father, and I am not *Veule* (which sounds like English or the German 'Foul'). Go out now and be Foul, but get my child back. Handcuff people to the radiator (tight) and turn the heat right up – do them good.

John is torn. He cannot altogether withstand a thoroughly German sentiment; an immense distrust of French police. He too uses a child's words; crooked, sly, underhand, cruel and cowardly. His adult mind knows perfectly that a German Orpo, Sipo or Kripo is no goddam better – lazy, inefficient, incompetent, profoundly corrupt, riddled through and through with fascistic right-wing *schweinerei*. As a student he had thrown stones at the police, and catapulted them with large steel bolts, and come under the water cannon for his pains. And what's more he doesn't regret it even while knowing it to be silly and useless.

He feels all his loyalties towards his Emma (who isn't in the least 'French'; who cares a damn about identity cards?). Loyalty and respect and liking for Emma's father. And self-hatred. Oh why did this have to happen Here? I wish I knew what to do.

I wish I could help it but the word is *Schlamperei*, that vile but French mix of the sloppy and the callous.

Perhaps Vera takes it the hardest of all. Torn everywhichway, as though by the barbarity of the medieval punishment for an attack on the king's own person, which is to be torn in pieces by four horses, roped to each of the four limbs. She can feel every torment that can be inflicted upon a wife, a mother, a grandmother – and upon the artist; for she has the strongest imagination among the four of them. That is her job. She is nearest to John, but music is so much more concrete – a note to be struck and sounded; one knows what it should be, it is governed by the rules of mathematics. The line of a pencil upon a piece of paper is a jump into the void, an abstract approach and attack upon a metaphysical non-entity.

Castang knows that one cannot reason, argue, talk. There is not much reason left in any of them; raw instinct. What can civilisation mean and how can it count? One can only see the barbarism, the inhumanity, the collapse of everything we have ever stood or hoped for. Africa or

Serbia, the ghastly nationalisms, the Moslem fatwas and fanatic self-martyrdoms, the hacking down with a sabre or the bomb lovingly borne on to a bus full of children and women, the hatred masters everything.

And with all this the police officer. What does this mean? There yes, everything is meaningless, but here? There is here a mechanism and a motivation, a chain of logic however crooked or distorted. But what is it?

Because, covered by the safety of anonymity, people say vile, absurd, morally imbecile things across telephone lines to people in circumstances like his (and one cannot do much about it; this is a means employed by wretches to alleviate their own suffering) he isn't answering the phone unless a pre-arranged code is used; and he isn't answering the door either; he was feeling the isolation. It was self-imposed – so, during plague epidemics, people barricaded themselves within their houses, refusing all contact with the outside world for fear of infection. He doesn't want anyone to speak to him (the police at least will use a tone and words disinfected as it were of the emotional charge). And he feels, too, the need to speak to somebody. Even if it were only the postman; an electricity bill and the Paris paper . . . but he has also a superstitious idea that there might be a letter – something tangible, evidential, and which would shed some light.

In this irritable and restless, slightly mad disposition he put on a hat and raincoat. It was drizzly weather and gusty both: the rain and the wind might both increase suddenly and without warning, just as both might die away to nothing.

"I'm going down as far as the dirty shop. Just to stretch my legs. Just to get a breath of fresh air." Vera nodded. Where was the need of saying anything? "Listen carefully if the phone rings. I'm funnelling every genuine item through the police. It'll ring twice and then stop – only then; otherwise you disregard it." She understood this fussy formula. In the past she too has suffered from the malice of the neurotic and the sadistic. Many people seek vengeance upon a police officer, do not at all disdain his family.

It is not above two kilometres; the laneway joins a road, itself a rustic affair, narrow and winding and with unkept verges but full of houses. Where this joins the main road is the 'dirty shop' which sells ice-cream and packets of crisps, and has papers.

In the laneway itself there are only three houses besides their own at the end, and the smallest. In the dip there are trees, and fields of neglected rough pasture, plenty of space besides the gardens themselves which are luxurious, lying behind tall hedges; rich people who like their privacy. He barely knows these people save to nod to. They keep to themselves and show no interest in his doings. Presumably they also own the strips between – there is nothing there of any value; a tumbledown shed where some peasant had once kept sheep; ragged thorny old bushes and overgrown brushwood, but where one can glimpse the houses they are trim and well cared for. They are not old, but in this climate a garden grows fast.

And there in the laneway where Castang couldn't dodge him is 'the neighbour' walking his dog, a rather nasty labrador. But expensive and obvious like the man's car, which is the dearest model of six-cylinder Renault, and this in turn resembles the man: prosperity is evident but without showing-off. A large pale man of perhaps fifty, peaceful and well-fed, with a big round face on a big round head and Vera calls him the fair round belly with-good-capon-lined. When he saw Castang he stopped, in a perfectly friendly manner but with that circumstantial face one assumes for 'Sorry to hear about your father dying' to people one scarcely knows.

"Sorry to hear about that – you know, I mean in the paper this morning." Castang has a vague idea he sells insurance, but whatever he sells he will do so cleverly, competently, and make a big profit. It is a friendly, pleasant voice and one cannot snub or disregard this buttonholing, which to be sure is kindly meant. "Nobody's exempt of course ... hooligans, lunatics ... I feel sure they'll clear it up very rapidly. One has to shake the police up, they never do anything unless it's made clear one's in a position to make a complaint stick." He stopped abruptly and coughed a bit, having just recalled that this might not be the most tactful of remarks, his new neighbour being like the old one a retired police officer. "Still," changing the subject in a hurry, "there are consolations. Juicy deal we got here on the ground. Be a fine investment opportunity into the bargain, one can glide over the inconvenience then."

Castang stopped, and smiled, and patted the beastly dog, and uttered the meaningless phrases appropriate to having no idea what the fellow is talking about and not in the least caring. "There's that," and "to be sure, of course," and "it's what I very often say myself." Even in France one is polite to the neighbours. One never knows; there might be a boundary dispute or something about the electricity line or this muddy pathway – 'Can't we get them to do something to clean this up?' There is never any good reason for quarrelling with people who share one's piece of ground and its rights and constraints: the drains are septic-tank but the telephone poles are in common.

A little further down he crossed the postman in his little yellow wagon but, "Nothing for you this morning but the paper and a few handouts." He put it in his pocket with a vague disappointment, but what had he been expecting? Besides magazines, pornography, various handy and probably illegal things like videotapes and shotgun cartridges, the dirty-shop has several useful items for people who've forgotten them while out shopping, but he only wanted the local paper and some cigarettes. The woman shook her head and said, "Shocking thing; all my sympathies." Too many children turn up weeks later in the woods, murdered, with foul details that he has known, seen, enquired into: it is not encouraging. He must control this, this ... god it's like some appalling mental illness. Having imagination – in primitive times one would at least have been respected as a witchdoctor. And in medieval times burned as a witch. Nowadays again the wheel spins and one could make a very tidy living as a fortune-teller. If that is, one didn't go to jail, which in France not many of them do: we – they – credulous folk. Right now he'd go for anyone who told him the child was alive, be it a gypsy mama with a crystal ball. See the small-ads in any local paper; they do a roaring trade.

He was well on the way home before it hit him, sank in. Only then did Capon's words reassemble themselves in his mind. 'A juicy deal on the ground.' 'A fine investment opportunity' and something about that took the pain out of the inconvenience.

Castang has remembered Monsieur Leclerc (was that his name?). Because What ground? – it could only be, look, the scraggly bit of 'common ground' between Capon's clump of trees and his own boundary hedge, that's no use to anyone. 'We' – We Got – would it be the whole, the four of them, down to the corner of the laneway? If that were the case it would account (assuming that he was the only one holding out) for the wheedling and the juicing and the half-stated hints – for Leclerc. No, can't you see, you fool? If he – they; who's they? some syndicate – has the rest; but I've got the smallest bit, but it's the key bit, the clifftop bit with the view. And I've refused even a stiff price plus – aha, that's what Capon meant, he's got a percentage on some development deal. Can't be yet another golf course surely, but some country club affair. And failing a bribe ... dear god could this be possible? If it were a mafia set-up. Am I just 'imagining' this?

But he was at home, and was he imagining a lightened heart? Anything – *any*thing – is better than the dead baby in the ditch.

Vera met him. Her face; a roughened, scrubby texture.

Like slum laundry, crumpled because never ironed, grey because never bleached, '*rêche*'.

"I've been listening for the phone. Yes – it rang the way you said it would."

"Martre huh? PJ, I mean, in Bayonne."

"No, a woman. Judge of instruction."

"A judge?" as though he'd never heard of the animal.

"Yes a judge," irritably. "So I begged her to tell me if she had any news. And she said she didn't, but she wants to see you. In person, not over the phone. What are you gawking for in that slack-jawed fashion? It's normal isn't it? You report a crime, the Proc names a judge to instruct a criminal procedure – no? Isn't this what happens? I suppose she got the code from the police. So do please go at once because there must be some good reason for this."

"Yes . . . Vera—"

"*What?*"

"No, only, try not to worry. I think I'm beginning to see something here. I only wanted to say, I don't believe this is as horrible as, as we've been worrying about. Tell the children that," hoping to God he wasn't arousing false pretences.

But it would fit, in a ghastly sort of way. However crooked the logic and distorted the mentality.

If I am right (bringing out the car) then only greed is at stake. And that is a million times preferable to the wretched cripple of my nightmares that steals, kills, and almost certainly rapes small children.

I am only a cop. I have no psychiatric or even medical training beyond the crudest of rough and ready. Doctor Freud might frown but we know what we know. Show me some sad fuck who likes to stick it up a girl's behind and I'll show you a sad little boy who had big troubles getting sat on the pot, and a mamma likely as inhibited as his sicky-little-self. Always look at the mammas, Richard used to say.

But if I'm right, and maybe it's as sicky and in ways I understand even less, this could be the dwarfish greed for dwarfgold, and the gnomes are ranged against me. They wouldn't go this far? I'm no longer so sure of that. The greed for gold is the greed for power.

Bribes and even big ones, because they see that as the easiest, the simplest, the frequentest – the obvious because they can't imagine anyone refusing. If you do refuse, and it gets home to them that you have and do and will, then what? Threats? For the ordinary hooligan yes. Give me your money or I'll bash your face in. But a dwarf could see this as troublesome, perhaps even risky. Might even be squeamish about 'violence'; that wouldn't be out of character.

(On the main road; stopped at a red light.)

It still seems an appalling Enormity. But a dwarf might see this as exactly what he wants: quick, easy, totally irresistible. The certainty that neither Vera nor I would hold on to the house a second if that meant an hour's delay in getting the baby back. Why then doesn't he declare himself straight off? The deal is simple. The house for the child and no further messing. But then that would point to him, wouldn't it? Can he be sure that there's nothing to point to him? No proof, no evidence, nothing that could have weight in a court? It's a commonplace to any judge, any police officer. We know perfectly it's you, but we've no legal grip so we're letting you go with a wave and a smile and there is not the slightest stain upon your 'character'. Yes, we ran you in ten years ago, charge of legitimate suspicion of corrupting minors, we know damn well your taste for little boys. We couldn't make it stick. Any more than we can make this stick.

If this dwarf, or dwarves but we'll say *Alberich* for handy reference, has not yet declared himself, there are several possible thoughts regarding that.

One – to make sure that he's covered. Wants no

open-and-shut cause and effect deal, dear me no. You
sell your house to the Agency Leclerc, quiet little deal
and no skin off anyone's nose, could be the child's sitting
in a pram on the seafront: dotty woman felt remorse.

Two – we're letting you stew in your juice twenty-four
hours; make sure you're cooked tender. Being an ex-cop
you could be pally with the local PJ. Think about raising
an uproar. Procs, judges of instruction. Forget about that
mate, withdraw any complaints made. The dossier is then
'classified without further enquiry': legally dead.

Smart, wasn't it? There were no Threats. Nobody (in
their right mind) would ever associate a property transaction with a little personal melodrama. But we're counting
on you, Castang, to be bright enough to add two and two.
We thought you a bit slow.

Rub-a-dub, rub-a-dub, rub-a-dub-dub-dub; what is that?
There are musical phrases which get into one's head,
won't be denied, repeat themselves interminably inside
one's empty head, drumming senselessly in one's head –
oh come on there, the light's gone green and the front
driver stands there sleeping – rub-a-dub, now shut up
will you.

The PJ, if not exactly an élite corps, is still supposed to
be more highly qualified, better trained, brighter in the
head than ordinary lumpen-cops. A high proportion are
'officers of police judiciaire' with powers conferred upon
them by the law, of enquiry and interrogation. Castang
passed a couple in the corridor. These are boys I could
have found under my command, if my own career had
followed its normal course. I'd never have got one of
the plums in the central direction at Paris, nor even
Versailles, traditional stepping-stone to the big time. I'd
have got, though, the command of a big regional service;
Nancy or Dijon or Strasbourg.

Like Richard.

One of them gave him a big wide empty smile. Another
switched his eyes away. What's going on here?

There are also powers which only Commissaires have. Retired or not, he belonged to the top grade. Respect is paid to hierarchy and his business is with the Divisionnaire, the chief; 'Le Patron' as he is known to the underlings.

Martre was very polite this morning. The signs would be read by those accustomed to working with him, knowing his little ways; or perhaps by those equal in rank, experience, knowledge. There was a feeling of his being a little hurried, not altogether impatient but call it evasive and one will not be far from the truth.

"Sorry about the press, Castang: as you know they're not easily reined in."

"Doesn't matter."

"Barring latterday miracles, I don't know but that they're pretty scarce, we can just about write off the frustrated-motherhood line. I've had two good women working on it. I've had informers out on the terrorist angle, there's the usual mass of insinuation and rumour but it comes to nothing.

"Woman carrying a baby – should have been noticed, attracted attention. All so slick and pat, I don't like it. Something premeditated, Castang, even carefully planned. Press hasn't turned up anything either. This is looking prickly. Almost like something political." Looking at his watch. "Like, uh, careful now where you're putting your feet."

This – overwordy – commendation towards caution is beginning to sound (Castang isn't unfamiliar with it) unhappy; like a man dragging his own feet. Showing absence of zeal until or unless the matter were to become a little clearer.

"You've hád no ransom demand. Why not, huh? Why no indication of 'this is what we want and this is how we propose to set about it'. Know where we stood then, huh? My antennae are telling me to lie low, wait and see."

There was nothing to be had here. Fellow acting as though he didn't know about a call from the Judge of

Instruction? When of course he had Castang's phone tapped? Come off it.

Rub-a-dub – there it is again.

Sure – of course – that's the 'Radetzky March', the inevitable last encore to the Strauss concert put on every New Year in Vienna, and they'd switched it on at the end to tease John . . .

"Those buggers in Wien, all asleep." There spoke the Berliner! "Dead conductor – oh you can see he's a musician, knows his job, can beat two tempi with two different hands, plenty of spin on it, plenty of *Stick-Effekt* but that's a dead stick, there's no forked lightning there."

Yes. A lot of Commissaires of Police follow this description, closely.

Or Ministers, who like to turn around during the 'Radetzky March' and lean up against the *estrade* and with great broad toothy grins conduct-the-public, which insists on clapping pom-pom-pom to an over-obvious beat, be they drunk, blind, or asleep.

The Palace of Justice was almost next door.

Madame Céline Fauchon. Rounded, comfortable woman. Late thirties and no young flibbertigibbit. Experience in the face, which was kind. Freckles. Small sharp white teeth. Got up politely to say hallo. Not pretty but 'nice'. Asked to guess you'd say 'Nurse'; you wouldn't guess 'Lawyer'. She sat back in her chair, tilted it to an alarming angle.

"Well, Monsieur Castang, I haven't a lot to tell you but I'm pleased to see you. I don't know much about you, but I've heard a thing or two that awoke my interest. Oh, not just from Martre. Been having a chat with him, have you? – ye-es, he was on the phone just a moment ago and as you see, I've cleared the decks for you."

"Yes," drawling it. "He was being a bit oblique. A scrap Opaque." She was smiling; knowing all about it. "'A word to the wise.' An excess of prudence is thought preferable to the over-fervent optimism." She nodded.

"You're of course a professional, of much experience. And you've been in Bruxelles. Moving among the Diplomats. Perhaps this is why it seemed particularly interesting to meet you."

"I agree that I have a large, and on the whole distinguished collection of examining magistrates." She put her head back and laughed full-throated.

"I won't be a Flamboyant addition. You notice we're alone. Officially my clerk is seeing her dentist. Nor is the recorder running."

"So I think you've something to say just between dentist and patient?" The smile touched her mouth again, and left it.

"Monsieur Castang, turn your mind back over your life and career. What would you find the most consistent feature of your dealings with judges of instruction?"

"That few of them have any sense of humour."

"I'm flattered but try again. In a political rather than a personal sense, and remember I said consistent." Well they're like this. They want you to reach a conclusion without actually putting the words in your mouth.

"In the light of your choice of phrase – I'm thinking. One makes an enquiry, one arrives at a conclusion. One forwards the dossier with some fairly clear recommendations. One then hears nothing about it for around eighteen months – ah, I think I see what you – that some dossiers travel faster than others?" She sat back, rolled the pencil on her desk, and said "Go on."

"The experienced officer doesn't ask himself the reasons for legal arguments which don't concern him. Ah – in this instance the matter does concern me. Martre's found out something? Doesn't tell me because he doesn't like it. You're looking for a way to tell me that you don't like it either. God damn it, we're talking about a child. Has she been found? Is she dead?"

"Hush. No, and no. Martre would have told you that. He's straight enough, when he's allowed to do his job.

Do not think personally. Exteriorise. Distance yourself."
She closed her eyes, began to speak in a hurried, colourless voice.

"Not long ago, it wasn't hereabout, the gendarmerie
made a dreadful botch of a murder enquiry. There
was loud press criticism, a public outcry – and strong
political disapproval. When that happens the next affair
is accelerated, the examining judge – my colleague – is
hustled; the whole thing goes to trial in two shakes of a
lamb's tail."

"What's the point?" exasperated.

"Keep an orderly mind, Commissaire. I'll find you classic
instances of cases most minutely and exactly prepared,
formidable presumptions brought by the instructing magistrate – my colleague – and most mysteriously, an
interminable delay in bringing such a man before the
tribunal for judgment."

Castang sat back too, closed his own eyes (feeling
suddenly tired) and said, "I see."

There was a silence. Then she said, "Not got a cigarette
for me have you? Doesn't matter what it is," when he began
feeling in his pockets. He was grateful.

"This is what Martre didn't want to tell me."

She lit it, blew smoke at the ceiling, looked after it, took
up again her rapid mumbled monotone.

"Martre, surely I don't need to tell you this, is a political
appointee and very sensitive to the winds which blow, and
if a secret message hidden in the filtertip says 'Absence
of zeal' he's highly alert to such." She opened a drawer,
found a saucer, put it on the desk, knocked her ash off
in it. "I want to smoke I'm supposed to go and do so in
the lavatory, something disgraceful, bad example to the
children. So I try to keep them for when I get home.
Understand me, Castang, this sort of thing isn't a directive
from the Chancellery. It's not said by my hierarchical
superiors. It's scarcely even conveyed in a tone of voice.
But in this job one gets sensitive pretty quick. Does no

good playing the deaf or the obstinate. Times I subpoena a witness, and that witness is somehow always unavoidably prevented from attending. I get medical certificates. I don't, you know, get a phone-call from the Minister."

Castang rubbed his forehead with both hands and said, "You got any advice to give me? Just while we're having a smoke together in the shithouse?"

"Yes I have," in her normal voice. "Don't go to the police looking for results. Don't come to me, I've nothing to say on any subsequent occasion, or on this one either. I have one little grain of an idea, that if a blockage exists it's not Paris, for what good that may do you. But you've been a cop, haven't you? It's something local. Truly, I don't know any more."

He had reached the door when she spoke again through a haze of the cigarette she had smoked too fast.

"Castang – friend – I think that baby is alive and well and cared for. You find something out, you bring it to the Proc. My guess is you'd find he'd listen. Something evidential, just a thread and I'll instruct it. It's what I've been looking for, for quite a while now.

"Ah, yes, I knew there was something else. Do you know an advocate, name of Bastien? Snuffy old sod out of Pau? Buttonholed me here this morning. Pleading some civil cause along the passage, but gist of it was if I were to see you he'd be glad to have a word. Crooked old bugger; breath smells something terrible. Rather you than me. But if you see him tell him I passed it on."

Outside the door, Castang thought of John. Who'd asked fetchingly, "Were you a good policeman?"

"Fair," he'd answered. "Beating people up is what they do best."

The Palace of Justice is not that of Paris – or not in terms of sheer size. There were still quite a few courtrooms for Castang to dodge in and out of, in search of his old gentleman, discovered in a nook with a few more of that ilk, smoking cigars in a conclave of perfect amity preparatory to being very cutting with one another in court. Maître Bastien appeared dirtier than when last seen even though the light was no better; imperfectly shaved, dubious round the neckbands, robe pungent with the legal distillations of many many years in places like this: Madame Fauchon says it's his teeth but – well, fearful smells are the policeman's lot in most corners of the earth.

Richard found friends in unlikely places; just look at myself. It was one of his skills; terms of the closest intimacy with some frightful old *clochard* as with the most aftershaved young whipper-snapper from the National School of Administration.

"Wanted to phone you," taking a hideously wet cigar out of his mouth, "couldn't get through, didn't matter, sure to be tapped anyhow. Bethought then, pleading here this morning, paths might cross. Might have a little light to shed." *Eclaircissement,* word also used of a 'sunny interval' on cloudy days, which today was.

"Nobody'll notice us here. Consultations with clients, common form, we won't be overheard. I've been looking at these papers of our friend. He got on the track of some business deals. It's nothing directly evidential, no leverage there, more in the nature of suggestive, that if – we'll say the fiscal authority – had grounds for pushing an enquiry into whitewashed accounts, one might get a few surprises.

"Now our friend was of course in retirement, with no mandate for pursuit. There was an area of conflict about the title to some ground. It isn't clear but the suggestion is that parcels of land were acquired in ways thought questionable."

"Open to misinterpretation," said Castang pleasurably.

"Nothing is illegal, until a judge has pronounced it so."

"Is anybody specific named?"

"Yes, but we'd do well not to name him, unless we wanted an action for criminal slander to lie against us. Our friend expresses the opinion that the police, if duly empowered by a magistrate with a mandate for search of business premises and seizure of documents, might well uncover conclusive evidence. A magistrate," dryly, "is not likely to issue such a mandate, without sufficient grounds for complaint."

Castang could hear Richard's voice saying 'Catch Twenty-two.'

"We're not likely to convince anyone," went on the lawyer. "Going to look would create a domino effect, involving local notables, all well entrenched in the power structure."

"I have a complaint," said Castang, "on a grave criminal charge."

"No way can you make it stick. How are you to link the one affair to the other? You've no shred of evidence. I can do nothing but pass on the conclusion our friend reached, that this is no better than tendentiously circumstantial."

Castang did not mention his conversation with the neighbour. He knew perfectly what Bastien would say. 'You think you could ever get a fellow like that to stand up in court? These people will think of nothing but covering themselves.' Nor would it be helpful to mention his little chat with Madame Fauchon. 'The buzz in the Judge of Instruction's office is that the Ministry-Public is inclined to be dilatory. And this confirms an absence of zeal, perceptible also in the corridors of the PJ.'

Bastien would reply 'Domino effect . . .'

"Where is this gentleman to be found when he's at home?" Bastien told him.

"I want to go out."

"Where to?"

"I don't know."

"Walk, you mean?"

"Yes. Miles and miles."

"I don't know if I can manage miles and miles." Vera has been limping more, in a day, than ordinarily over a year. "I'll do my best."

Two consecutive sentences; that was a lot. Since the moment of the child's loss she has scarcely spoken at all. She has talked with her daughter, Castang thought. With John. With, to or at himself, no. She has not asked whether I should prefer to be alone – 'thinking'. Her place is beside me, that's an automatic assumption. Her silence, now, was a support. Indeed, a comfort.

He thought about Bettina. A Swiss woman well known in Brussels. Tall, blonde, and beautiful; blazing hair and a lot of diamonds. Married to a mild man in Ag and Fish, greatly liked by all as both man and colleague, and whom one didn't ask to dinner – because of Bettina.

But at a formal party, a Community-cocktail, her aggressive manner and strident voice was inescapable. Her huge shattering tactlessness had been known to strike a table of twelve or fourteen dumb, writhing with embarrassment she never noticed. Even Harold Claverhouse, famous for effortless mastery over man, woman or child, had withdrawn in confusion, producing thereby a memorable phrase – 'I bruised myself badly on Bettina's shinbones.'

Yet, and equally as well as for the waving fields of ripe corn hair and sapphire eyes, she was famous as a devoted, arrow-straight wife and an excellent mother. Shouldn't this outweigh the little failings?

The most egregious bluntness or colossal shouting rudeness is known throughout the Community as 'Doing a Bettina'. Her man will go nowhere without her and maintains an impassive mask of Stout Denial.

Vera can be very tactless indeed, and extremely brutal. Perhaps all women of very strong character are. And with it, humble, vulnerable, wretchedly over-sensitive.

They climbed hills outside Biarritz and Castang said,

"We could have lunch at the golf club." He could see she was at the limit of her tether.

"Will they let us in when we don't belong?"

"Nothing stops us asking." He wasn't sure himself. The enclave of wealth and élitism has a forbiddingly exclusive look to it, but it was nearly midday. In and around the neighbourhood there are three or four of these seaside courses, all rather grand. He didn't know whether this were the grandest, perhaps because oldest, nor whether this had been Richard's playground, because he'd never asked.

No problem at all; "more than welcome; you can have one of those little tables by the window". Vera went off to the lav and he asked for a beer. "Belgian?" There were several stewards and all of them pretty girls with wide smiles. One gave him a menu, extremely impressive and remarkably low prices. "This is something more like it" he told (a washed and combed) Vera who looked about her and was impressed by everything.

Only a few steps away, across raked gravel and clipped box, was (he knows this much) the eighteenth green. Rich men, and women too (they wear, carry, and are surrounded by expensive paraphernalia) are approaching the house, thinking about lunch. They are trying to get the little ball to fall in the little hole: it struck him that they mostly seemed bad at this. Indeed, little balls clattered about, reprovably inaccurate. Of a sudden, a missile struck apparently with immense and surely unnecessary force, banged on the wide bay of glass – it seemed an inch from his ear. He gave a jump and said, "Jesus".

On his other side there was a loud chuckle. Nobody had seemed perturbed and the glass was obviously armoured, so that Castang turned, with a face of protesting innocence.

"Often happens," repeating the chuckle. "Some of these boys . . ." only semi-indulgent, "shouldn't be allowed out without their mothers."

It was a sight familiar in Biarritz, a 'curry colonel' with a beautiful silver moustache and a soft well-pressed tweed suit. And he had spoken English – not that one needed telling. He was by himself at the next table, eating shellfish (with a curry sauce).

"Forgive me. Rude of me."

"Not at all," said Castang politely. The truth was that he welcomed the distraction. One couldn't think all the time, and even a very good lunch (and a bottle of Meursault) could not stop his mind from squirrelling round in useless circles, while a silent Vera opposite offered no slackening of his tension. "I want to learn. Please instruct me."

"You don't play this silly game," wiping his mouth with his napkin and taking a drink (red Bordeaux), "those little balls are elastic, built for speed. The little dimples lessen the air resistance."

Castang fell readily 'into conversation'. Even Vera became fascinated. The 'colonel' had the good manners of his generation and talked well – and amusingly.

"One could make – probably has – an Agatha Christie of it. Most unpopular bugger in the place laid low; if that ball took you upon the temple, say, it could perfectly well make an end of you. One would have twenty suspects and a row of red herrings."

"Took me between the wind and the water I'd feel it more and enjoy it even less." The colonel looked a little prim, as though his generation had been brought up not to make questionable jokes in front of women. Precautions had to be taken: he explained about 'Fore!' but Castang thought he wouldn't like this game.

Was that how the subject of football arose? Which Castang found plain boring in normal times. But charmingly, the man found himself remembering his youth.

"I'd quite agree nowadays. Player with talent, their one idea is to saw his leg off for him. Not to speak of the ultra-defensive, so sterile, playing four-four-two or even a four-five-one – but when I was a boy, d'ye know, they played two-three-five and it was a real attacking game. It's true that the pastime was slightly looked down upon but we used to collect the cigarette cards. Do you know, I think that even today I could name you the Arsenal team of thirty-six or seven. I suppose they did get beaten sometimes but damned if I can recall when."

"Try," amused.

"Let's see – Moss in goal, was his name Frank? No matter – in front of him George Male and Eddy Hapgood, no defenders like that now. Midfield, the incomparable Wilf Copping. Didn't he have red hair? Oh dear, I've a blank here . . . I've two; that's really bad. But up in front – on the right, the splendid David Jack. Inside him . . . devil take me, it's on the tip of my tongue.

"Nevermind, because out on the left is the wonderboy in person, our very own Cliff Bastin, and inside him is the Scottish magician with the baggy trousers, the one and only Alec James. While in the middle is the most dangerous head there is and that's Ted Drake.

"Come now, eight out of the eleven, that's not half bad at my age. Course, there were villains who claimed Dixie Dean was the better but you see, we were Londoners. Oh dear, am I being the most awful bore?"

"No no no," said Castang laughing, "you've come up to scratch – I say, is that English?"

"It is, it is," delighted.

"And fairly beaten I must beg you to allow me – what shall it be, cognac?"

"A bore," said Vera speaking for the first time, "wouldn't ever admit it, doesn't even know, and the dreadful thing is it's very hard to tell them without their getting vexed."

"Tell me, Madame, tell me, I beg of you," with gallantry; the colonel was greatly enjoying himself. "My wife doesn't hesitate. Alack alack, and my only excuse is that Americans are just as bad about baseball."

"And in Hamburg," added Castang, "they'll get very

heartfelt indeed telling you there's nobody now like Uwe Seeler."

For a whole halfhour he had forgotten the black pit of despond.

"Here's my card," said the colonel with some splendour, "and if you want to join let me know and I'll put you up."

Castang managed a phrase or two. He was thinking that the sooner they were out of this part of the world . . . Would he hesitate an instant? Would Vera? A house, what's a house? He liked it, and she liked it more. Set against the child it was not worth a snap of the fingers (English expression?). The only real, live question was how to set it up. Through Bastien, probably . . . he hadn't yet told him so, and wondered why he hadn't.

At home they found John, sitting slumped, and Emma distraught.

"There was a phone-call." Castang took a deep breath. This is now the high dive. You are shaking: there is no disgrace in shaking. Breathe slowly, concentrate well. Keep your legs straight and your feet together. Enter cleanly; it looks like concrete from up here, but it's only water, and this isn't wind. Just a nasty cold draught.

"No!" said Emma. "D'you think I'd be here? No, better, in one sense, and in every other sense worse. A job for John. Which we cannot possibly take. How could one . . . ? I left your number with a friend at home," she finished miserably. "Of all the stinking coincidences . . ."

"There aren't any coincidences," said Castang. At lunch he had drunk a lot. The walk had cleared his mind. He went and got a bottle, poured out four glasses. "What kind of a job?"

"Repétiteur," dully. "Nothing much and one could still say," with all the bitterness that was in her, "too good to pass up. And turn it down there won't be another. And we cannot . . ."

"Oh yes you can. And will. Because you must."

Emma got up, and stood stiffly, to look him in the eye.

"Not if I were to live a thousand years."

"I'm going to make you a solemn promise. Which I haven't made you often. When I do, I keep it. I'll have your baby. Inside a week. I'll have to stay here, or it's probable. Your mother will bring her to Leipzig. It's an oath. On my life."

"And on hers."

"Emma. You must trust me."

John got up, then. They were all standing in a group together, stiff, in the centre of the room.

"I'll take your word," he said.

"No," in a hoarse shout. Castang took a stiff, awkward step and put his arms round her; age-old instinct and the best one can do, and words do not strengthen it. She cried, grinding it deep within her, wringing herself out, until one cannot breathe and the effort must go to living, to getting air back into the exhausted lungs. Then she stood again on her own feet, braced herself to pick up the glass, drank with her teeth clattering on its lip, and said, "I'll go and pack." Vera hugged John, looking for something to say, finding nothing.

Castang was left to fumble with the anticlimax, floundering across to his desk and opening drawers. Had he dived, or was it only a clumsy, despairing jump? He didn't know what he was looking for. There was his pistol, neatly laid away. He didn't want a pistol, useless object, try again; came up with a handful of German money, marks saved from his own last foray across frontiers, pushed this in John's hand muttering something about small contribution to help with the piano maybe.

"*Abrazo*." His shaved cheek touched John's, unshaved.

"I've your word."

"I've only one." It isn't the upper lip that needs stiffening. Castang is not the first to be exasperated

at this being inaccurate as well as the world's deadest
cliché.

"Drive carefully." This one, phrase of every mother at a
parting, since the invention of the wheel, refuses to die.

"I do," said John.

"I will," said Emma. Castang was blithering about think
of the fools and the criminals on the road. When, mercifully quick, they climbed into the Volkswagen (Vera has
kept some baby clothes, with no word said but "I'll need
these") Castang raised an arm, dropped it when they were
out of sight. The picture which had come to his mind
was that of an English officer many years ago in Ireland.
He was about to be shot, in reprisal for the execution of
hostages. The British conducted a dirty war there in 1920,
and so did the IRA. He looked around him and said, "Fine
hunting country." Ernie O'Malley tells the story; a man
who knew and respected courage when he saw it.

Vera had gone 'to clean out the guest room' and Castang
sat by himself.

It had been a day or two after the New Year. Lydia had
come down for the weekend, 'late as usual' said Emma;
she hadn't seen her sister in two years. Both now grown
up, squabbles forgotten. The family together, thought
Castang; a fine moment. Here in this room, listening
to music. Undoubtedly Lydia had wanted to tease John,
saying, "Put on some swing, a gutsy bit." He had hunted
about (John saying, "Why not?" with an innocent face),
found the Carnegie Hall Concert. Benny Goodman 1938,
apogee as they say of the big-band-era. So stiff and
self-conscious at the start. "Well," kindly, "technically
very competent." Skip on to the Quartet; John's eyes
began to shine then. "But who is that man?"

"Lionel Hampton," and at the end of 'Avalon' he was
under the spell. "Only the very best are like that."

"Skip to 'Sing', Pa," in Lydia's 'commanding' voice.

Gene Krupa's drumming, as vulgar as always and here

so compelling. And what's vulgarity? wondered Castang. Harry James is appalling, Goodman himself can be unspeakable: here both are perfection. They have all been heated and hammered into plasticity and now the sound has a spontaneous cohesion . . . what good here are words? Where else do you get this? Even the best symphony orchestras reach it rarely. One must be lucky. The man with the stick; hardly any of them – so that every single human being present, yes, even the firemen, are wiped clean. When the world starts again, it will be from scratch, and even original-sin no longer exists. This sudden, total silence, cleared there for Jess Stacy.

Nigh sixty years on now we have this, the rough casual old microphone pick-up of the time so crude and blurred, full of coughing and laughing, and we have it by accident.

'Somebody should have recorded that.'

'Somebody did.'

I dived, Castang told himself. Or perhaps 'I had jumped; it seems.' How? Because of this moment? Jess Stacy died, this last year was it? People die, in California, ninety years old, and the last actors of the swing era, of the glad confident America, have now all gone. I remember one day in Paris, when I was still a boy, he went on thinking. A lot of laughing and drinking, with even the police joining in. I didn't know, I shook hands with a man with a lip, which tells you he is a trumpet player. Yank Lawson, they told me. Others too maybe, the names Lydia swaps about. We've had moments; this was a perfect one.

"You won't often hear piano-playing like that," agreed John soberly.

On that shitty old record, a hundred-and-eighty degrees from the sterilised operating-theatre of today's recording studios, you hear the yelling of the audience, you hear Krupa shouting, Lionel's liquid bubbling ey-yey as he gets hotter and hotter, the laugh when Goodman moves the mike closer to the keyboard. Stacy doesn't care or even notice. He is gone to the land of Avalon and if he doesn't get back his life has not been wasted.

"Isn't that Something?" said Lydia, leaping about: one has to laugh at the child's carefully-fostered New York accent.

This moment of happiness has given Castang courage.

He – who was this? He, one-time Divisional Commissaire in the Police Judiciaire; now in retirement: mm, very. He, formerly an Advisor upon affairs concerning criminal law in the European Community, now hopefully named the Union; legal experts for-the-use-of. A counsellor, in the drafting of proposals towards unifying the codes of criminal procedure. It all sounded quite grand: it amounted mostly to being a dogsbody for Mr Suarez. 'Whom God Preserve,' Harold Claverhouse used to say; 'he's Professor Strabismus of Utrecht.'

These were positions; he was a somebody of some consequence. His skills were supposed to be worth something. Dammed if he could see any use to them today.

He sat on a bench by the sea, smoking a small cigar; it tasted good in the open air. He turned up his collar; he had a viewpoint here, but a draughty one.

This scruffy little public garden is called the Atalanta Plateau; a rocky point, the oldest part of Biarritz. From here on top, spread out before him, was the town centre, the nineteenth-century florescence. Or what there was left of it: the railway age (but the station has long gone) and the nouveau-riche grandeurs of the Empress Eugénie. Now mostly knocked down and replaced by the newer, still nouveau, riches of many eager dwarfs: one or two of the Monuments remain.

Over there, halfway along the Grand Plage, the immense neo-classical pile of the Hotel du Palais, and beyond it the modern Aztec temple, wedding-cake in white concrete, of the Miramar. And here almost at his feet the neo-gothic splendours of the 'Empress'. This had been the other grand hotel, rather smaller than the Palais but just as ludicrous; even fancier and more impressive to those with a taste for such things.

For years and years it had stood empty, a white elephant nobody wanted; as a hotel unusable since the days when servants outnumbered guests. No cook would work in those basement dungeons after the war, no waiter would climb the slippery pierced-iron stairs to the dining rooms, no chambermaid would ferry chamberpots along those twisty stuffy passages. It was not the broad and massive English Gothic of Saint Pancras but a tall and narrow – very French – invention whose architect had been looking at the Mont Saint Michel; a wonderful and quite lunatic affair of crockets and pinnacles and improbable flying buttresses. Much admired, and had engendered several more Hatters-Castles only slightly smaller along this coastline, all with many iron grilles and fences looking like instruments of medieval torture, all with this dark blood-boltered look.

Granitic, terribly cold in winter – iron furnaces roaring like the crematorium of Auschwitz. A remark in extremely bad taste but what other comparison can be found to describe this? A good dash of Scotch-baronial, distinctly monster-of-Glamis; a reminiscence of Hearst's San Simeon. One wants to burst out laughing; one would and one does, but Castang isn't laughing. He's using binoculars but there is no penetrating those narrow lancet-arch windows.

It was never knocked down. True, it was immensely solid, a fortress for all the flimsy-seeming flibbets – decorative gibbetry; one could hang traitors on the portcullis, stick heads on spikes; sea birds would pick out eyes. Any Gothic fantasy is permissible.

It wasn't allowed to knock it down anyhow; some loony in Paris had it classed as a historic monument. The people of Biarritz viewed it with something like affection – now that they no longer had to work there. And then – and then . . .

Castang had done some homework. Hereabouts one had to conjugate the verb (a modern one) 'to tangent'. Originally an Italian verb, which has replaced many clumsier phrases about pots-of-wine or palm-greasing. Or how to cover a crooked deal with bribes, and how to cover the bribes so that they look like an innocent invoice for value-received. Pork barrels; feather-bedding; Laundering. Skilful tangenting makes an inextricable muddle of private and public finance; judges of instruction tear their hair, if they have any, over what went in to the social-housing project for the poor and what got siphoned off into somebody's country-house swimming pool. Tangenting is as old as the island of Corsica and as modern as the newest marina, and it's the especial skill of the Dwarfs: you can know them by it.

As far back as he had got, with Bastien the main and often the only source, Monsieur 'Edmond Framont' was no more than the usual shallow-water shark, and probably his name was Bloggs. A tribute to the deftness of his hand? It is illegal to change names in France: deed-polling doesn't exist. Of recent years a tendency has shown itself to add the 'de' particle, and given the French passion for acronyms – he is often known in the 'Economy' columns of newspapers as E.d.F. Since this also stands for Electricité de France one could speak of an adroit scrap of self-publicising.

So he'd been, for a good few years, a fixer of the commonplace municipal sort, in the Bordeaux region, a specialist in picking up decayed or defunct small companies, injecting energy, and an undoubted talent for finding cheap homely objects which appealed to the public imagination, and reselling at a large profit: the skill is in knowing when the fashion for such things has just peaked.

"We know a few more bandits like this, no?"

"Not quite the same," said Maître Bastien, blandly. Well, he would know. Been consulted often enough, no doubt, by such, anxious to perfect the art of sailing close to the wind. "It mostly goes to their head."

Castang understood; megalomania is the characteristic affliction of banditry. They start buying antiques, yachts, football clubs. Then their debts catch up with them, the banks foreclose on mortgages and the tax authority becomes stroppy. Some are in jail, and others have fled to South America.

"This one was cleverer than that. Humble; low profile. No big pyramids. Never tried to leverage more than it would bear."

A reputation for being sound. A great prudence. Never raised his voice, never sought to be popular, never appeared on television. But knitted, steadily, pleasant and friendly relations with people in power. Always sufficiently distant and never asking for any favours.

Not as easy as it sounds. The self-made man is familiar in fiction and not very believable as a character: a caricature like Mr Merdle, as superficial as Flora de Barral's father. Castang, who doesn't bother with fiction, asked a few pertinent questions.

"Politics?" Many of them, in France, have built empires as mayors, senators, even ministers.

"No. Close friends, wherever possible, but doesn't dabble. Not even a regional councillor."

"The technocrats?" That was more complicated. In this country the new aristocracy is that of the High Schools, the mathematicians gifted for abstraction, who lose touch with the light of common day and become aridly, boringly dehumanised.

Hasn't even a university degree and probly despises those who do. But who 'dressed the part'; English suits and a polished, slippery exterior.

No confidence tricks. Nothing as coarse, as crude in the Merdle-Barral sense as inviting the public to invest in a phony enterprise. The Framont affairs were dull nowadays, as unspectacular as they were unpublicised: in a word, Sound. He had long divested himself of manufacturing interests, which were too much trouble for too little result. Nowadays these are all financial holding companies, and Castang to whom words like investment-trust are so much Chinese doesn't even try to dig deeper. How did he . . . ?

"Yes, that was extremely astute. There's a Paris office still, but it's something small on the fifth floor. Take a look at the top of the Empress and instead of a statue of Saint Michael the Archangel, there's aerials; he Listens. Strong on communications; he's well into any Internet you can think of. It's a satellite world; who needs offices in Tokyo when Seoul or Singapore are closer by than Bayonne?"

He had chosen a smallish world, and a pleasant one, as gateway to Taiwan or South Korea. Not for him the big towns with their perpetual manoeuvres and assassinations within the power structure. It pleased the local people; it buttered up the notables; it trod on no one's toes; it gave just the right touch of eccentric folklore publicity. A kindly, cultural-minded Maecenas, who bought pictures from local artists. He had bought the Empress for an apple-and-an-egg (earthy Flamand phrase that Castang had learned while still in Picardie) and without changing anything of the exterior structure had turned it into the cave of Ali Baba. There were offices – sure. There were guest suites. Monsieur 'de' Framont lived in a flat at the top. There was a private dining-room and a small very expensive restaurant down below, where the dungeons used to be and with a pretty view of the waves breaking on the rocky point. Really, it ought to set Castang's mouth watering.

If it be so . . . if it's just remotely possible . . . since there isn't any shred of real evidence. But then, then this is an adversary the likes of which he has not encountered.

The Mafia picture collector in Lugano – brilliant in his

way, a formidable manipulator of events, and of people, but in that very theatricality not real. The solitude and isolation, the contempt and the vanity – there'd been a great basic crack there. And instinctively, while drunk and angry and not even thinking, Vera had gone straight to it. This was a man more real and thereby the tougher and more resilient. There would be no doubt of his vanity but it would be the less neurotic. A greater self-knowledge?

Castang was saved from these ridiculous, and pompous speculations by thinking of other men and women, as – apparently – impressive. Some had also been wealthy, powerful. 'You've quite good fingers for the rich,' remarked Richard at one of these moments.

Richard – what had he in fact known? Had he been close to finding the evidence his nose and experience told him would be there? Had he abandoned from fatigue and illness? – from cynicism?

This man had been aware; he had suspected that Richard might have more than just a message from his nose. He would have made an offer for the piece of land, as he had for the others in the parcel, and met with refusal, and told himself that this was nothing but the obstinacy of a dying man. He could afford to wait.

And then Castang had shown something of the same tranquil immoveability. Had he inherited any damaging facts as well as a house? Richard had decided, and Bastien had confirmed, that the facts weren't damaging enough. But the man did not know that.

And this would be at the bottom of the whole thing. Why would such a man adopt so crude, so melodramatic, so violent and even so risky a means to squash an obstacle?

Richard's last joke . . . he had respect, and he had affection for Vera, for myself. Mostly, his mind was clear; it was possible that the treatments from the doctor clouded him betimes, towards the end. He was paying us a big compliment in trusting us. And if his judgment got clouded; if he thought what he had better than it was.

The man Framont does not, did not know. Finding me, as he thought, over-confidently cocky towards his bribe he became angry because frightened, and decided upon something this drastic to make quite sure I would be beaten flat.

I don't see how this is to help me. The man has good friends, here and in Paris, powerful enough to take all the juice out of a criminal enquiry and its legal process. One need not be astonished at that quite frequent occurrence. There are people in this country still alive, who have enjoyed immunity ever since Vichy days. There is one, a notoriety, who has been charged with crimes against humanity on half a dozen occasions over these fifty years, who has never been brought to trial and never will, who will die peacefully in bed and in perfect comfort. The instruction of a devastating dossier was never allowed to gather impetus. Twenty different Ministers of Justice have been aware of a minute written in a margin recommending that zeal be not shown. For this man was one of ours.

Castang was frightened. He felt his impotence like a scalpel touching the scrotum. He had been sleeping badly, and had no courage. His life was a failure, and now it was as good as ended. *Qué*, a fucked-up police officer who got unstuck. A PJ Director in magnanimous mood. Find the fellow a cupboard; make it a Comfortable one. There's this sinecure in Bruce we've been asked to find a body for. Ach give him that, he can do no harm and he's bright enough we don't have to be ashamed of him. He comes recommended by the *sous-chef* for criminal affairs – an old friend. Look, over there he can't embarrass us. It's only a theoretical job, advisory blah-blah in the Communauté.

Both those men had been replaced since; euphemism for being sacked. But that's all in the game; a new Minister of the Interior loses no time in filling these posts with his own creatures. A job in Bruxelles – it wasn't thought important enough to have Castang unstuck again.

He got up. He went on down the hill, feeling a bit tottery on the pins. Rheumatism no doubt, goes with my age. He felt that he was inside a familiar dream, in which he was pushed out upon a stage, facing a huge dark auditorium full of people looking at him. He was brightly lit. Worse, from over there in the big black pit someone turned a spot on him, blinding him, a fierce light beating on him. He shuffled forward to the centre. Was it a speech he had to deliver? Or was he supposed to do something? No word or idea came, and he stood there like a fool, waiting for the catcalls to begin.

But he had promised. He had given his word.

The gateway had been cared for, the rusty old iron grille replaced by some elegant wrought work. Logo of the company; it didn't say *Arbeit-Macht-Frei*. Grass would not grow so close to the sea but bushes and plants had been found which would be comfortable here. There was pavement, and there were rounded stones in sizes between pebble and boulder, and there was a pretty fountain, and there would be a gardener to keep it all clean and tidy. Over to the side was the entrance to the restaurant: that wouldn't do him much good. On the left was the office entrance, where there would be some damned terribly helpful and certainly pretty girl receptionist. These were estimable qualities; not, perhaps, quite what he was looking for. Assuming one knew what one was looking for.

Between was the café, and perhaps one wanted a second breakfast. This was made fairly obtrusive, to beckon people in off the street if they felt exclusive, and expensive, and were beautiful. There was a broad terrace, where people would sit in summer. Not now, but when the tables and chairs were set out it would be pleasant, with a glass roof to keep the rain off and sun blinds over that, and glass against the wind, but not so as to interrupt the view. Inside, it was nice too. The management would rather have a few of the pretty people than a mob. The tables were spaced, and their tops were clean and shone; the chairs were rattan, cushioned and comfortable. It was quiet and cosy, with thank-god no music.

There weren't a lot of customers. Two business men in dark suits were having a good tuck-in but most of their attention seemed to be towards the pink pages of a financial newspaper. A thin elderly woman in dark glasses was drinking black coffee, but her purpose in life had been to take her dog for a run along the beach; it sat beside her, disappointed that there was no cake. And then there was him. There was only one waitress, doing her housework behind the bar; no barman this early. She glanced up, gave him time to settle in. He looked at the menu, which said 'Breakfast' – helpful in four languages: he understood fairly rapidly why those handsome briefcases looked well-stocked – need to be stuffed with bank notes going by these prices. The eggs came 'any way you'd like them. We will recommend the classic Au Beurre Noir, or En Cocotte à la Crème.' Further down it said 'Sausages' and below that 'English Sausages', and then the waitress was by his table, and he said, "Good morning. I think I'd like a beer, please."

"We've Belgian, German or Danish."

"Belgian," said Castang feeling patriotic, and she nodded and moved away; there'd been something vaguely familiar in her face, or was it her walk? Extremely smart, with starched bows to match her apron, and with an embroidered badge on her breast (plastic is low) saying 'Ilse'. Good legs, elegant walk; gave one an appetite. Middle-aged, but the bottom going away was – come, Castang, this is not the purpose. Then she came back, and while uncapping the beer and pouring it carefully she broke into a sudden smile.

"I thought I recognised the face." So did he. It was the woman in the dress shop, what seemed like a long long time ago. The smile which did it.

"And did the nightie fit? She enjoyed it?"

"It did, and she did. How clever of you."

"I remembered because – there was a picture in the paper, a bad one but – a story about a missing child. A baby stolen, some girl who'd lost her wits – did they? . . ."

"Not yet, I'm afraid. It turned out more difficult." The smile vanished.

"But that's awful. Is it – is it your baby?" He understood; she thought he looked a little old.

"My granddaughter."

"Oh my god, just as bad. Why is it? – we exchanged two words and straight away I feel involved. I'm sorry, I'm being intrusive."

"Don't be sorry. On the contrary. But I'm holding you up."

"No no, I'm not busy. They're good for a while yet. The old dear comes in every day." It had given him time for instinct, if not for the laborious little clockwork wheels of thinking.

"Ilse—" She made a face.

"Waitress name. Sounds more like a prostitute to me but no matter, I've got used to it. But my real name's Lisa."

And now he'd had the time to think.

"If you like to, you can help me."

"Like to! Help you? . . . I mean, of course I would but what on earth? . . ." His eye was travelling round; she mistook this. "Oh, I'm gossipping with a customer but 'sall right, there won't be any manager before eleven." A rather hangdog young man had come in, sat irresolute, was gazing at the card. "He can wait a minute."

"What time are you off?" It knitted her brow a scrap; she'd be wary of even a remote pick-up sound.

"Three-ish, this time of year."

"I have to do some explaining. Could I give you a beer or something then?"

"Let me just take that fellow's order and I'll be back." Only coffee. She walked across, the face professionally 'Ilse'.

"Do a bit of the explaining now."

"I'm a painter and I'd like to do a picture of you." She frowned until she saw that he – "The paper said you were a retired police – I see. Or I don't but okay then, any time after half past two." A small grin of complicity, and then the more distant 'Ilse' smile and she moved off upon the duties of a good, well-trained waitress in a high-class establishment. More people had come in for breakfast when he had finished his beer. A barman had come in, and took his money without looking, and she did not look up either. Perhaps she would be already regretting her unprofessional admission of a mere chance-acquaintance into her off-duty hours.

At a quarter to three outside the gate, for he wasn't anxious to compromise either of them, there she was in a winter coat and her shoes changed, carrying her traps in the anonymous bag, a woman you might notice on the street, but only if you had a painter's eye for unordinary faces.

"I have to pick up a child from school in a while, gives you a good hour. That enough?" It was to underline 'respectable married woman', but a touch of humour to tease him, too.

Another café, a good deal dirtier; he liked it that she made no comment. A corner free, and two beers. Sitting across from her, no regrets. Diamond-shaped face, a high narrow forehead with a bit of fringe over it, wide-spaced eyes, one with a slight cast, a matt biscuity complexion and a broad thin mouth; mouse hair but the good ears which Castang always looks for. Neither a French nor a Spanish face; he could find himself attracted to it. Remotely there was something of Vera there: when he thinks that a girl appears desirable, there always is. Men are like that. There would be, he thought, 'a Polish granny' there somewhere.

"Can I say Lisa?"

"You can," Like that; it wasn't an encouragement to be familiar.

"I'll tell you in a nutshell. I want to learn more, a lot more, all I can about your employer." Inside an hour one can say a lot. In half an hour, come to that, since she didn't interrupt. Even the 'sleepy' eye grew larger and burned at him.

"But this is appalling. Has he the child there, d'you think, inside? It would be possible. Oh yes, in fact distinctly, no trouble at all. There are so many ways in and out."

She didn't try to 'explain'.

"Have you a piece of paper?" Yes, one habit which has never been lost: the ex-police officer always does have the notebook with him. She's like him, makes little drawings. The hotel is the lower floors. Not many rooms nowadays, maybe forty and most are suites. The offices are above that. Separate lifts. We don't go up there. Evguenni, that's the maintenance man, he might. There are two cleaning women, sour types they both are.

"The office people come downstairs, conference room, dining-room, next the restaurant. Sometimes they come to my café, and I might be called to serve inside too, the odd time. So I know them. Not well. There aren't over about twenty, counting Paris, New York, it ebbs and it flows."

"The thing is," said Castang, "do you believe it?"

One could see both Lisa and Ilse thinking about this. Things seen and heard. A waitress is not seen, nor heard. Often she stands still in corners, the good ones alert to a gesture, a tone of voice.

"One can't say one knows him. Probably no one knows him well. Those eyes, like poached eggs. I suppose too I know him. The office people don't, you know. He's always friendly, a good listener, and always cold, always distant."

Yes, he lived there. A flat right at the top of the Gothic pyramid – must be a marvellous view. There's a wife, one really sees very little of her. Often in Paris or wherever.

Has meals sent up sometimes, but nobody gets in to the flat. There's a secretary. Middle-aged, very confidential indeed. That really would be blood out of a stone.

Castang was thinking that here, at the least, was a witness and a good one. A chink in the door, and how could he make use of it? That was a bad phrase, 'make use of'; it had a manipulative, crooked sound. But any tool whatever, that he might find to his hand . . . There were things now to think of, which he could ask her to look out for. It wouldn't do to be seen often in the café, where he would quickly be known and remembered. He could ask her phone number.

Lisa was thinking.

"Yes I could believe it, dreadful though it is. And dotty, a horrible dottiness but I think it fits. So – utilitarian. That's what fits, to use a human vulnerability because that is seen as weakness." She turned her head, away from the street outside, to look him straight in the eye, staring; her own eyes as though focused on something behind his face. "Give me your book again, a sec." A good waitress can write very rapidly on the pad in her hand, keeping it legible, where a man will make a scribble like the one that Castang was paying for – a cop looks carefully at the price of a beer and this was a lot for two Kronenbourgs. She pushed it across. Ilse, it said. A street, a number, a floor, a phone. Clear as print: she was trusting him. "I have to help you, don't I? Because I must. I find this odd."

"Odd, you can say that again."

"Not that way odd." Buttoning her coat, gathering her affairs, the bag, the umbrella; she hadn't a car, or she didn't bring it to work. "Odd, you're not one of us. We are the stupes, the poor silly working class, the idiot – ducks." She had been about to say 'cunts' and delicacy stopped her. Vera, over the years, had acquired the habit – from the police – of using what she called rough language. Even today she'd need to be fairly wound up before she'd say cunt. Because, in her mind – 'I feel respect for my cunt'. So – wasn't she making it plain? – did Lisa, and Ilse too.

"They all feel such contempt for us. You've only to look at the television – one can make those idiots jump any way one wants, they're dough, plastic, utterly passive. Put some stinking aftershave on Joe and she'll pull her knickers down without even being told to. Well we don't, you know, and among us there's a sort of solidarity. You, you're a bourgeois, and you don't have the remotest clue. It just so happens that for once you've done something which throws you across the electric fence. You're inside Auschwitz."

A highly Polish remark, he thought: nobody was ever there but themselves. But she was sensitive enough to see, and correct herself.

"Fascists are the same everywhere. Look, come to my place, this evening – around nine, I'll have my daughter in bed by then. No, I've no man. Skipped out on me years ago. But I'll have someone for you to meet, maybe." She swung off abruptly, crossing the road as though she didn't want to be seen with him. Quite right, he thought; you don't want to get involved with me. Your employer wouldn't like it either. In the dwarf kingdom, the social classes do not mix.

One wouldn't say anything to Vera. Not yet. It would only make her the more anxious, the worse strained. When – in times gone by – the police officer had to go out again after supper (a very odd meal, eaten almost in silence and Vera's cooking was peculiar; he was careful to make no comment) she had known how to live with it. It happened often enough to be all in the day's work, and if she hated this above all of the job's unpleasant aspects she closed her teeth and did not speak of it. But alone in the house, and while the children were still tiny, she suffered every time. Too much imagination. When he got back, and however late, smelling certainly of drink and probably of thieves, prostitutes and policemen, she would be in bed but always awake. He had the habit then of taking a shower before doing his teeth; symbolic in a way.

So that he said only, "I haven't worked too badly. No real light yet but I begin to see some things. I have to go out again. It shouldn't take me too long but don't try to wake up." She nodded, cleared the supper things, switched on the television: if any inanity could be yet more inept than the French senders then the Spanish would fit the bill. Halfway through the evening informations-bulletin – or that's what they call it – she got up suddenly and left the room. A few minutes later, above the sound which was turned down to drool-level, he heard something like a sob. He got up then too. The door to the next room was not quite shut and the light was on. He pushed it just a little. Vera paid no attention and perhaps did not even see him because her eyes were shut. She was lying back in a chair, her throat contorted by effort, her jaws clenched but her breath coming in gasps. She had dragged her clothes down and was masturbating in the jerky violent way of someone who only desires to be finished with it. He didn't think there was anything to do: volunteering to help wouldn't be welcomed.

He took a piece of paper off the phone table, wrote on it. 'Bathe perhaps? Or a vervain? Trust me. H.' The commercial tisanes which come in teabags are too dry to have any real flavour. Better than nowt (make a note, to look on the market for fresh). Vera never took pills. By herself she wouldn't drink either – at least, she never used to. He looked at the level of the cognac bottle; seemed low but he couldn't remember whether that mightn't have been him. He put his hat and coat on; before leaving he took a stick too. At night one was never altogether sure of the encounters one might make.

Ilse-Lisa lived in quite a reasonable street; narrow, dark, dingy, by day at least noisy. But these were old houses, solidly built, a bit lacking in the modern conveniences maybe, sinks and washbasins decidedly antiquated, but less cheek-by-jowl than the run of post-war social housing. She lived on the third floor; stairs to climb and an unaired smell but it would be preferable to the rackety blocks with every television set blasting and outside in the shadows the young, restless and aimless, bored out of their minds and spoiling for an excuse to kick someone's kneecap. She had released the catch on the street door the moment he rang and was waiting for him at the top. She looked trim and welcoming in ribbed white tights and a loose smoke-grey top; hair with a healthy shine under the feeble landing light and white teeth in a broad smile. Inside was warm and crowded and comfortable: cheap 'Ikea' furniture from the Scandinavian supermart but smart and well cared for with cotton Tunisian rugs and primary colours and smelling fresh as though she'd had the window open. He made an appreciative face and noises; she was pleased.

"I've only this and the one bedroom – 'sall right, she sleeps well – but we manage and it's quite close for work, and schools or whatever; even the market's not far. Like a beer? And I've someone for you to meet." In the 'Man's chair' was a massive figure; a broad ham of a face and a broader belly, close-cropped iron-grey hair and hands like machine tools and a smile as broad as hers and a beer glass, and already two empty cans. Ilse went into the kitchen and came back with two more and a 'pretty glass' from Beck in Hamburg for himself.

"This is Evguenni but here we call him Eugène. He's like me, a Polish bastard or maybe Ukrainian, he's none too sure himself. A blood-thirsty old bastard too, he did a hitch in the Legion and that's how he's in France."

"Légion look after their own," in a placid rumbly bass. "Moi do plenty dirty jobs. Not talk about it. Got two wounds," holding up a hand with a missing finger. "Légion pay well. Eugène not speak much French but good for action." Castang understood perfectly. Ilse had served herself an apricot juice. Keeping her figure trim meant an eye on the beers.

"The thing is, back in Sidi bel Abbès or wherever nobody gave much of a damn about his French; action's what counts. He's the day maintenance man at the Empress. Plumbing, electricity, what-have-you. And electronics, there's a great deal of that. Security systems up to here. Eugène knows how to open doors for you. We're old friends and we don't like fascists. You might even say, bring Polish whores and beggars this far south we get quite Anarchistic."

"Eugène fucking Communist. Monsieur Pasqua think bad type, throw him out. But can't," laughing heartily.

Castang's eyes have opened wide.

"I've also another friend for you. Give me one of your fags, would you? Jacky can't be here tonight because he's on duty. He's the fish-cook, pretty good one too. You could maybe meet him by tomorrow. Are you going to be cross with me? I've given away a few of your secrets. We have a few secrets of our own. I had better leave Jacky to decide whether he wants to tell you his, but knowing yours he'll be likelier maybe to trust you. I don't know how well you know this town. I've been here ten years. We're not as provincial as we seem. We used to have a lot of Russians and we still have a few. We've what you call the dwarfs and they have the place by the balls and make money out of everything. All that's unimportant really. Odd if you like; what you mustn't forget is that peel off all that golf club shit this is a Basque town. I say no more, but Jacky is Basque."

"I'm quite good friends with Basques," said Castang. "In fact I lost my job on their account, a few years ago, and on that account too I'm sort of a sympathiser." He told them a little of the story of Robert, and of Velma, thinking it might interest them. It did. And—

"That'll interest Jacky," said Lisa. "One wonders whether he was around, thenabout." She was suddenly deep in thought. Contemplating, this could be called, possible consequences if Castang turned out crooked. Shouldn't she have learned by now, that it never did to trust anyone, anyone at all? Pretty slick talker and so had been her own one-time man, now by the mercy of God firmly her ex. To listen to him you'd put your hand in the fire for his honesty. And she had listened, several times, each time telling herself she was a fool, and each time fool enough to go on listening. What was it people said? – Once a cop always a cop; blacklegs every fucking one. Suppose this one were an infiltrator – wouldn't he come with just such a pathetic hard-luck story to melt warm hearts? Ol' Lisa always trusts every sweetmouth twister and always finds herself the piss-post. This was why she'd turned herself into Ilse – a woman she didn't even like much but it was safer that way. Not turned far enough? Snakes change their skin but (confused, this, but she knew what she meant) leopards don't change their spots. Piss-post you'll always be, girl.

Eugène sat there stolidly with his hands across his belly, wondering whether it would be all right to ask for another beer. Lot of talk . . . there always was.

It wasn't too difficult, thought Castang, to know what was going there through her mind. The French are forever asking for things to be made clear. 'Transparent' they call it. Word much used by politicians, and by which they mean the precise opposite. But in Poland, perhaps? . . . he'd known a lot of Poles in the days when he'd been on post in the north; they're thick on the ground up there.

"No no, I haven't been feeding you a lot of bull-shit – back in that dress shop I wouldn't have known, would I?"

"Hardly. I suppose." Cheering up a little. "Just remember though would you? Tell even your wife and I get kneecapped. Or something worse. Course, so would you. But you'd have plenty of protection. Even so . . ." Jacky didn't look dangerous, she thought – but he sure as hell knows people who are. "You're to meet him, if I say I'm satisfied and I suppose I am. That woman. You talked about. Sounded as if I'd have liked her. Anyhow . . . tomorrow afternoon. You know the pub in the village? Opposite where they have all those African antiques? He'll know you, and he'll pick you up. Now Eugène here is my witness." That gentleman smiled peacefully.

"Ol' Eugène know your face. He not forget you."

I seldom bet, thought Castang, but I'd put my money on this, that in the old days in the Légion you were a pretty good bowler with the hand grenade. He got up, and said,

"Thank you. Both of you." She held her cheek up to be kissed.

From here it wasn't much of a walk, ten minutes maybe, to 'the village' clustered round the point, and the far side of the point the Gothic castle, Monsieur 'de' Framont's extremely well-organised fortress. And no doubt exceedingly well protected, but he'd have a stroll around to get the picture clear. The front one knows, with the wrought-iron gateway and the landscaped forecourt and the flowers – and some discreet but efficient floodlighting. It was near midnight and the restaurant was closed, but lights inside the hotel entrance and a night-porter on his rounds. Guests would get given plastic cards and they'd have to show them, and maybe they'd open some doors and others they wouldn't. You'd still have to show '*patte blanche*', the whitened paw of the wolf in the children's tale of the little pigs . . . But what about the back?

This was found too, where one would expect, down a steep narrow laneway just big enough for delivery trucks. Near midnight the kitchen was of course shut and the back barred up like the Santé prison. There'd be a little pantry open where the night man could make a smoked-salmon sandwich for the belated hungry guest, and a cup of coffee for himself: a good possibility too of a night security man who'd check the electronics every hour or so. And

Monsieur Framont would have seen to it that he did. A little cabin, behind the manager's office, with a row of blue lights saying all was clear, and would wink red at any malfunction or interference? Back of the accountant and the safe for guests' valuables. Hm, it might be a little less simple. To be sure, there is a master switch to all this, and Eugène might know where it was to be found. Was all this supplied by the municipal electricity cables? Or was it like a hospital and they have their own generator, just in case of a big storm and an – even momentary – power cut? There would be ways of finding out this, too. One couldn't expect Eugène to give away information that would compromise him: this is a good job he has here. One would have to see first what 'Jacky' thinks about it all. The tricky part is to come. But this wasn't a bad evening, was it now? It took a moment's effort to recall where he'd left the auto.

Vera had slept quite well, woke up fresh; it was still dark, but morning coming there, or was that the false dawn still? Looked at the little window of her alarm clock, redly digiting away there; oh well, wanted to go to the bathroom anyhow. She opened the window, dressing-gowned against chill, breathing a still sweet air, and she heard the owl call, down there in the wooded dip below the headland. She didn't know much about owls; this one wasn't the Whoo-hoo kind: the distant, clear, menacing call was confident, a little hoarse – Ohhh. Paralysing the mice with terror.

She could not see it of course, but she stood still, picturing. A leisurely, even laborious flight; the deadly stoop. An omen. I'm not the one who's paralysed, she thought. She closed the window quietly, wrapped herself more tightly in the gown. I've been paralysed; I know what it's like.

In the kitchen there was a note on the table. 'I was fairly late,' it said. 'I'd just as soon you didn't call me, o.k? I'll want the car this afternoon so if you've shopping? Love

H.' A homely detail – 'mundane' is the word. Like him, somehow; always wanted house-keeping things planned, and could get very vexed indeed if she forgot and there was only a tin of ravioli for supper. And when she *had* planned, the supplies assured, he would appear carrying a piece of fish or some spinach, saying vaguely, 'Looked fresh so I thought I'd pick this up.'

She put water on for coffee, turned the paper over and wrote 'Works out well. I might not be back for lunch, so forage.' She drank a cup of coffee while it was very hot. Thought she might like a boiled egg; the innards needed staying. Sat, a while, thinking. She'd like a cigarette, a thing she seldom does. Didn't want to disturb the sleeping beauty, but there would be a packet on or in the bureau. Here indeed – and a lot more junk too. Thinking about this she sat at the bureau and wrote a short letter, thought better of it and went to throw it away, thought better of that and put it in her handbag, had another cigarette back in the kitchen. Planning – not the moment for planning.

She took a deliberate sort of shower, making the water hot and turning it at the end to cold, jumping about but this was what she needed. Dressed, carefully; no raggedy undies with holes in them. It must be ladylike on top too; neat but not gaudy; no, better than that. She spent some time on her hair, which was always a pest, being limp, and never really nice whether short or long, and she'd never been able to make up her mind which was the better. Made herself up. No jewellery (she has very little) but perhaps yes earrings. It all took a long time, what with peeing, finding her handbag (she'd left it in the bureau), changing the earrings, couldn't think what she'd done with the car key. In Biarritz she had to find a place to park the car, never easy with the morning rush. But of course, this damned hotel has space. One mustn't be intimidated. There was a silky grand *concierge*, and there was a young *chasseur* with his mouth open; she offered a lavish tip.

"For long, Madame?"

"I expect I might be an hour or so." It was exactly a quarter past eight.

"Madame?"

"I'd like to see Monsieur de Framont."

"Monsieur de Framont?" The tone contained multitudes. Never heard of him, as well as That will be exceedingly difficult, and You hadn't an appointment, had you? He looked her over at some length, appeared satisfied with the outward aspect.

"I think, Madame, that if you have a word with the receptionist – over there – she'll put you in touch with the secretary."

A very pretty young girl, her real beauty spoiled by the eye, hard-boiled and then put under the cold tap.

"Well—" much astonished at the words 'I wish to' – "I suppose I can always ask. You hadn't an appointment, had you. Your name?" Surely much too rudely. Holding the phone with the tips of her fingers, as though it might make them dirty. Vera felt sudden irritation, reached over, took the phone from the painted nails and said in her deepest voice "My name is Madame Castang. My business is personal and confidential. When he knows who I am, he will find the time." She felt astonished at her own efficiency. The new voice was soft, clear, spaced; plainly an older woman and one who knew her job, because perfectly polite.

"I have that, Madame, and I'll tell him. But I mustn't hold out much hope, because he has to go to Paris and has a very full day. Perhaps I can make an appointment for you, tomorrow even?"

"No," said Vera.

"Madame, I have to ask you to show patience, and I can give you no guarantee. I will pass on your message."

"Thank you, I'm grateful." In the halls of hotels there are always a great many chairs which nobody ever sits on. The girl looked at her with unconcealed hatred and to save her face embarked upon a long conversation, apparently with the housekeeper about a changed booking. Vera lit a cigarette; it was a good idea to have brought the packet with her. A waiter glided across, put an ashtray in front of her, bent down and whispered, "Did Madame wish for anything?"

"*Merci.*" Then she wished she'd said yes, but it was too late by then.

It took ten minutes because she had two cigarettes; her nerves were burning her up and she felt ashamed: she didn't even want them. Two or three customers pottered. One had a bill to pay, giving the girl a chance to tear off the computer print-out with a lordly gesture. An unnoticed lift door opened. A man of fifty or more in clothes of English cut, even here rather extravagant, walked across the intervening space. Not slow, not fast, not looking. To the *concierge* he said, "Now where is this car?" The voice was not in the least raised, but carried very clearly.

"I don't know sir, I'll find out." A classic answer. Vera thought it almost a Police answer.

"When you do find the driver," there was no breath of sarcasm or impatience in the level, even voice, "you can tell him to waste a little more of his valuable time in waiting for me. I'll beg you to employ your own meanwhile. Ring the airport. Tell my pilot that I may have shall we say thirty minutes delay, he's to adjust the flight pattern according."

"Certainly sir. The driver is to wait?"

"To wait," with quite a royal inclination of the head. He turned with the same deliberation; the eye rested on Vera and he took a few steps. "Is this the lady," to the reception girl, "who wished to see me?"

"It is," said Vera. He made a faint formal bow.

"We don't seem to know each other. Edmond de Framont. And your business you said was confidential; we'll make it so. The little conference room" – to the girl "– is it free? As you see Madame, some small hitch has occurred in my own employments; shall we make use of it?" a hand movement indicating that she should precede him.

Castang would certainly have suspected that the scene was staged entire, for his benefit. That this man was adept at manoeuvres and that quick thinking lay behind the stately manner, he knew already. Vera thought of herself as slow and innocent. That was only partly true, but it did put her at a disadvantage.

Dark blue velvet, pale birchwood furniture, an impersonal space. There was no window but a whisper of air-conditioning kept the atmosphere fresh.

"May I take your coat? We'll sit down, shall we?" A small oval table and six straight chairs, a cabinet for papers and another for drinks; he smiled at her look about. "Just a place for discussions, perfectly suitable." She put her gloves and bag on the table and he sat down opposite her with oddly old-fashioned and mannered gestures, sleeve and shirt cuff just-so, the hands folded under the chin; small white hands well-shaped, a narrow wedding ring and a wrist watch, both plain gold. "There now. I will make the time that is necessary, we can speak quite at our ease. The room," smiling, "is not wired. It is possible of course that you are wearing a wire." The move was sudden, and so swift that he had her bag before her own hands were off her lap. "This is heavy. I conclude, a gun. Many American women carry one. Here that is not prudent, and the police would look askance upon you. With your permission I shall return your property when you leave."

She realised her own foolishness. Henri would be simply furious. Now she was still further at a disadvantage and she had to fight to control her voice from trembling.

"I am wearing no wire." Level, at least, but it was like listening to her own voice recorded, the accent much stronger. Like some Arab – talking pidgin. She felt small. Framont did not go on smiling but spoke as to a child.

"Not everyone I meet is my friend. I follow elementary

rules of prudence. I am also what is termed courageous. These two qualities put me where I am. If you pointed your gun at me, that would not impress me. Supposing even that you fired it. You would probably miss, but in any event you would go to prison for a longish spell, and where would you be then? Now let us speak sensibly. Who are you and what do you wish of me?"

"Who I am you know very well. What I want is simple. I want my grandchild back unharmed." Now her voice was getting stronger with her resolution. "I know who you are, and what. My husband would prefer no doubt to build a legal case against you, and both the evidence and motivation are clear. I don't see things that way.

"You want my house, for purposes of your own. They don't interest me. Nothing here interests me, not even your own inhumanity – that you must live with, and settle for yourself. I'll make you a straight deal, one for one and nothing further. You today, put the child unhurt here in my arms, that day you get the property you wanted conveyed by the notary at the face market price – you can afford that," her only effort at something like sarcasm, "and that attracts no notice. I suppose legally that takes a week or so – you're in no hurry, you say – but my signed promise to sell will keep the notary quiet, and I'm so sickened I have no wish to stay here knowing that you appear able to bend an entire town; the municipality as I understand, and even the state apparatus of justice. So let's make no further bones, lose no further time in admiring your own cleverness. You get what you want and I've no doubt you'd know how to arrange the matter with nothing to point to the empty mask of your nothingness. Do we agree?"

There had been no alteration in Framont's face or attitude. Sitting in an English sort of fashion with one leg crossed over the other the most he did now was to cross the other leg: one must not interfere with arterial circulation after the age of fifty.

"My dear lady, an impartial witness would be forced to conclude that having constructed a theory, paranoid though that might appear, in quite a feminine manner and that is always appealing, you stick to it through thick and thin.

"As so often in these tales of grievance is to be found a tiny grain of truth. Certainly I had wished to acquire that piece of land to which you have as I gather title. I had instructed agents to go about that in the habitual fashion; to offer if need be a generous sum. I am never impatient. People refuse; very well, sometimes they change their minds. To jump from that to a suggestion that I would somehow countenance a criminal action – if I understand you rightly – is of course preposterous. I must urge upon you that to make known such fantasies would do you further harm, would indeed invite a suit for defamation. In private I hope I can take a kindlier view.

"A moment's calm, my dear lady, for this tempestuous approach puts you in a delicate position. Hypothesise, that I should agree to your proposal that I buy your property. People could be found to give credit to your supposing I had held some threat over your head, prejudicial to your peace of mind. One cannot give effect to a business transaction with quite the simplicity you find desirable.

"Consult your husband. Some instrument could be found whereby a lawyer might state in terms that would satisfy a court that no such supposition existed. That would remove one obstacle to an amicable arrangement."

Vera climbed to her feet. He stood up at once, courteously.

"Give me back my bag please."

"Let me help you with your coat."

"It's always said that in France one should never do things simply. Not when a complicated means can be found." He smiled, put a finger over his lips, opened the door to let her pass.

"Not in public, I beg of you." In the hall the reception

girl, the concierge, a probable security man – or was that his driver? – were doing the obsequious hover.

"*Voiturier!*" The young man hurried forward but Vera said,

"Don't bother, thank you," and took the key from his finger. Framont was bowing. They were all bowing. She should be on stage having flowers thrown her. 'Ladies and gentlemen this is the happiest moment of my life.'

Utter humiliation. Perhaps much worse. She might have compromised, and fatally, the plans Henri was making; she didn't even know what they were.

She parked the car, nicely, facing outward, so that he need only get in and drive away. Only then did she notice that she'd forgotten to do the shopping.

Very well, it will be something beastly out of a deep-freeze and who cares? I'm dead on my feet, anyhow from the neck up, and it's likely that he won't even notice.

The foolishness! And I saw myself walking in here with the child in my arms saying rather casually, 'Henri, you might fetch in the shopping for me.' Sitting down to give Berlin a ring.

My vanity! It's true that I have done silly things in the past and the sheer outrageousness of them took everyone by surprise, knocking them off their balance. How could I for a single instant have imagined I could do that here?

And the gun! Supreme silliness (put it back quick while he's in the lav). She didn't know what she had thought of – 'Have I perhaps gone right round the bend?' *What* bend? – the one in the siphon? Some vague notion of frightening the man, startling him, and he'd smiled and said, 'You'd miss.' Probably, now that she thought of it. If she were ever to pick it up with Henri in the room he'd say, 'Put that down, silly'.

Perhaps she *wouldn't* have missed. She has been friendly, betimes, with policewomen, and they had even shown her how to handle the thing. Henri didn't know. He'd only have said, 'These girls can be alarmingly casual with firearms.'

She must control herself. Up to this morning she hadn't managed too badly. Now she must start again from scratch, that's all.

Three

"It doesn't terribly matter, I shouldn't think," on Vera's confession that she'd forgotten about lunch, forgotten the shopping, wasn't very sure about anything. He did though have vague feelings of hunger. They were both pretty far out, he supposed, from the secure shores of reality. Known as being At Sea. "We'll go out and eat somewhere."

Fidgeting with the driving seat of the car – no not like that; try again – he remembered his sea-water cure: there'd been a lovely quiet girl, name of Frédérique, who used to massage him. 'Your back is hard like a board.' What would she say to it now?

Vera's heart sank when he took the road out to the point, lurched into a deep abyss when he turned the car into the parking she had left half an hour before. But she had said she would control herself. Now's the moment to show she meant it.

"Food here's said to be good. Won't be a lot of people. Are these my keys, or yours?" He had no thoughts at all. The sketchiest notion that knowing nothing about an adversary, anything you learn about his familiar surroundings is to the good: for what good that may do ... but he'd have to have something to eat, before tackling Jacky. Which was close by, and it might as well be something good. Try out Jacky's cooking. Expensive place but wasn't it the moment to put out more flags? Poor Vera, might it take her mind off the misery? There wasn't a table free 'with a view' but a blandly varnished headwaiter escorted them – this is better really; one can see the room. Comfortable, Castang? Nobody can sneak up in your back. Like something out of Ernest Hemingway.

It would be some decorator's taste: yes but Framont would have approved it; thought it necessary, but felt at home with it. This made the difference, to one's own morale.

A bad room, badly proportioned: the food will never taste really good without a properly high ceiling. Good restaurants are simple, and for preference even shabby. This was a thoroughly French vulgarity, of shot silk and cut velvet, of gilded wrought iron and morocco leather and none of it better than a micron thick. Every detail that minute fraction wrong. Veneers of exotic wood instead of honest native walnut; the curve of a chair leg that scrap too far. The certainty that it isn't real gold leaf, that the leather has been split and planed and chemically faked; no honest Moroccan goat but a cow that dropped dead of old age. Castang felt contempt and this was what he needed.

But the food was a pleasant surprise. The mode in such places for pederast dainties – *les Mignons, les Délices* – has passed but pretentiousness has only changed costume. There were some horrors, and when he asked for water there were eight different sorts including the one from Wales, but the fish had a robust local sound, and he had to eat fish because of Jacky. A good wine to gladden Vera's heart; he'd have just one glass of it. He had more; this was marvellous fish, neither overcooked nor over-seasoned and he began to look forward to meeting Jacky. And the wine waiter is a girl, and points to things which aren't shockingly overpriced, and these are all happy surprises and here, Monsieur DE Framont, is to a lot of dust in your eyes. Castang in his fairly faded suit (Lanvin but several years old) had not noticed Vera's clothes. A sensible woman: she has decided sagely to get drunk, in the nicest possible way: 'this is supposed to be salt-cod; nothing more peasant than that, and I've never known anything like it.'

"Do you remember a thousand years ago, eating fish in Pruniers? No, in London. Saint James Street, come, sharpen your wits. Hats, shoes, Brookses and Boodleses. English fish, very good it was. It's been a long time . . ." Becoming a bit maudlin, is she? Did it matter? He knows her meaning. That they've eaten fish – together – in places grand and humble, and almost anywhere you care to name – for many many years. All the time we've loved each other.

"We ought to have a fish," he said, "on our coat of arms."

Together, he thought, we'll get through this, too. I've come no further perhaps towards a man like Framont but I've come closer to understanding myself.

"Let's have some pudding," said Vera. "Help sober me up."

"Yes. I want you to take the car. I'll walk home. I'm meeting someone. I may be some time."

There weren't a lot of people in the café; a simple little place of bare boards and wooden tables, where no tourist would ever set foot. A housewife gossiping with the man behind the bar, a few old boys playing cards. A momentary lull in the undertone of conversation when he came in. None of Framont's people would ever come into a place like this. A plain-clothes cop might, but they'd have him rumbled inside ten seconds. Even if he were to wear the leather jacket and bedroom slippers (winter and summer wear of old countrymen) and have failed to shave these last couple of days.

A man slipped quietly into the chair opposite, offered a (very clean) hand.

"Mister Castang. My name's Dolf." An old tweed jacket. A ragged open-necked shirt. Two pullovers – it's hot in the kitchen, and cold outside it. So he looked like an off-duty cook, which of course he was. Then one looked a little further, one saw a man of fifty with remarkably good features and two penetrating greenish-grey eyes. So – one would say – then a good cook. Which he was, and Castang knew that already. "What's that you're drinking?"

"Rioja. They say."

"It's no good?" It was revolting; what wine-growers call 'fat'.

"It would make a camel switch to Perrier." A small smile. Dolf got up.

"We'll go in the back room." Passing the bar he said quietly, "Bring this man something fit to drink." The 'back' was a cosy frowsty little den with a lot of worn-out leather armchairs and unemptied ashtrays, a violently patterned carpet (one could drop ash without its showing), a gaudy brass-and-veneer television set and on this a crocheted mat; on that a vase of plastic flowers and an Andalusian dolly in a flounced skirt. They made themselves comfortable. Two glasses and a bottle appeared of wine with a lovely colour.

"Here's to you, Jacky. I ate your fish, bloody fine it was. Ah – this one's good." Another small smile.

"That Ilse's name for me, is it? He brought you that shit not knowing you. Now you're with me all the Policia in the Pyrenees can walk in and be no wiser. You ate fish there? Quite right, I'm a good cook. And that's a good job. I'd be sorry to lose it. Which doesn't mean I like the man who owns it. I don't. But I'm careful, with my fish, with that man, with policemen. All right, let's get to business. I'm here, and I agreed to meet you, on Ilse's word, that's a good girl. Nothing more than that; I was curious. I know a bit about you and I propose to learn a bit more. It means nothing. You couldn't even prove you've ever seen me. Nor am I any sort of terrorist. I'm a man who knows a lot of people and now I'd like to know you, I might be able to help you and I might not. So we might both be wasting our time, that's up to you, I'm just a cook having an afternoon drink between two shifts."

So Castang spoke and Dolf listened. Good listener. This, thought Castang, is a 'smoke-filled room'.

"You know Martre? – the PJ chief in Bayonne?"

"I know him and I don't. Younger than me, we weren't at school together. We've crossed paths a couple of times without noticing. It's clear he'll do nothing for me. May have orders, I couldn't prove it. He knows my name isn't bright and shining, in PJ circles, now or ever, much. He reckons that getting involved in private business of mine might not do his career any good. Won't get his feet wet."

"Has danced with a man who has danced with a girl who has danced with the Minister," said Dolf indifferently. "You don't know any of the RG boys? They sort of frequent, around here."

"Not my territory, ever. Was one a few years ago called Morosini, nice fellow. I got up his nose on a little job of my own." Nod.

"I know about that. Thing is, you're a loose cannon. I don't mind particularly. Some people I know wouldn't want you as an au-pair girl. Or even pen-friend. Once a cop always a cop, they'd say. Now this man Framont, apart from being a turd, which he is, however gold-plated, what d'you make of him?"

"I don't know him much – yet. My information's pretty one-sided. He's very well dug in around here; in Paris too. He's plainly confident he can put the lid on any sort of police enquiry, legal process, administrative interference. I don't mean anything crude like building contracts, feather-bedding the street-lighting for the city of Nice. But these are all small towns along here. He's big enough and wealthy enough he doesn't have to kick back to any local machine. My guess would be he contributes to everybody's funds, whoever wins an election the odds are on his side, nobody would want to cross him and any little favours he'd like done he'll get, because he has good friends in Paris and in Barcelona and no doubt Madrid too."

"I'll fill you in a little bit," said Dolf gently. "You're thinking of some little shit, got a nice job on the Social Housing and getting paid off like in Nice by all and sundry. In with the Masons, got a nice country house, taxpayer put in the plumbing and the swimming-pool. This man's a lot more than that. Knight of Malta, that mean anything to you? – very exclusive. Big with the Vatican – *That* mean anything to you? *Opus Dei.* Now they can manage their affairs very quietly indeed.

"I listened to Ilse because this is one I'd quite like to see slip upon the banana skin. We could arrange that. But apart from you there'd be a lot of complex political considerations. Is it opportune? I'd want to talk to some people. I better not hide from you I'm cold on this. Dry. You're a good chap and I like you; that means nothing at all. Personally I can do something for you. I work in that dump, I can find out if he has your baby, if he's got it there, how he's looking after it. His wife – Solange – she's not a bad woman but she's putty in his hand. That I can do; be a pleasure.

"Anything more, I'll hold out no hope at all. I'll talk to some friends, I better say my own vote would be no, and unqualified, there's too much heat in the kitchen right now.

"But let's go this far, you know the rugby ground? Aguilera? You know the pub, opposite? Big deal, they've a player there coming up for the Equipe-a de France-a, and the match this weekend is sort of fierce. So you be there around this time tomorrow, I might have some people for you to meet. Wear an Olympique scarf and make sure they aren't Aviron colours, place is full of fanatics and any cop there, likely to get himself lynched. Okay?"

"Understood," said Castang.

I think yes. I think that asked to give a formal opinion after listening to the evidence, hearing the arguments, giving my full attention; weighing the matter; I do have to come down on the side of insanity. Since we are in committee; this is a private deliberation. We are not in Court. I am not a judge and we are not a jury. My colleague across the table has psychiatric qualifications and any opinion I may form is based only on my admittedly broad experience as a police officer. I'd like the secretary to make a minute to that effect. I don't say the man can't be treated. I believe he'd respond quickly enough to the obvious remedy. Take away the obvious source of anxiety and he'll be as normal as Herr Schmidt and Doctor Schumann; I suppose I've known twenty just like him. A man lost his living and walked in to the manager's office with the gun openly in his hand. A woman who'd lost her unemployment benefits went for the social assistant with a kitchen knife. They both sat down immediately afterwards, perfectly reasonable and consequent, to wait for the gendarmerie. An injustice perceived as being without remedy save by direct action. They had attempted legal remedy and been denied it. No no; the Court won't recognise this as insanity.

Castang, stop fantasising. In all that you'll only find one relevant fact; that I'm an experienced officer. So I'm retired now. I remain bound by my oath of fidelity and obedience to the Republic and the authorities duly accredited. Which as we saw in wartime Germany can only be put in question by crimes against humanity.

No look, when I took those people into custody to prevent them doing further harm to themselves or to others, that was as far as it went. Investigating officer takes a brief statement on fact. 'Are there children at home?' – that sort of question.

States of mind are not within your attribution. A bit of common sense. 'Mention this to anyone beforehand, once you formed this intention?' You are there to see that the law is respected and nevermind about injustice.

Calm discussion over a couple of drinks. Is or isn't it

advisable meaning opportune to – it wasn't said. They weren't spelling out the action proposed. Nor the method they might choose. All that they're concerned with would be a deliberation whether the political timing is opportune. You don't talk to them about injustice either. Fellow is a good choice; in one and the same breath you're putting the boot into the French government, the Spanish infiltration, and the Vatican for good measure. Fellow's no loss, anyhow. Arranges the affairs of friend Castang here, so much the better for him.

You are drinking with these people. You're not about to go running very fast to the PJ in Bayonne. The only result there would be the loss of Castang to the world, pretty rapid. Would scarcely even interest Martre: this sort of talk is three a penny. The police want and need a 'commencement of execution' because that's the only sort of proof that a court will consider. What's this? Pub boasts, for no other reason than to puff up our credulity.

Friend Dolf – he's not carrying a gun or planting any bombs. He's a communications man. Sure we can pick him up and put him on ice awhile, and all that happens is that a restaurant loses a good fish-cook.

This is very good for you, Castang. Nice long walk, almost into the country. Some gardens, some green lanes before you get home. Clear your head, after sitting in the smoke-filled rooms; drinking a lot too. You're a bit mad; probably about to be more so. Because you promised Emma, and you have to keep your promise.

It had been overcast all day but a clearish sky, a grey like a veil through which now and then the sun could be perceived: look, you can stare at it. It wears a mask but it's there. Be reassured, good people; we don't think the world's coming to an end just yet – not anyhow over the next half hour.

Which should give him time to get home. Step out smartly, for seaward here come these big cumulus clouds a-sailing in, and they look pretty dark. He was wearing his trench-coat, it's a genuine Burberry, and one of his better hats. Bogart could play the part but ol' Bogart wouldn't want to get Drenched. Castang lengthened-the-stride a bit while indulging a new fantasy involving a 1939 Packard coupé with a canvas top, and a flat pint bottle of goodish blended whisky in the glove compartment. Come to think of it, these roads are not altogether unlike the way Laurel Canyon Drive must have been in the thirties. Those pre-war Packards were beautiful pieces of precision machinery. Would no doubt be much prized nowadays; worth a heap of devalued dollars. He had never been much interested in cars. The Sultan of Morocco has five hundred of them in his garage, and the Sultan of Brunei will always go one better, and both of them scared out of their wits of a little bladder cancer going creepy-creepy. Come, Castang, diminish your madness. Put it into reverse.

At home there was a Surprise. He opened the door and heard voices and there was an overnight bag dumped on the floor and one knew who did that. Light, and warmth, and whoopee, and drinks being poured out, and a loud enthusiastic yell, and extraordinary trousers tight over a bony behind, and weird shoes with very high heels, and Lydia.

"I got home," said Vera, "and the phone was ringing, and so I drove out to the airport, and Guess who's coming to stay the weekend."

It lasted about five minutes. A new job – and some new clothes to go with it – and perhaps, um, a new flat; there's in store still, in Bruce, a lot of Goodies in the way of furniture, I'd like to Rescue. And then, "Any Progress?" in a sharp bossy voice rather like a warlord demanding news of the secret weapon.

"Some ideas."

"Walk in on him, is what I'd do. One can't let things drift. All right, I know – Ma's house. And it's quite ignoble. But who the hell would want it, if that way we could get her back?" Vera didn't say anything at all.

"In theory, I suppose," said Castang at last. "There are a number of objections. We don't even know for sure, we've no real evidence. He can laugh and say he knows nothing about it. How do you do a deal with someone who is capable of a thing like this, who thinks of it, who carries it out? You've nothing to bargain with, you're powerless to prevent him doing as he pleases, you don't even know if he'll keep to an agreement. You're like Whosit, Chamberlain, thinking I'm a businessman, I'm a reasonable man, I'm an honourable man, so that Hitler must be one too. The moment it was clear they wouldn't fight he turned around and ate Czechoslovakia. All the warlords are like that. Something for nothing. They'll only respond to force. Where you've no legal constraint . . ." his voice tailed off; he didn't want to go into it. "I've thought about this, of course. Can't go oneself, one would send the lawyer. An hour or so of meaningless talk, ending with you hand him everything he wants on a plate and dead cheap – that's what he was after in the first place. Maybe a few days later, when any coincidental ideas of cause and effect have had time to evaporate, you Might get our baby back. By pure chance, found in the ditch, oh, the gendarmerie will say, must have been Stolen by the Tinkers – the legend that the gipsies steal babies is alive among the backwoods to this day, and they'd pretend to believe it. It's perfectly true that the Gitans live by shoplifting and nobody adds that so does half France.

"Believe me, I've thought of it," wearily. "It may come to this in the end. Is it self-respect, or is it just foolish pride, that stops a man giving in until he can no longer get up off the floor? Under law," he said slowly, "there's a referee and he can count you out and you're finished; that's it. Here, under a very thin skin of pretended luxury and polite manners – your mother and I went to look at it this morning – there's a man who takes what he wants by craft or by force. Down in Calabria kidnapping is still a commonplace. And do you remember Baron Empain?

To hurry things up they cut his finger off. A tiny child – the man knows I'm helpless. But while I can still get up, or while I've still a knife in my hand, I won't lie down and roll over with my paws in the air. And that, my girl, is where we stand."

Silence fell. Lydia said, "There must be something . . ." When she had said this a second time with even less conviction Castang answered.

"Oh yes, there's something. I won't tell you because I can't. And it's so thin I can't believe in it. I can't see where it might start and I wouldn't want to think about where it might finish. I'm supposed to be a police officer. So I'm not going to talk about it at all and don't try to ask me; that's flat."

There was another long silence. Lydia cleared her throat.

"It wouldn't be the first time you've done something illegal."

"No, but I hoped then that at least I had some moral law behind me. Not just an eye for an eye, a blood vengeance. And yes, I've thought about that too. No evidence, but my own certainty.

"I could tell the bastard I was going to get him, and make him believe it. I could have him scared shitless to go outside his own front door. He'd never play golf again. He could never take a plane. I might be there with a hunting rifle."

"Why not?"

"I'm not just outside the law then, Lydia. I'm outside humanity – I'm on his level. I hadn't wanted that. And now I don't even know. I think maybe I'm a bit mad."

"Do you remember when I was just a little girl?" Timidly, if that were possible. "You dressed me up in dolly clothes. You'd conspired with that film director woman, pretending I was to get a part as child-actress. It was to give me confidence. You sent me in to seduce that horrible star of the literary world."

"Vividly," and obliged to smile at the 'little girl' of so long ago – she'd been fifteen.

"Couldn't I try the same thing again? I can make myself quite glamorous. He might well take a fancy. I could maybe get inside, and who knows, I might be able to steal our baby back."

He felt joy and relief at being able to laugh. Wholehearted, and with admiration. This was not whisky boasting. Lydia had never lacked courage.

"Darling – it wouldn't work. I know quite a lot about the man by now; he doesn't fall for girls. In fact I think he's frightened of women. Recall, my darling – that other pig was just a dirty old nothing, practically impotent, a bordel voyeur who could only get it up if he had his hand up a schoolgirl's leg, it's not an uncommon type. But this is a much tougher proposition, a competent, disciplined businessman who has learned how to harden his weak points. I don't say he hasn't got any: everyone has. But it would take too long to find them out. I promised our Emmachen. I've got to move fast."

"What are you going to do?" The bleakly direct question with the emphasis on 'are'. She has always been like this. When she was a little girl one could say, 'Shut up, Lydia' more or less as though one meant it. Quiet; acid; an exasperated bellow. One had to establish parental authority. Or something of the sort. So that whatever answer one had given to an inconvenient question, it didn't matter whether she believed it or not: she had *better* believe it. Damned child would put its lips together tightly and give him a Look; the face known in the army as dumb insolence.

"I don't know myself. I've found some people who may help me in cracking it." This too – when he said such things to the girls when they were small . . . Em would believe it. Holding the big trustful eyes steady on him, while Lydia would be looking into corners with nothing there, 'whistling a tune'.

Vera still hadn't said a word. There was a horrible silence and the doorbell rang, startling all three of them.

"I'm nearest," said Lydia; Castang was saying, "No," but she was already out of the door. There came a loud "Wow". He was up and through the doorway but it was an astonished noise rather than a frightened one. Emma stood there. The two girls were hugging each other. He stayed in place as though turned to stone. Lydia was exclaiming. Emma clenched her hands and put them in the pockets of her tatty teddybear driving coat.

"I'm sorry, I wasn't able to stay away." Vera had got up too, to throw herself into the arms of her tall daughter.

"Is John with you?"

"No he's working thank god, he wanted to, I made him stay but I—" No, that was all right, a jumble of loud noise, the have-you-had-anything-to-eat, the would-you-like-coffee, the I'll-make-up-the-bed, Vera would be all right, the two tall daughters were there to look after her. Castang stayed in the hallway, slipped on his own driving coat since it would be quite cold outside, shut the outer door quietly. Emma's dirty Volkswagen stood warm and companionable cuddled up close to his own only-a-little-less-dirty joybug. What Vera would like most was the little SL coupé, or better still the cabriolet; a model already many years old but the last time stupid Daimler-Benz managed to build a Pretty car. Laughing, she had said, 'Dark green paint, and pale green leather.' Not really all that extravagant, the motor's only two and a half litre and one should be able to get a nice one secondhand. One can be sure it would be stolen, he had said primly. Anything remotely luxurious and I don't go together.

He parked on the Biarritz seafront. A quiet night, not many people about this late. The harsh whisper of waves on sand; no wind and the tide was out. He stared back at the gothic pile of the Framont fortress, the outside comic and even pleasant. But inside – he'd been no further than the restaurant but that was enough: a traditional, unimaginative French luxury with no life in it, a vulgar copy of *grand-siècle* splendour. No sense of design, of invention or creativity, all a parody. French taste has been a steady downhill slide. Nowadays it is as though the last shreds of juice and flair have left us, leaving the dry hollowness of the gnome-palaces, the gnome-kingdom. Shot silk, and brocade, and cut velvet, green and gold or red and gold but all dry and dead; leather and gold leaf, marble and mahogany and *maroquinerie*, the traditional skills and none better than a millimetre thick. A book with nothing inside, a piano which doesn't play. Germany, sticky with ostentatious vulgarity, making lots of money and loving it, but that's the big-black-piano-appassionato. Energy!

He looked in front of him, at the dreary muddle of concrete cliff built by dwarfs, for dwarfs – no headroom. He thought of John's piano. One only wanted a little one. A Steinway, he'd asked, a Bösendorfer? (not knowing the first thing about the subject). No no, said John, the uprights are no good, those have to be the concert grands, what we want is a little Sauter, a little old Steinberger, in Germany there are a dozen good makers and in France there aren't Any, we'll settle for the little Czech Rösler or we'd look for a Yam.

Still, in the silence he looked at the Society-Anonymous behind the Gothic façade. There is a hotel, and who stays in it? There is a starred restaurant and who eats there? Dwarfs, and has he turned into one, himself? Money; the great piles of the Nibelungen gold. This is a mafia, but not the classic old-fashioned kind, we've met those, we know them, he couldn't bend them but they could be broken. This is the modern kind; it has weight, it can move markets, it buys up Deutschmarks and waits for them to rise. Doesn't even bother with risky stuff like coffee futures. As for production firms, which actually make things, who the hell wants them? Much too much trouble, for no real profit. Ever since Mime kept making swords, and Siegfried busting them, throwing them away, dwarfs are much too smart ever to make anything. Even if you happen to acquire something-made, then you have to spend a lot on publicity persuading imbeciles that they need to go out and buy it. Money is the only real commodity. That and human beings, if that should prove absolutely necessary. Like this poor stupid Castang, and his silly little family. They can be used; put us in the way of a pretty little investment. Concreting the seacoast, the littoral, that's forbidden, it's against the law. But who cares about law, as long as we're good friends with the Ministry of the Interior?

Does Castang know any human beings, outside his family? Yes. Perhaps. A long way away, and most of them seem to be dead. Richard, what got into you? Apart that is from the beetle, there within, burrowing unseen. Death, yes, gets into one a good deal. We meet people in the street, stop for a chat, nod sympathetically and blow our noses. Lot of it about.

One would prefer it to happen in other places. Blacks chopping each other with machetes, in large, really abnormal numbers, mean to say, gets into the press. Japs, too, go in for death in a big way, seems to be a popular pastime. But not in France surely. Always saving Aids, which became fashionable; caught on, you might call it. We don't much like the expression – sarcastic? – facetious? Being French we call it the *sida* and to listen to us you'd imagine nobody ever died of anything else. Having been a policeman, Castang was familiar with anything-else: death in France is fond of grotesque devices, jumps about dressed up as a clown, riding a one-wheel bike and blowing squeakers.

Like in the winter, stop up every crevice with rags against those Draughts, then turn on the heating, carbon monoxide poisoning, that's very French. Or in the hunting season, sally out with the brother-in-law and blow his head off with the shotgun; looked like a wild boar there in the bushes. Road deaths, the most French of all since every man will tell you he's the only really safe driver in the whole country. Adolescent suicides; nobody understands French children and least of all their parents. If we run short, there's always alcoholism to fall back on. And should you be young, dark-skinned, and bored with basketball, your chances of being killed by the police are always excellent.

Even when Castang got away to Bruxelles he brought the clown with him. Eamonn; Iris; Jerry. Mathilde. Even people he'd barely begun to feel friends with: Margaret Rawlings or old Klaus.

He left the car where it was, and went for a walk in the late night streets, moving in an aimless unpatterned way that brought him abruptly back to where he'd just been. Only mad north-west. He'd been thinking a good deal about the police these last few days, and if he were the PJ chief hereabouts, well, he might have been told to keep quiet for good sound political reasons, but he'd still be keeping an eye on friend Castang. Neither would one want to compromise Ilse. Knocking on her door there at eleven at night, one didn't want to bring anyone along with one. Dolf wouldn't be pleased about that either, and that's not someone to get on the wrong side of. Call this France but Basques have a different name for it. A pause, and "Who is it?" said the voice-box.

"Man about the gas."

"Oh . . ." and she thought about that for a longish time before the release clicked. He climbed stairs slowly, wondering whether it were Ilse he had come to see, or would it be Lisa?

She was in a dressing-gown, pale blue and white stripes like an Argentine football player but the resemblance stopped there. Even if they had long fair hair tied back with an elastic, which they do sometimes, it would be rare for them to smell this nice.

"I was going to bed. No, it's alright, I've a free day tomorrow."

"I've been going quite gently and steadily out of my mind."

"You met Dolf. Jacky . . . oh, I see. Bastardly Basques . . ."

"Lisa . . . what am I to do?"

"We'll try to think. Take it easy. I've nothing much, in the way of drinks."

"No . . . cocoa or something. Jesus . . . sorry, my back."

"Oh I can manage that. Cocoa I mean. Is it warm enough here? – I switched the thing out. The back . . . I've got some stuff. No, not wintergreen. Smells nice. From Peru or somewhere. You have to lie flat. I'll try not to hurt. No, I'm afraid you'd have to take your shirt off, does that bother you?"

"I've too many other bothers, already."

"You'll have to try and forget about them for a bit. Not very helpful, I agree . . . It's only cold at first."

Vera had never been any good at this. Her hands were strong, yes but . . . just not one of her talents. Lydia, when aged about ten, had been much better. But had to be bribed. A franc for five minutes. And a very sharp eye on the clock.

"Look out, this cocoa's going cold." Plain chocolate in fact dissolved in milk. Spanishly, she'd added a bit of cinnamon.

"Less bad."

"You're fearfully stiff."

"Yes."

"I'm terribly sorry. I thought Dolf might know of something he could do. I didn't want to let you down. Is there now . . . anything you can do? Don't move about so, or is that getting easier?"

"I know what I have to do. Frightened to try, that's all."

"I have to work this stuff right in, till it absorbs. Is this room warming up?"

It was better, and it wasn't better. He sat up, and peeled back the dressing-gown.

"Oh dear. I was afraid of this. I'm afraid, I'm not at all good at it. Are you sure this is what you want?" Her nightdress was an odd colour. Not flame, not pink. A cotton material with a nice touch, a funny name. He had it. He had both. Seersucker, which is probably Indian or something. And Campari mixed with orange juice, which is not Indian at all. In an effort to keep the record straight – "This is not in my habits."

His back had stopped hurting, and he found his voice. He wasn't going to act the hypocrite saying, "Not in mine either," and promptly said so. As Richard used to say, when faced with a remark both stupid and unnecessary – 'The phrase is otiose'. It did occur to him that they had met over a nightdress. The acquaintance was ripening over – no, under – another nightdress. Likewise an otiose remark, but mad or not, there were still two sides to his head. The Observer explored a typical northern body; the white fine-textured skin; the breasts small, soft, a little slack; the hair fair, and not much of it. But – was he regressing into extreme childhood? For this might be the earliest memory he had. Of being in bed, very warm and very safe; a bliss made total by a radio playing, and a comfortable drawly voice which he did not know was American and which said, 'Midnight in Munich and it's time for "Heartbreaker".' Near his bed burned a little lamp. It had an orange shade. Lisa's voice spoke softly in his ear; this was not with the accents of the American Forces Network in Germany.

Poor Lisa wanting to be sensible and painfully aware of being less so with every intake of breath, horribly afraid of spoiling her good will by her clumsiness. Yes, Castang, if you insist on going to bed with Polish women – probably Catholic and certainly still of child-bearing age. Gasping, agonising, saying pathetically, "I'm clean." For what you do, you are answerable. Bear that in mind, will you?

An hour or so later the voice spoke again.

"This is horrid of me, but I don't want the child to come in, in the morning, and find a strange man fucking Mum."

"No no. The cold ground for me. As soon, that is, as I find the courage."

"But I won't let you go like that. Don't be guilty; accept. I'm refusing guilt, and don't be guilty for me. Make me ready, please, anew." Small thing to ask, of a man feeling grateful, or did that too sound a bit pathetic?

And at the street door – this is cold, here. Take a good look, slip out silent. The street was as bare as the bones of a Roman soldier.

Lisa did not say, 'Maybe you've made me pregnant and that worries me.' She did not say 'I worry me' because of making love with a man she hardly knew. She said, 'You worry me' and there wasn't any answer to that. Except that if he wasn't to feel guilty then he wouldn't be so on account of his grandchild, neither.

Dolf did not turn me down. Didn't turn anything down. Chilly he was, sticky he was. But he gave me an assignation for this afternoon. Did so in a way he meant me to take seriously. And before I get any madder I'm going to keep to that. Right now, going home, at three in the morning, I'm pretty clear. Not mad at all. Thanks to Lisa. Thank you; my dear.

"Where have you been?" Not about to get back into bed with his wife, and with both spare rooms full of daughters, he'd had a kip on the living-room sofa, got up early and had a quick shower, made the coffee for all – thought, even, of going to fetch fresh bread. What would one say? London to see the Queen? Out conspiring?

"Working. Talking. Thinking."

"You had better tell me, you know," said Emma, resolute.

"I don't think I should. Not even sure I could."

"But you will. I'm your daughter and I know, when you do promise you keep your word. And I'm her mother."

"I don't know myself yet, for sure. I'll know more this afternoon."

"And I'll come with you." Flat. "So now just tell me this.

"We've been talking too. Of course. Lyddy, Ma, me. Ma's a bit fey, I can't blame her. So are you – I notice. I'm not a bit fey, I'm over all that. I'm perfectly clear and controlled. So cough up. Her theory is that you're in with the Basques. I want to know about this."

Castang cleared his throat, pushed the plate away, used the edge of a hand to collect breadcrumbs into the palm of the other, poured out some more coffee, coughed a bit, went to look for one of his little cigars. Vera came in, looked at them, gave herself a cup of coffee and went out again, all in total silence. Emma waited with inexorable patience.

"Have to be didactic. It's so confused I don't know myself. Probably they don't know either. There's an ETA political, and another military – like the IRA. There's KAS, and there's Herri Batasuna, and there's the old Basque national party, PNV, and these arc like French acronyms, don't ask what any of them mean.

"Briefly, terrorism has got a bit discredited and there hasn't been much recently. You could say that like the IRA they haven't got very far with terrorism and a good few of them now think it better to talk; diplomacy, peaceful means, and so forth.

"But all this got complicated by the GAL. That's an underground gang, suspected of being organised and financed by the Spanish Government, a dirty-tricks-brigade, idea of infiltrating all the revolutionary movements, destabilising, that's the modern jargon, polite for getting in close, denouncing people to the police, treachery all round, and assassinating several of the revolutionary leaders. You see? Nest of snakes.

"So sure, the tougher among all these groups have been hardening their line. Blood for blood. I'd have to say I know little and understand less. So where do I come in? All right, I'll tell you. I had a little to do, and tangential at that, with these people years ago when you were small, and they've good memories. If it weren't for that – what, a cop, ex-PJ? – they'd tip the pisspot over my head, and laugh heartily."

"They sound," said Emma with distaste, "exactly like a lot of Corsicans, forever shooting people in the back out of a dark corner and scuttling very fast."

"You're a European," he said. "I brought you up that way. Since living in Berlin and marrying Johannes, twice as much again so. You've contempt and rightly for these paranoiac old colonial powers huddled in a corner quacking about their sovereignty; so retrograde, and so out of date. But we have to try not to be too complacent: this is a genuine people, like Kurds, who had the misfortune to have their land cut in two by a frontier planted in their midst by two fat old dominant powers who couldn't care less about Basques or Kurds either. If some abject little Corsican gangster with a gun in his pants told you he'd help get your baby back, and strictly for reasons of his own, what would you do?"

"I'd go down on my knees," said Emma, "and kiss his behind."

"If you're going to have anything to do with these folk you had better remember that, and be very humble."

Commissaire Martre of the Police Judiciaire in Bayonne was doing a lot of thinking. Sometimes he liked what he was contemplating and sometimes he thought it a quicksand: you put your foot on a nice grassy patch and went straight in up to your arse in a stinking bog. This business, any way you look at it, it's iffy.

Castang now himself, nice fellow. Good cop – well, technically, that is. Politically not a clue, but a good colleague. One knew about – that is, one could find out; he had. One had got a friend to pull (well, get a sight of) confidential stuff in Paris; there was a (what's confidential?) report from Old-Foxy-Richard (whom he hadn't known at all, except that everyone did; bit of a byword and even a bit of a legend in the old days). Which said if you knew how to interpret Linear-B that Castang was a bloody good second-in-command and perhaps would never be better because he was at his best when brigaded with a Fast Brother, meaning some sly old bastard like Richard himself. And it would be a pity to fail to make use of indubitable talents, so don't block his promotion but find the right hole for this square peg (an insurance policy, that).

So they had given him an antenna up somewhere in the north, Amiens or Arras or whatever, and there he'd done very well except that he would go poking his nose into things that didn't concern him, chasing butterflies all around the countryside (including right here on one occasion). They'd got fed up, yonder on the Quai, and found him a nice hole in the Beaux-Arts, faked old-masters, bits of historic cultural patrimony getting flogged out the back door to foreign museums; smashing job, lots of money in it, brigaded with that woman Whatsername, she must have done something dodgy too, to get sent like that to Corsica! He wasn't quite certain What Castang had done to fuck that up; he'd antagonised a few Powers over an old boy touching-up little girls: if you're an Academician And a big television-personality, that's barely a misdemeanour. And Still Castang had dodged getting-sent-to-Djibouti, must have had friends of his own to get a lovely feather-bed in Bruxelles . . .

But those friends were past tense, very. The Minister was notorious for cleaning out old stock, replacing them with his own nearest-and-dearest, and the entire directorate of the PJ had been renewed. Castang had seen the wind change, no doubt, to ask for his pension, smartish.

But one had to be fair. Castang had yet again struck it lucky here, somehow fiddling that house of Richard's which turned out to be an oil well. Bringing one to the affairs of Monsieur Edmond de Framont. And there one had to be mighty careful because that's not only very good friends with local mayors, deputies, senators; he's got lines up to the Ministry, and the Chancellery too over at Justice: the message had been unmistakeable.

Well, that happened, and quite frequently. Just fr'instance, look at the Dear Old Man who back in wartime had only been secretary in the Préfecture at Bordeaux; he'd put packs of Jews on the train for Destination-Eastward. They'd had a cast-iron case against him for war crimes these last thirty years, but never yet have they managed to bring him to trial, and now he's nearly ninety. Which is what comes of having good friends.

He had himself felt a real sympathy for Castang. Warm. A baby kidnapped; who wouldn't put one's energies into sorting out a dirty trick like that? But when a word got passed, that the Chancellery would just as soon see an absence of zeal . . . When indeed one had a word oneself, that Monsieur de Framont's speculations in land aren't viewed as illegal (what is it anyhow, only the law about protecting the Littoral) we're all lying a bit low.

Oh yes, he'd found out, one only needed a friend over at Land Registry. Richard had refused to sell that house, plonk in the middle of a nice little development scheme. But Richard was an old man, plainly dying, so just have a little patience and it'll come loose like a ripe apple in your hand. It hadn't: you'd Castang playing the obstinate instead, just when you were all set up, your banks, your contractors, your planning permissions, the lot. So to stop it going rotten-ripe you had to do something radical. Get the gipsies to steal the baby. Goddam inhuman, yes, but you can always tell the French that Les Gitans do such things, and get believed. It may be filthy but it's extremely Efficacious when you're in a hurry. And 'Mossieu' de

Framont would take damned good care to see to it that his hands stayed snowy white.

Except that now this infernal woman had come along claiming the contrary.

He'd seen to it that nobody had any clue to anything but himself and Desclaux. Orders had been discreetly given to keep an eye on Castang. That was bit of a loose-cannon. Chap like that, has known a few things in his life. Having got the message, nobody knows and nobody wants to know, might go taking the law into his own-hands. So one watched, ready to move in if need be and block any 'ankypanky. And there was, worryingly, just a shadow of a suspicion that Castang might have some connections among Basques. And that is a pot which is always on the boil, ready to boil over. In fact one of these chemical pots full of sudden reactions; overheat that, it can explode like a nuclear reactor. Chernobyl-Effect. Shit, one wasn't Jealous of Castang, was one?

If one were to be very scrupulous, yes maybe one was, a bit. Fellow fucks up, gets posted to a feather bed in Bruxelles or Berlin, not Saint-Pierre-et-Miquelon this time round. Whereas oneself, got given Bayonne: if ever there was a hell-hole. Basques likely to go pop any second, and I'll get blamed, and it will be *my* arse gets shot like greased lightning to Kerguelen Island. Leaving Castang here playing golf without a care in the world, exactly like Ol' Foxy before him. Not fair. Damn this woman.

It was Ilse's day off. She had been lying in bed milling, since three o'clock that morning. The hours between three and seven, she'd made her mind up. Got her daughter off to school: showered and dressed in respectable off-duty-Ilse clothes: tidied-the-place-up, and went to Bayonne. Offices of the Police Judiciaire. Name, address and occupation? So what's this then – witnessed a crime, have you? Knowledge of crime committed? Information then, about crime planned, that it?

"I want the man in charge." The habitual defensive blockages; Le Patron isn't here. Somebody – at last – called Commissaire Desclaux.

Chief of staff; the all-purpose man. A job Castang knew well for it had been his through hard-bought years, in the Richard days. A commonplace in officialdom, a man already dry and grey, who will never be promoted any further, but of much experience and real competence, much weariness, much boredom; a decent man but dulled down to an old piece of iron these twenty years. Still, no fool.

"Sit down, make yourself comfortable, tell me all about it. No – I take his place. Very busy man. Put it that I'm him to all intents and purposes."

"No," said Ilse. "This is personal, and it's important."

"Well Madame, that's just talk, isn't it. Give me something concrete."

"Tell him; it's about Monsieur Castang." He put his glasses back on. Mature woman, properly dressed and neatly made up. No sign of instability or hysteria. And he knew a little about her. He looked at the papers on his desk; nothing there bar bullshit. Locked the drawer where he kept his gun; only on television do they wear guns in the office.

"Just sit here, Madame, for a minute quietly, d'you mind?"

Martre's office was bigger, altogether grander, furnished as near as possible like a sitting-room. Le Patron was sitting behind his nice clean desk and smoking his pipe. But he knew his job.

He stood up politely and shook hands, pointed to an armchair and took the other, offered her a cigarette; would she like some coffee? He knew quite a bit about her. Desclaux knew only that a lot of effort and manpower had been going into Castang, and his view was that it was a waste of both. Martre thought not, which was the boss's privilege. She was a bit of a puzzle. Waitress in the café, there in Framont's place: what was Castang's interest in her then? Sure, nice-looking woman, and was that all? He made himself a father-confessor; bland, tolerant.

"Sleeping with him, are you?"

"No," with so clear and calm a look that she must be lying, but it didn't matter.

"Very well. So you're friends. You don't come to see me on that account."

"You know about the baby. And I know you've done nothing about it."

"No evidence. These things can take time. Need delicate handling – let's keep to the point."

"This is the point. The baby's there, where I work, I'm pretty sure of it by now." Martre had ado not to be startled at that; took refuge in the well-worn cliché, 'the servants always know everything'.

"That would be a pretty grave accusation and how do you establish that?"

"I'm in and out of the kitchens, you know. A chambermaid heard something and Madame told her some tale of looking after her sister's child."

"Not evidence. You have to be very careful."

"There's such a thing as being too careful. I'm frightened. I don't know him well, and I'm frightened of his doing something violent."

"And what d'you suppose that would be?"

"Isn't that up to you, to find out?"

"Don't be cheeky with me, young woman."

"I don't know. You don't imagine he tells me. It might be soon and it might be sudden. You must know that he feels – well, strongly." ·

"Do you know of anyone else, there where you work, he might know? Might have approached – as he did you?"

"No idea." Not going to mention Eugène, and very certainly not 'Jacky'.

And when you told him this piece of gossip, which one must treat with great caution? And did he confide in you at all? And do you realise the harm that can be done by repeating this slipshod sort of hearsay? Martre pushed her, but when these women start being obstinate! ... The most he could get was the repetition, that Castang had gone very tight and silent, that it frightened her, that she thought he could be suddenly unexpectedly – what does this word mean, violence? Shouldn't one then go to the police? Isn't that their business? Yes, she calls herself a woman of intelligence and common sense. Yes, it is a good job, she earns a reasonable living and it gives her the independence she values. Her employer? Monsieur de Framont? She knows him by sight. He has occasionally spoken to her; he is always polite, and could be called a severe but on the whole considerate employer; she hasn't the slightest reason to feel spite or animosity and she doesn't want to lose her job, which she has held, as far as she knows to everyone's satisfaction, for nigh on three years: she's sorry but she's an honest woman and a good waitress.

The commonest of police techniques is to get people to repeat a story, with a pretence at confusion or uncertainty. You look and you listen for the holes and variations, the hesitancies and discrepancies, the lies, the evasions and the prevarications. Martre got nowhere with it.

Which isn't surprising since Ilse had only told him the truth and had made up her mind about the things she'd decided to suppress. And if he had this written down, would she then sign the statement? No, she would not. Hadn't he said himself it was just hearsay? Hadn't she said at the start that her business with him was personal? She'd done her civic duty in coming to say what was worrying her. Beyond that, it was his affair, he could decide for himself whether he cared to believe her.

She left him a much vexed man, and unwilling to admit to himself – unhappy.

Castang might be destabilised (useful word); yes. Enough to take a tale like this seriously; one couldn't rule it out. For chrissake an operator like Framont, so smooth he does everything at two-three removes, he can't have that baby right there in the sanctum – or has he had his arm twisted by his wife? A woman one knew nothing of, she couldn't be more anonymous. But he'd better take it seriously and the hell of it was he didn't see how to cover it: there's sure as hell nobody to carry this can; not RG, not nobody. The best would be to fake a scenario involving a few terrorists; he could always say 'an informer had let slip' . . .

Might be true, at that. He'd always suspected Castang to be a bit more pally than he let on with a few of these Basques. And Jesus, that place is a fortress (maybe that's why Framont feels it safe to take a risk, this lunatic). Castang can't possibly imagine he could get in there, not even with two guns and a certainty: that would be plain Insane.

Where the hell is Castang anyhow? Desclaux had kept complaining about the waste of manpower and inefficient into the bargain. Always the same stupid story; light surveillance is both too light and not light enough (and Castang himself might well have said 'Lots and lots it is and none at all').

His eye fell upon the draft of a confidential report.

'Some ten young men' – no, not ten; put 'several' – 'masked with scarves, attacked the central police station' – not ours, thank heaven – 'with cries of "Txakurak Kanpora".' He took his pen and added 'check spelling'. And add the translation: 'Dogs Out' rather than 'Throw the fuckers in the harbour'. His eye travelled down the page; mm, fires, explosives; barricades . . . And before they could be apprehended had melted into the crowd. This would cause frowns: WHAT crowd? Er, some hundreds manifesting against er, collaboration (add 'suspected') between the French and Spanish authorities: it is, er, alleged that the so-called 'GAL' – shit, death squads said to be fomented by the Spanish parallel police – have assassinated twenty-five persons upon the territory of the Republic within the last five years. Mm, windows broken, molotov cocktails. 'Slogans were shouted highly injurious to the persons at the head of both the French and Spanish governments.' The Préfecture has been requested to make available and place on standby extra squads of Republican Security Companies. With dogs, please, and guns, as well as anti-riot equipment; in fact armed to the bloody teeth.

Good, yes, but is it good enough? Would one keep this paragraph – a recurrence is feared of politically-motivated assassinations by the terror-extremists? Because that's just begging Paris to come smartly back at one, asking what is being done to infiltrate and suppress these illegal nationalist organisations. The Minister was said to have been so cross last time as to have threatened to disband RG (the 'parallels') altogether and make the PJ responsible for the entire mess, and God-Bloodywell-Forbid.

As though one hadn't enough already, now this infernal woman . . .

One would have to admit, thought Castang, that this is cleverly thought out. Aguilera is the football ground, home of the Olympique de Biarritz, the sacred local rugby team. A home match, and what's more it's the local derby, against the nearest as well as dearest of the enemy; the Aviron Bayonnais (since 'aviron' means an oar one wondered whether this in origin was the Rowing Club.) Seems unlikely because rugby is a devouring passion throughout south-western France and on occasions like this swamps even Basque fanaticisms about Pelota. Everyone is here, and can talk and think of nothing else: everyone but us. And furthermore (if that were needed) an international is coming up in a fortnight and at least two players here on the field are under consideration. Said to be 'too old' but man, the French rugby team is a dead-bloody-loss and has been so for the last three seasons. Fanatic? – boy, they're raving, fair foaming at the mouth.

Nobody could possibly have marked our coming here: the whole pub was just one yelling scrum. Now that they've all gone off to the match we are left quiet and unobserved: even the barman is glued to a mobile phone. And when they get back – win or lose the pastis is going to flow in rivers and every policeman from here to the frontier will be swept off their great flat feet. Both our assembly and our dispersal will be noticeable only to God, since even his stand-in is busy yelling. The England rugby team keeps winning because it's so efficient, yes, granted, but sweet-Jesus it's so Boring.

There was Dolf, who had organised this, silent in the corner and as though unconcerned. There's this elderly, soft-spoken man with the hair cropped so short he could be a Benedictine monk, which is just as likely and maybe more so than the Mafia Dom: nobody's kissing his hand. There's me. There's Emma, whom I had seen as a universal turn-off, but though Dolf looked a bit sour the Dom didn't as much as twitch. And there's the tigress. Who is the proof if one were needed that we can all feel perfectly comfortable: her face is on Wanted posters in every police-station in France – Mairies – roadside petrol pumps – public lavatories. Even I recognise it. And here she is, laughing and joking. Newspapers and television announcers, who of course cannot resist the most cow-plop cliché, call her 'La Pasionaria'. She's killed three men to certain knowledge, and talks a great deal less than dear old Dolores ever did. She's taken a great fancy to Emma. I don't think this is lesbian, and plainly Emma doesn't either. Having introduced herself, simply, as "I am the mother of the child," everybody has shown their tacit acceptance of her essential part in this play. Hearing me introduced, the tigress gave a great beaming smile.

"A year ago arresting me would have got you a big big medal. And shaking hands with me now will steer you arse over astragal into the salt mine."

Very nervous; she was chain-smoking and drinking a

lot but had plainly hollow bones. Has been a beautiful woman if you like the Andalusian-*gitana*-type. Still is very fine looking if unkempt, battered, the clothes thrown on anyhow. Smells beautifully clean and across the room you'd swear she stank of sweat and fish. Yes, she has more than a look of Mathilde. She drinks beer and hasn't a surplus ounce on her body, which is as fast and controlled as any dancer's, and she's surely well over forty.

The madness, in Castang, has mounted again high; has this also to do with Mathilde?

The tigress spoke the pure French of an educated person, and with no accent. No reason not to; she had an economics degree from the University of Toulouse and had been brought up in an atmosphere of the most sheltered bourgeois respectability. She had done 'Sciences-Po' in Paris with no trace of the ridiculous affectations found often in the speech of this milieu. Oddly, when she dropped now and then into Spanish it was with a broad country accent; a voice harshly metallic but low in pitch, soft in volume. Her name was Elena and whatever she was, thought Castang, you couldn't stick any cheap labels on her. Sneers about 'Marxists who have never read Marx' would be to miss the point entirely.

She did the talking; Dolf did not utter, and neither did the Dom.

"Don't think in cliché terms. 'The blood-thirsty indiscriminate killer.' Six months ago I killed a policeman. Two men were with me and both were dead. We got off a train. We were ambushed; they opened fire without warning; the plan was to kill us, nothing else. Can you credit my word for this?"

"Yes, I can."

"I killed the first, two years ago. I was sitting on the lavatory, having a shit. Is that crude? He kicked the door in and stood laughing at me, paralysed there with my knickers round my ankles. He made a filthy joke. He turned round to call his mate to come and see the terrorist in her bare arse. I had my first gun under my blouse, very uncomfortable it was. A magnum twenty-two, a woman's gun. I put six bullets into the two of them and I went back to what I was busy with. You're a police officer. You're retired but after all these years you can't be anything else."

"And I've done some very filthy things. But I've never called out to come and look at Shitpants in front of a woman."

She turned around, to Emma, who didn't hesitate.

"A boy at school made a big joke about sanitary towels. I didn't have any gun of course but I'm glad to say I kicked him straight in the bollocks."

"I never knew that," said Castang.

"It was kept from you," said his daughter.

"We understand each other," said Elena.

"We aren't wanting to kill anyone," she went on. "It's not our purpose or intention. We aren't satisfied that it is – perhaps ever has been – of genuine service.

"In practical terms, they of course have killed three or four of us, in the ways I have described, over the last twelvemonth. If one of them came in at this door, he'd draw down on me that second, without hesitation. He wouldn't worry about either of you."

Castang like the tigress was drinking beer. Dolf was the sort of drinker who can make one pastis stretch the entire afternoon. Emma drinking pastis – this he'd never seen before. The Dom – austere with a barely-touched cognac.

"If, now, we decide that this man is a legitimate target – he stinks as much in Bilbao as here or in Bordeaux, where he has been buying vineyards – we see taking him out as a brake on this.

"Indeed a thrust, back" – pushing against the air with her opened palms – "against greed. And social injustice. Against unconcern for human lives or liberties. Against inhuman cruelties and naked, cynical exploitations. And all this has nothing whatsoever to do with you."

"I don't think I can go along with killing him," said Castang, "I don't judge you; I ask you not to judge me. It isn't in my, my police attributions, you know, ever to judge anyone."

"You won't be armed," said the tigress. "You need not even be present. You're only concerned with getting your child back."

"I'll be present," said Emma. "I don't want any gun because I think I might kill him and I don't want you to put me to the proof."

"I wouldn't give you any gun. They are horrible things. They leave unhealed wounds.

"I don't think it'll be necessary," she went on. "Because we knock the bastard's house of cards over, with as much noise and ostentation as may be. We aim to show him up. The baby's there. Dolf here has found out. We'll see to it, that he gets plenty of press coverage. After that, the Procureur de la République, my excellent friend, cannot stop himself having questions to ask. Because this clever business man who thought he could do anything made the mistake of intervening in reality. He has no idea of reality. None of them do, they live their lives behind micron filters. I have no child," she said to Emma. "One cannot have a child and a gun. Also a child needs life. I shall not live long.

"He has people, who can kidnap a child. They know nothing and to them it was meaningless. Only a bonus. Money. These people could not keep the child. They would not know what to do with it: they would lose it, or throw it away; it would be most unsafe. He had to keep the child himself. His wife insisted upon that. The sequestration, that she has made her affair. And she made a great fuss. That is how it was found out. In the kitchen," with a charming, brilliant smile.

The barman came, to wipe the table, to ask whether more drinks were wanted.

"Because they'll be in, within minutes now. We've lost," in a high voice, presaging Doom. "By one point, by one fucking point and that a penalty in injury time. That referee is going to need police protection."

'Mary Murphy is a killer.' You might wonder what they were talking about, English being a notoriously imprecise language, and French which is supposed to be more exact, or why do they say four-twenties-ten when they mean ninety, very much the same. Are you going by the foot-of-the-letter, or are you being metaphorical? Maybe she's a chess player, a ballet mistress, or a competition skier. Or she has dazzling looks.

But in the PJ they mean it quite literally, except that this isn't her name and nobody can remember how she came by it. Perhaps that she's quite plain, very ordinary-looking, and once went to Ireland on holiday and came back with a taste for bottled Guinness. Killer is what she is. She has shot three men, all fatally. In the PJ they are proud of her.

It happens a lot in France, where they have a solid, one had nearly said republican tradition of bearing arms. It isn't a right: there's no provision in the Constitution. There's a lot of complicated and confusing legislation, some of it observed; you can't walk into a gunsmith's shop and come away with an armoury. But somehow everyone has a gun, and might think of going for it too, in any situation where violence gets beyond the talking stage: a car is also a favoured method of hitting people. It would all look rather 'foreign' to the English, who don't as a rule romp about with firearms, not even when drunk on a Saturday night. Here there are several categories of prohibited-offensive-weapon. Some officious policeman could make your life a misery for carrying a nail-file, while from teenager to granddad everyone has

a twenty-two. Journalists use the cliché 'a pistol 22 Long
Rifle', unaware of being ridiculous.

So the gendarme – waving you quite politely in to
the side of the road – has that great big .357 on his
belt. Even the cop doing nothing outside an official
building, and known thus as a green plant, Leans on
his Musket: place is full of loonies with long-rifles. It's
a notorious scandal that all this officialdom is ill-trained
and badly-disciplined; at least fifty per cent of it is unfit to
be in command of a peashooter. Castang, who has been
deploring the nigh-daily calamities known as slip-ups for
thirty years, and hasn't worn, much less used, a gun above
a dozen times in the last twenty of them gets tetchy when
reading the paper. Here's one said he thought pulling his
fucking cannon would help intimidate a drunk. This other
pisspants claiming he felt threatened; it was dark, you see,
and an Arab boy with a beer bottle looked to him like
Scarface O'Hara.

Sighs, turning the page. African child of twelve. Bare
feet. Kalashnikov. We sell them, on the pretext that if we
don't the neighbours will.

The Police Judiciaire which Castang has been ornament-
ing all these years is supposed to be an altogether more
professional body. It's a banana army, with a lot more
officers than men, because under the criminal law only
an Officer holds the rights of judicial interference thought
needful to maintain public order. Ordinary cops are slow
to tell you your rights; or theirs either, because they
haven't any.

Thus Mary Murphy, also known as Maggy Rouff. Officer of experience close to forty and has seen a lot of
rough trade. Square heavy face (from peasant stock near
Rouffignac); square lean body. She's a pillar of the rowing
club – 'Aviron de Bayonne' – as well as a rugby fan.
Because of this awkward figure she wouldn't be found
in the ditch in uniform. PJ people wear plain clothes
and carry their guns concealed. The uniform of women

police is as preposterous as it is unbecoming. Idiotic pot hat. Behinds stick out of their trousers. Giving these drag queens a gun is asking for trouble. Packet of tampons and they're a public menace yet. She's a nice woman, a kind and gentle woman, self-educated, sensible, and sober. She drinks, and hard. But not on duty. As sure as she could be she'd seen the tigress outside Aguilera. "Not a damn thing I could do about it. What, get lynched for my pains? You don't imagine I wear a gun to go to a rugby match? You do, yes, I know. Because it's the only dick you've got."

Nobody, ever, had questioned Mary Murphy's courage. And yes, she's a killer. Best shot we've got, says Commissaire Desclaux. Utterly reliable, will never panic. Put her in charge of the second team, said Martre.

One ought to fill it in a bit. Feminist, sure. Unmarried. No. Not butch, not a bit. Would have got married, but not fair on a man, not fair on the children. This job, one's at risk. Apart from the lousy hours.

Coquettish even, on occasion. Looking at a picture of German policewomen she said, 'What, lousy Boches? That green and khaki's nice. Their trousers fit. That high-peaked cap looks good, gives them height. I wouldn't mind, wearing that. They can even have long hair. Big long thighs, why are we all so squat and butty?'

Martre, too. A mistake to see him only as an anxious and even timid man (Desclaux thinks of him as an old maid). He was resolute when it came to a scramble. Like most men happiest with paper work he would not go out of his way to provoke a rough-and-tumble scene; one would rather leave that to the Corsicans. No lack of physical courage though. In that at least Castang would have felt some fraternal fibre: one has a dislike for being shot at, for Martre too has some imagination. But if that familiar cliché arises, of push coming to shove. For he felt pretty sure now, and was making his arrangements. It is also a mistake to see him as only a hair-splitter, a balancer of risks and probabilities. He would like to be human, and if Castang is a gone-goose he's sorry for it. Fellow's off his rocker. Commissaire Martre has no intention of going off his rocker. There's a very distinct likelihood here of getting the tigress, and a few more. Pin a few of them to the cork board and it might be a ticket out of this hell-hole. An ambitious man, Martre and he has a dream, of getting the command at PJ Versailles, the traditional antechamber to the lush jobs in Paris. Political jobs, but he'd know how to handle them. This would be a big big feather in the hat. No Minister was going to be ungrateful to the man who took the tigress out of his hair. One would want to be able to give the baby back to Castang, because Then one would be able to shush all that potential scandal way out of sight.

The operation here is tricky as hell. Two teams; Desclaux and Mary Murphy, and one will hope for plenty of firepower because these Spanish madmen . . .

He wasn't very happy with the gang. All these boys, they're all called Jean-Pierre and Jean-Paul and Jean-Marc. They're all, what's that American phrase? 'Loaded for bear'. Yes, but. Thing is – he told Desclaux – we don't want anybody getting in on this act. No parallel police. We want to be on our own, risks and all.

"I don't at all like the way Castang might be mixed up with this. He's a loose cannon. But he has no official standing whatsoever, and if he's in any conspiracy with this fucking crowd it isn't the Bishop of San Sebastian will bring him to heaven. Not even the Cardinal-Archbishop can save his arse this time round, he'll go to prison his life long, that is if he doesn't leave his skin on the ground. A great talker but No Way will he ever climb out of this."

Desclaux said nothing. Castang is or was a Divisional Commissaire and this is going to make a mighty big scandal. But if we win, we win. I could do with a promotion out of here my own self.

'To say goodbye is to die a little.' And upon this remark

a writer, one of 'Vera's writers', annotated, 'The French have always a phrase for it, and the bastards are always right.' Oh yes? She found it a boring, platitudinous, Stupid remark.

Anyhow, it is '*Partir c'est mourir*' and '*partir*' is simply to *leave*. But to leave is to say goodbye. The tearing-apart is implied, and the more dreadful for being left unsaid. He had left. There had been no goodbyes. Emma – he, she, they had left; they had not come back. No word had been said.

A man had written that phrase. Those who leave are generally men, and they it is who dramatise their partings; occupied with and even enjoying their emotions. No word about those who stay behind, and those are the women. To stay behind is worse than to go. As anyone who has had to stay behind can tell you.

Henri had always made a joke of it; quite right, what else can one do? Intoning, doom-laden, a for-whom-the-bell-tolls voice. 'They stay behind, in Casablanca, and wait – and wait – and wait!' Quite so. She has had to do it, a good few times. From the outset, from even before her marriage. Her marriage! – knowing perfectly well that marrying her was an administrative ploy, a check upon any ideas the French might have about deporting her straight back to some highly irritable Czechs. Marry her, she'd have French nationality and be safe. Not a good pretext for marrying this silly young girl.

She'd been pretty as a young girl. Too pretty, and flattered by French jokes about the Cattleya. Less pretty and perhaps she'd have been a better gymnast – And less of a feather-head. She'd gone to bed with him straight away. Nothing surprising there; it was all she had to offer. She'd have been perfectly happy just to be his mistress. Odd – is it? – this is the only man I've ever been to bed with. Even my daughters look with indulgence upon this extraordinary display of virtue – no, that's not exact; Lydia does but Emma is like me, a

one-man woman. Emma has gone out with her father. I
have been left here.

She, it is better to think of oneself as she, had made
up her mind to be a good wife. It was the least she could
do: there was all this awful having to be grateful. Faithful,
and a good housewife – it didn't seem much – and a
conscientious careful mother. One learned. That police
work is dirty, squalid and depressing. One invented jokes,
rationed the drinking. Nobody thought about smoking
in those days; every French man and woman lived with
a permanent fag on the lip. One can see it in all the
old films. And girls . . . knowing little – knowing nothing
– surrounded all the time by prostitutes. Coming home,
he smelt very odd.

So that one fought. That the home, they'd been pretty
poor at the start, should be happy, pretty . . . even when
poor she'd spent a lot on flowers. Simple-minded, you
know. Warmth and comfort, food and sex, books and
pictures. Yes, I've been naked on a lot of hearth-rugs.
Total faith, total trust, total giving. I won't, I don't
have an instant of denial, over those years. I have been
astoundingly fortunate in a man who gave and gave and
has not reproached. There have been some very rough
moments. But he has not added up bills of costs. He has
not said 'Look at all these debits'. It was instinctive, it was
spontaneous.

And to this day Vera tries not to go psychoanalysing
herself. Lydia who is rather given to staring at her own
navel can be so tiresome. Telling one to think, all the
time. There are areas of one's existence one should and
has to think about. Some are better left to instinct, and
one would wish to be a perfectly stupid woman. Low
intelligence-quotient; go put the kettle on, woman.

If one Has to go thinking about it, there are simply
several Veras. There is a technical one, much concerned
with the artisanal, the craftsmanly aspects of pen and
pencil, paper and canvas, the eye and the hand. There's

a creative one – she would like to suppose – and this one too has nothing to do with thought; it's a has or hasn't, a do or a don't, one doesn't Think about being creative, you might as well think about hitching your skirt to sit on the lav. There's a philosophic one who reads and thinks – yes, and mostly it's like Emma's pianist, wrong, all wrong, go back to the start and begin again. There's to be sure the now a-bit-educated, even highly-sophisticated one who looks at a book or a play, listens to a concert or a picture (yes one listens), says 'In Bad Taste' (and what in God's name does that word mean?). And there's the wife, Henri's wife. Even sex, I'm getting close to sixty and I like taking my clothes off. Like it better still when a man tells me to take them off.

"Lydia!"

Lyddy has been so sweet. So patient. We've never got on all that much really. Always her father's child. This last twenty-four hours hasn't she been marvellous! So much love. What is there, buried? She is the child of the ghastly time. After I was paralysed, when I could still scarcely walk. Yes, that scraped me down to the bare bone. A cliché. One can cut and scrape at skin and flesh and nerve and muscle, but do things to the bone and only morphia . . . when Lydia was tiny it was down to the bone and there was no morphia: in the little bundle, what went on? What got communicated? That wasn't bacteria; virus; ADN – whatever. That was purely metaphysical, that part of myself which went into Lydia, and I don't understand it because nobody does.

"Yes. I mean here I am."

"Do stop me. I mean going about tidying things."

"Nothing much left to tidy, I should think."

They have cooked a meal, which neither ate. Well it'll do for tomorrow. They have tried reading, listening to the radio, and even turning on the television. The Spanish senders would be even worse than the French, if the French weren't already rock-bottom. Lydia had put on a swing record, and said "Let's dance." That was lovely, but not for long.

"I have to go out."

"That's for you to decide."

"Lyddy."

"What?" Short.

"I can't find the key. To Em's car."

"It's probably in her pocket."

"No I remember finding it and putting it somewhere safe. I can't remember where that was." The search, at least, occupied some time.

"And I was sure I'd already looked there, too."

"Don't do anything silly."

"No. Of course not. Not badly silly."

"I have to stay here. By the phone or whatever. Hold the fort."

I did that when you were small. With your first milk you sucked in my courage. Love. Fear. Solitude. And now you are the adult and you have the courage . . . When you cried, and Henri walked about holding you, he used to whistle a silly thing, you liked that, it kept you quiet.

> Oh Mam-ma, how happy I should be . . .
> I want to marry the butcher's boy,
> The butcher's boy for me!

Left to herself Lydia fell asleep at last on the sofa.

"Who's got the cards?" asked Castang; an old joke and at best a poor one, but classical in all 'waiting' situations and the police have more of these than most trades.

They'd bundled into a car, two or three cars but the tigress had suggested politely that he stay with her, and get down on the floor in the back, which wasn't comfortable and still less so when she threw a rug over him but he hadn't complained. It was understandable that she didn't want him to know where they were going. Some houses are more safe than others and one might want to use it again, and it didn't do to let him see: simply, the fewer who know the better. They hadn't gone very far, and he could make a guess that it was in the old town; it had the smell of an old house – fish, predominant – and the feel of an old house, and a small house. His instincts about these things were rusted, and he could not be sure. A sort of basement kitchen; an oilcloth-covered table and some wooden chairs and some battered antique cooking arrangements. The table had been wiped but not very thoroughly, and there were still fish scales sticking to it. He scraped at these with a dirty thumbnail; not the moment to worry about hygiene.

"I'll make some tea," said the tigress maternally. It might even have been the below-stairs of the café he had been to with Dolf. There was a room next door, and from this came electronic sounds, whistlings, hummings and scraps of murmured conversation in Basque. One felt comfortable in understanding none of this. One felt even safe, or as safe as one would feel anywhere. Emma was produced soon after, wide eyes and hair dishevelled, but no more than looked natural. Certainly, she was in perfectly good command of herself. They smiled at each other. She said,

"May I pee, please?"

"Certainly," said the tigress, "we've every mod. con. here."

"But you'd better tell me what else is going to happen." He got a cup of tea. There were plenty of cigarettes but no alcohol; the tigress was plainly more professional than most policemen about slow reactions and false euphorias.

"That's straightforward enough. I'd prefer working by day myself. It's so much easier to create confusion. People stand around in numbers, clueless, getting in the way of the police. Afterwards, there are a hundred different versions of whatever is supposed to have happened." From a broad experience Castang nodded agreement. He'd gone out of date, and there'd been much progress in electronics but this fact remained constant; the bewilderment of the public, and also police stupidity. Try as one may, it's a lousy job and has never attracted people of high quality. Those that are have a few screws loose; like him, he supposed. It pays a lot better than it did, but this hasn't made much difference: so do other jobs. Notoriously, it is a haven for right-wing people who dislike Arabs and believe in the death-penalty. 'Terrorists' will have a similar sort of problem.

"So we wait awhile," giving him his tea. "That's hard but we want the movie to be over and people gone to bed. Even your friend Framont, safely asleep. Another point is that your baby will be sleeping too. Peacefully, one hopes."

Castang's mind went back to a police congress of two or three years back. The usual gabfest, and Our experience has been such-and-such; to this one had been invited three senior Russian police officials, in the charge of a delightful, slightly overweight girl interpreter: the sim-tran hadn't run to Hungarian neither.

One had gone; one often met old friends. There wouldn't be much of interest, and that would get published anyhow, in the standard, illiterate, and enormously lengthy sub-American jargon common to such affairs. An absence of enthusiasm for seminars and discussion groups, shared by Russians, who tended to appear around eleven at night, fresh and rested. Catching a glimpse of the girl people would ask after them. With a dazzling smile, in her pretty accent, 'My Russians are sleeping.' This became a leitmotif, since every policeman present longed to share this alcoholic insouciance.

Elena lifted the lid of a pot. A pleasant smell, of chickpeas stewing with a bit of bacon. From the fridge, a bowl of calamars.

"*Garbanzos,*" said Castang, "*con polpo.*"

"You'll need a meal." He didn't think he could eat. "Ballast."

"I would like," said Emma, getting up, "to learn this."

The tigress gave her brilliant smile. One could see her with the machine-gun but now one saw her with the wooden spoon.

"You can make the *sofrito*," digging in a basket; tomatoes came out, onions, peppers. "Don't cut it too fine." A lemon, some greenery he did not recognise. Herbs and we call them weeds. "Careful with that chilli, don't get it in your eye. Use this, it's sunflower. You don't cook with good olive oil, spoils the flavour, you slosh it on afterwards." Good; we are Learning.

"You still didn't tell me," he said politely.

"If I plan at all," sitting down with him at the other end of the table to Emma, "then carefully and thoroughly. At a given moment all the electricity goes *kaput*."

"The whole town?" startled.

"I'll let you guess at that one. All you need know is that the dwarf fortress" – she had enjoyed this definition of Castang's – "has extremely good and elaborate electronic protection. Which we can put, all or in part, out of action any time we like."

Evguenni, thought Castang, but it was better to say nothing. An ex-*Légion* armourer, and the hotel handyman, good combination.

"Dwarfs are good at keeping their secrets. But the insurance company, and the fire brigade, and Electricité de France have rules they lay down, and one is to know where things are. Like a prison; it can be formidable but there's always a key, and a man who keeps it. It may all be highly confidential but sorry Monsieur Framont, in an emergency we have to know."

Basques in the fire brigade. It is their strength; they own this town, the dwarfs only own the buildings. Under the concrete lies the beach.

"Second is geography. I've no time to show you that,

so you stick closely to my heels, I've made it my business to know it well. Our friend Dolf is also good friends with chambermaids . . . Hold it in the pan until we're ready," to Emma, getting up. She concentrates upon one thing at a time. Electronics: chickpeas.

They could put nerve-gas in the metro, but that is hardly their style, or make the sewer system explode. Shit would hit the fan then, dwarfs haven't yet learned how to avoid sitting on the throne.

What money can do, that the dwarfs can. Make Marie-Antoinette's diamond necklace appear in a jeweller's window. Change the entire face of the town. Make the peseta worthless – or the dollar. Buy it in as waste paper and hold it for a rise. There's almost no limit, or wouldn't be, except for the poor. Dwarfs have contempt for the poor. Lotto tickets or football matches, elections or television publicity; make them believe anything you like, push them any way you want them to go; plastic like putty. Not quite all, yet; not altogether. Not yet all the without-fixed-domicile, the long-term out-of-work, the unmarried mothers and the too-old-at-forty. Not all the good for nothings.

We're going to attack this stinking dwarf kingdom. And we're right. Don't anybody say No.

Stick closely to my heels, said the tigress. Yes.

Left sitting there, quietly by himself, it was as though his temperature had dropped a little: he could think about his legal insanity. You are conniving, he told himself, you are conspiring. You are an active party in a proposed assassination, and under any legal code you are as guilty as though you pulled the trigger. Accessory before, and after, and on the spot. You made some feeble-minded little mutter, you didn't approve of see-ing him killed; what d'you want her to do, kneecap him or something? The dwarfs produced those slobs in Brussels: one they perverted into a sadist and the other they held at subhuman level. The dwarfs killed

Jerry, and they killed Mathilde. I don't feel guilty. I do not care.

They ate the simple meal, three peasants round a plastic-covered table; out of the pot on to the plate. We're rich, said Elena. Plenty of fish, lots of vegetables, la Reina Sofia has not a better dinner. If you're poor you can thicken the sauce a little; in the south with a bit of bread, in the north with a potato. He and Emma did the washing-up; there wasn't much. The tigress went into the other room. There was, she said, an unusual amount of radio traffic and one would like to know what to make of that. And sit on the lavatory before you go; nothing like a good clear-out before action. A piece of advice Castang has both heard and given to young nervous policemen. Don't drink too much coffee, it'll over-excite your bladder.

When she came back she was tight, cold, angry.

"There's a lot of police talkytalky. They've guards on this, they scramble. We can penetrate some, and one can tell a lot from the volume. They're nearby. It looks to me like they've got a big operation afoot, right on top of us. That means a leak. Where comes that leak from. I wonder."

Castang only shook his head; what would be the point in speaking?

"What word have you got, that I can take?"

"I've only the one." Terrorists have to live in a world where honour counts: it's all to them because it's all they have. Perhaps it is why they hate politicians, who have no word to give and no honour to lose. Where would be the use of a complicated explanation? In stealing the baby, the dwarf had stolen honour. The dwarf has no honour, no manhood. In this world the word has no meaning because it has no market value. One cannot buy it and one cannot sell it. So that Elena sat down at the table, saying, "What do you think has happened?" levelly.

"I don't know, I wasn't there. Not going to speculate."

"Who knows? Or could I make an informed guess?" asking it of herself rather than of him.

"Elena, obviously my family, whom I cannot attack and refuse to defend." And 'Ilse' whom he cannot mention.

"Elena ..." Speaking reluctantly since for Emma how could there be any question. "I've asked to go with you. You aren't forcing me. In fact you think I'll only be in your way but you haven't said so because I'm the child's mother and you recognise my right. But I'm your hostage, aren't I? We both are."

"I could wish I had a daughter like you."

"My mother's not very different from you. Do you think they're lying in wait for us? I see no reason for that to change my mind."

"There are things they may guess at," said the tigress. "My face is well enough known to them, and they want me badly. All the more reason ... there are also things they don't know."

A great deal too much I don't know, Martre was thinking. A lot one can only guess at: he hated guesswork at all times, and he had very cold feet on this one. On the word of a waitress ... he was risking his own career, and lives. Even his own, and while a brave man he was finding it difficult to avoid calculations, and this is not the sort of sum which has a right answer and a wrong one. Too many things marked x, too many unknown factors. On the word of one – reliable, it's admitted – man, the tigress is here in the town, and he was gambling on what he knew of the lady, that this was the sort of opening to attract her. But Castang; who can guess what he will or will not do? Nor even what he's capable of. You couldn't tell anyone about this. Certainly not Desclaux, who would find the entire chain of reasoning much too tenuous. Martre told himself that command means solitude, and for a man who has got where he is by making sure responsibilities are limited first and split afterwards, it's a comfortless thought.

And Framont – there was another loose cannon; there are many and this the biggest. Not a man one could approach privately, saying here, you're sailing a bit too close to the wind here and you risk capsizing. A fellow who can get the Minister on the phone by picking it up. You are only a Commissaire of police. Fellow wouldn't even tell you to mind your own affairs, he wouldn't even Laugh. He'd say nothing at all, and next week you might find a word on your desk saying go to Corsica, count some of those non-existent cows the peasants are getting Community subsidies for. Quite a good way of getting yourself shot at dusk from behind a gate; on the whole one preferred to be here.

That this would be an inside job seemed obvious. Someone who could get the keys to the door, and it would be the kitchen door. He didn't like that nasty alleyway. Nowhere to hide people. You could block it, yes, but only after people had gone inside. He wished this was a goddam bank they were planning to hold up, with only one way in, and plenty of buildings around from which to oversee it.

Here at the front – unlikely but possible. This narrow roadway curving round, the little forecourt and the underground parking opposite; overseen, likewise, by too many spying Basque eyes.

Taking a lot of trouble, he had got together ten men; two are women but you don't spell that out, in a case like this they're all men, or had better be. Of the lot there are two you can feel real confidence in; Desclaux, who doesn't lose his head, and good ol' Mary Murphy who asks what she has to do and does it, scrupulously, woodenly. The others are all these damn boys who may be good and who might be bright; brave, ambitious, all that: yes but is it good enough? They have all these names (a whole generation, in France, has lacked imagination and is called Jean-Pierre, Jean-Marc, Jean-Paul: one perpetually gets them muddled).

He couldn't post people too close; they'd be noticeable. The idea has to be to hold back, wait for the classic beginnings-of-execution – without which nobody, and least of all some damn judge, will be satisfied if china gets broken – and close in fast. So he has Desclaux covering the back, from some way up that alleyway everyone complains of (gets blocked a dozen times a day by the laundry truck, the vegetable truck, you name it, they have to back down to the service entrance). And he has Jean-Marie there in the ticket-office of the parking-lot; just about the only place where you have a sightline and still stay under cover.

All this has meant a lot of radio traffic. One doesn't like that, because try as one may it's a giveaway. You impress silence upon these gabby boys, but they're nervous. So am I too, nervous.

"Auto, chief. Behaving a bit funny."

"How, funny?"

"Drove past slow, hesitated, gone on round. Now circled back, stopped right in front of gates. One occupant, woman, at present sitting there." Martre has a nightmare, shared with every police officer in Europe. Auto-bomb. The huge indiscriminate charge which is waiting for something to happen, someone to pass by – or just to cause an enormous, terrifying catastrophe.

"Describe."

"Small Volkswagen, oldish model, black, dirty, German plates."

"Idiot, that's Castang's daughter."

"Woman getting out. Car not locked. Standing there. Looks a bit old, to be the daughter." The cliché 'a flood of relief' applied. He was right! If the *frau* Castang were here the man would not be far. But puzzlement too; why so openly?

"Wait a moment. Tell me if she moves." Was this a blind, simply to distract attention? A trick even, to draw a watcher out of cover? To make into a target? This space, hardly more than a widening of the road in front of the hotel forecourt, was overlooked by some high buildings. He walked fast; one didn't want to be out in the open, here.

Vera stood by the elaborate wrought-iron gate. The short, steepish slope up to the hotel entrance looked different at night: the landscaping into miniature terraces was dramatised by lighting cunningly placed at ground level. One would indeed expect dwarfs in their most banal guise; the fishing rod and the wheelbarrow, the lantern and the mushroom. Idle thinking. She raised her eyes to the entrance level, where modern armoured glass had been fitted, not too awkwardly, into the moulded archways. The 'café' and round the corner the restaurant beyond, looking out to sea, were dark, the venetian blinds drawn and closed. Behind the hotel door, scene of her ridiculous humiliation, a gleam of dim yellowish light. Guests, this late, would have to ring here at the gate. Would their card give them entry or would they have to wait for the night porter? She couldn't see how anyone could get in without passing the scrutiny, the verification the rich exact. She knew of Paris houses so heavily fortified that even with an eight-figure code . . . ! How could Henri possibly imagine? . . . but she was here for a last effort at sanity, an appeal to wipe out the whole horrible episode – give them anything they want. Just let us have the baby back. The lawyer, surely – Henri, whatever you are planning, stop here, stop now, you have gone mad and Emma too. Where are you? I know that you are here somewhere. I don't know when your horribly dangerous plan is due to happen but I know it exists. I'm going to walk round and round this dreadful place, until dawn if need be. I've put Em's wagon where you cannot fail to see it. You'll know I'm here.

"Madame." She gave a startled jump; the man had come silently up behind her. "I am a police officer. I must ask you to come with me. Come on," irritably, "I want you out of this light, we stick out here like a – yes I'll explain.

And I have questions, and I want the answers, now and at once and with no query, I'll admit no obstruction or evasion; where is your husband?"

"I don't know," said Vera. "You seem to be guessing too."

Elena saw no need to modify her own plan all that much. And assuming, seems a safe bet, there's a pile of PJ types staking the place out, thinking to give us a surprise – it won't be a strain to arrange a few surprises for them: the French have a phrase for this one too. Reply of the shepherdess to the shepherd: one knows it was quick, apt, and in pretty coarse language.

Forces, of the Ministry of the Interior, Charley's Army, do not underestimate us. But no, there won't be any army; a smallish group, I'd hazard. Nor will the terrain help them, they'll have to split, to cover the front as well as the back. Hampered further; they won't dare say a word to Framont. That brave baby-snatcher is a sensitive plant, wouldn't like attention drawn to himself. There are the grimy little tricks he'd hate to see made public. But it's not in his style to be flamboyant: his whole reputation is built on being discreet. There are some who'd flourish on an exhibitionist siege with plenty of photographers. Publicity is the last thing he wants. We'll arrange to give him plenty.

Nor has Elena told Castang her intentions. Thinks of me as the frigging *Pasionaria*, shoot down one and all. Hysteria, hysterectomy, thank you, I still have all my marbles. This is not, whatever Castang imagines, a thing we've thought up on the spur of the moment because we felt sorry for him and his daughter. For nigh on a year we've been studying the type of operation we'd want here in the Republic, and for nearly six months of those we've been thinking that Framont would suit us nicely. Yes, he's an unsupportable prick, and I suppose this may have turned the scale. Castang may imagine I came here to Biarritz to give him a helping hand! Big coincidence.

We had four targeted; four slimy fascist bastards. But the others – knock all three over and there'd be six little National Front heroes ready to step into their boots.

Had you perhaps thought that Framont was just the usual crooked mix of international business and municipal politics? They come in all sizes. Thickest on the ground are the little village mayors, a finger in some local fiddle, recycling or road-repairing; they get ambitious. Even the biggest, who get to be deputies to the National Assembly, hope for a Ministry; unscrew them at the middle they're Russian dollies, and at the bottom you'll find the boy with a following in the ward, the family that bought up land, the head of the gang on the school playground, a racket going already at the age of fourteen.

Mafia, what's mafia? The word is used so loosely by journalists it includes the Russian black-marketeers, come storming down to the Côte d'Azur 'cause that's where Russians have always come. Their first holiday; wearing their first real pair of shoes, carrying the suitcase full of dollar bills. Mightily impressed they are too, first time they walk into the Carlton or the Martinez: boy, this is it, the lush life. Being yobs, find themselves high-hatted by some headwaiter, a piss-vinegar *vendeuse* in the clothes shop; all right then, we'll show them, the sister goes out to Boutique Vanessa still wearing her Prisunic frock, spends twenty thousand in greenbacks inside the next quarter of an hour. Boy tramps straight in to the Fiat agency, smells of sweat, didn't know which way the taps turned, where d'you keep the Ferraris?

Framont's not like this. Went to a good Catholic school and knew his knives-and-forks before he was six. Sure he's friends with Charley, because there's a man who understands Power, but he's better friends with the Pope. *Opus Dei.* Gold miraculous medal, keep you from all impurity, was the first thing the godmother hung round the baby's neck. That one's never missed early-Mass, Granny always thought he'd go to the seminary.

I don't have to, I don't need to guess at the psychology. You've seen Wojtila, shake hands with a woman, he thinks he's caught some horrible disease; the family doctor still says you get it off lavatory seats. They found him a girl, docile, submissive and crosses herself even with the light out. And sterile.

You know, I wasn't at all surprised to hear this story about the baby. I don't think I need any psychiatry – pathology, more like.

Castang's a man who likes women. I've seen his wife; she was a barefoot girl from central Europe; we've plenty like her in Spain. As a girl, ravishingly pretty. You can see it still; good bones. Two daughters; I've looked at them too. Youngest has a German man. I haven't seen him but all is said. Vatican likes Germans to be properly-Cath, meaning deeply reactionary. They've a baby girl, hit them there. Hatred was purely instinctive. 'Out of character' for a man like Framont? Only on the surface. Deeper, all that crowd, Pope foremost, women are filth, stamp on them. That poor bloody wife, she's looking after that baby. Probably thinks it's hers, by now.

It's interesting, I suppose, yes, in a sick-making way. A type like Framont, in the business sense he'd never have done a thing like this. Find something else. He wanted that piece of ground, needed it badly because it's the clifftop bit and without it the rest isn't really worth the trouble. It's in the hands of a cunning old bastard, I never knew this Richard, a tough ex-cop they tell me, knew damn well. Found himself dying of cancer, made a deed of gift. To a Woman! That must really have got up Framont's nose. It would be interesting, would it? – to know how the stunted perverted thought-processes take shape? There's a Woman in my way. Hit her where it hurts, through the baby. How dare they have babies? And a girl too. Young unmarried woman, sleeping with a filthy communist-anarchist Berliner musician – that's Dirty. Hysterectomy is the kindest thing for her! This has indeed simplified our decisions.

"Blindfolds on, If you please." They were back with the public vision of the tigress; a cliché-vision. Cold, or cutting; a voice and a hard hand adjusting the scarf, pulling it tight. "It won't be for long but this you haven't seen." The door opened; the air of the street was fresh and cool after the stuffy kitchen. The hard hand pitched Castang forward, stumbling on top of Emma into the back of a car which smelled worse than the kitchen. A detective could tell that the owner – better say habitual driver – smoked Marlboros, didn't empty the ashtray, and often had a dog in the back. It was also excruciatingly uncomfortable. The doors slammed and they took off in a hurry, turned three or four corners, stopped with a lurch and a screech of tyres and they were going backwards at what seemed an appalling speed. Blinded, vulnerable, he had time to go cold up the spine before grinding to a stop and Elena snapping, "Out. Out. Move. Bandage off. Fast. Fast." They pelted through doorways. It was pitch dark but they followed her flashlight. "Stop. Wait." She flicked the torch round quickly. Castang knew at once they were in the kitchen of the hotel. Tiled floors and stainless steel. No smell of food but the unmistakable taint of hot oil. The silence was total. The familiar hum and whir of ventilating and refrigerating equipment was not there. "Quick, Dick," grated Elena, and was rewarded by the patter of steps and the gleam of another flashlight. Small, compact, dark man – they were running, again.

Commissaire Desclaux, coming to with a jerk, said "Wow" as the car went past backward and fast down the alley to the hotel service entrance. Good driver!

"Stay still, all. Black Renault or dark blue," into his mike.

"Straight down to kitchen entry. Two women, a man.

Can't be sure it's her. Red jacket with a hood, carrying a large bag. Second man, doing something to the car – don't shoot. Useless, and it might be – smallish, broad, short dark hair. Wait." He looked through binoculars and said "Shit." A cardboard notice appeared behind the windscreen, rough black letters saying simply 'MINED'.

"Autobomb, patron." Using the cover of the opened doors Dick whipped through the high metal gateway, leaving it open. "So much for bolts and bars," muttered Desclaux, picking up the mike again.

"Back gate wide open. Inside job obviously."

"Doesn't matter," said Martre's voice, quiet. "They may get in, they won't get out as easily. Bluff or not, don't risk the approach."

"Re-shit." From the opened doors of the Renault a thick greasy greenish smoke was beginning to uncoil and spread. "Bomb query, smoke canisters certain. Look out at your end."

"Full alert," said Martre. "Both sides. You there, Jean-Marie, keep your eyes peeled."

"You don't say, I was just thinking of a kip," said Jean-Marie cheekily.

"That's not gas, is it?" said a voice behind Desclaux. "You know, phosgene or something."

"Shut up you silly-looking prick."

"Silence there. I want a car there, block the alley at your level, office acknowledge."

"Right, patron, roger."

But of course! No electricity means no lifts either. They were running up the service stairs; one could tell because uncarpeted, much narrower, an anti-skid strip on each tread. Fire doors on the landings, big numerals saying 2, 3. Aren't there five? Castang was suffering. Almost sixty after all. Emma, a strong young girl, running like a deer. She was wearing soft, high leather boots. A full, wide skirt which came down to their tops; it floated attractively and he concentrated on keeping his eyes

glued there to the back of her knees and holding out,
holding out; his own knees were hurting like hell. In
front of her lit by the bobbing flashlight Elena, very
sturdy legs there, clad in jeans, setting a fearful pace.
He wondered why she wore that bright red jacket with a
hood, seemed conspicuous but we're not mistaking her for
Little Red Riding – the basket for the grandmother! Over
her shoulder she had a wide square bag slung on cord.
Very nice too – Castang was gripping at anything which
would help him forget his lungs which were beginning to
scream out loud. Afghan or whatever, they are. Originally
camel-saddlebags. And just behind him – good, that's 4
– Dick running effortlessly, lightly, even with a sack over
his back like Father-fucking-Christmas.

Castang. Just hold on with one hand to the red jacket.
The other to your daughter's big loose-knit black pullover.
You're nearly there.

At the landing Castang's knees gave way. He clutched
at an obstacle for support. A linen-basket. Tried to close
his mouth. "Stop whistling," said Elena crossly.

Up here, at the penthouse or whatever they called it, the
two flashlights lit a short passage. They hadn't changed the
service area of the original hotel design. Climb to the top
of the Mont Saint-Michel, it's still the 'Merveille' and here
it's the private suite for the owner. The door marked 'Fire'
they had just come out of; door to private lift, doors to
the service-rooms, chambermaid, valet, waiter; cupboard
of electronic machinery – and the DOOR.

So with all the electronics on fail-safe this ought to give
way to a gentle push. No? Elena gave it a gentle push: no,
it didn't.

"Damn," she whispered, didn't like delay. Mechanical
lock. Monsieur Framont puts keys in boxes, locks those,
puts boxes in cupboards and locks those. Paranoid sort
of type. Castang was still fighting to get breath back, wait
for his pulse to come down to about five hundred or so.
"Take a look, Dick."

Dick put his heavy sack down, shook his thick shoulders loose. Middleweight arms, on a welterweight body. Whistled noiselessly between his teeth. Hereabouts you breathe light and easy and you don't want your hands to shake. They had been almost perfectly silent even if to Castang it's noise enough for those angels rolling back their big stone.

"Just stand back a bit. Into the cupboard there," pointing to the linen-room; feeling in his pockets. A bit of plasticine there in the big elaborate wrought-bronze lock. A little terminal to plug in a length of wire. Perhaps it all took ninety seconds. Dick's flashlight, a police model (quite handy too for knocking people on the head with) has more than enough power to create as much spark as one wants.

Small bang, quite an anticlimax. The 'sharp dry splitting crack' of cliché; that's just literature, people who've never been there. About the noise made by a small-calibre shotgun, like a four-ten, to keep those goddam birds away from the ripening cherries. Dick was a good artificer; knew his job. That heavy door is now supposed to swing open; so it did. There is hardly any smoke; a rather nasty smell. Elena went in full tilt.

What with the sound-deadening on the inside, buttoned padded leather such as you will see in the consulting rooms of French psychiatrists, by rights Framont shouldn't have heard anything.

Cliché clings to phrase, gummily, stickily. Perhaps especially the phrases of violence, which are of conventional banality. 'Full tilt' yes, but she stopped at once because she felt something was wrong. It was a large room with a lot of furniture. Nothing should have been moving there: somebody was. 'By rights Framont shouldn't': he had. In sleep people are aware of things. A movement sends out waves. A hostile purpose can be felt. Certainly the man awoke. Awake he was instantly alert. He had switched on a light and there was no light? He knew the position and distances of things. Probably he had a gun in a bedside table.

It was pitch dark. The tigress had twisted the focus ring on her flashlight to throw a broader light rather than a beam. Experience – or training? – she dropped it at once since it provided a target; on the floor it threw still a crooked, diffused light. It was Framont's bad luck to be wearing white pyjamas. The bluish white called oyster; Chinese silk; came from Hong Kong. If he had fired at once he would probably have hit her. He hesitated, and when he did fire she fired back: he hit nothing. She did. Dick's small explosion in the confined space had sounded loud; this one was deafening. In her camel bag she was carrying a twelve-bore shotgun with the barrels sawed.

Stunned by the noise Castang crawled forward on his hands and knees. He picked up the flashlight; he didn't think there would be any more shooting. Behind an armchair a bare foot stuck out, resting on a fine oriental carpet. Travelling up a little – only a very little since it's not a sight to show even to the man with the guillotine – one saw a piece of Chinese silk. On this was a print, in blue; spidery sort of calligraphy. Superimposed on this was now more calligraphy, of a bright arterial red colour. He used the flashlight to help himself, laboriously, to his feet.

Shakily he raised the flash, to know what else could be seen. At the far end of the big living-room were two doors; both would lead to bedrooms, dressing-rooms, bathrooms, but from one came the faint irregular cry of a wakened frightened child.

"There," said Elena abruptly. "There is your child." The room was full of the stinging smell of shotgun cartridges; he sneezed. He went to look for Emma. 'Dick' had held her back, pushing her into the little kitchen just inside the front door, but Dick was gone. When she heard the cry of the baby the freeze left her; she held her father by the arm.

In the far corner of the bedroom a woman in a

nightdress was crouching on the floor, her arms wrapped round the baby, crying quietly. She did not resist at all when Emma bent down and took the child from her. Nobody said anything.

The planning for the feint at the front had to depend upon timing. This went just right; it was Elena who had lost time, not a lot, but it was worrying her. Two men with a car drove in fast and stopped it by the gates. Jean-Marie, the lookout posted across the street, could not see well because Vera's car was in the way. Monsieur Martre, warned by Desclaux' experience, thought it possible if not likely that this one too might be booby-trapped: this caused some hesitation, a slight delay. Prudence was needed. After all, these terrorists wouldn't find it easy to get out. The whole building was pretty well bottled. The forces of order in the front closed in, but cautiously. The plantations in the forecourt, mostly low bushes of the azalea type, did not give much cover. It was disconcerting that the two men got in so easily. The front doors offered no resistance at all. It is all so much easier to understand afterwards.

It was seen then that the plan had been a good one. The job of the two men in front was to neutralise the night staff, who had been fumbling about wondering what was wrong with the lights and the power. Only the larger of even expensive hotels nowadays carry a real staff at night. It is too difficult to get good ones, and they cost a great deal. This place was expensive, but there were at best fifty 'guests' and Monsieur Framont saw no need for more than two reliable men, in winter. There were thirty-seven people in the house, and the breakfast waitress came on at six-thirty. The porters were still tinkering with the electricity circuits behind the manager's office when villains seized them, hand-cuffed them, put sacks over their heads and locked them into a staff lavatory.

What the two then did was simple enough, obvious when you thought of it. They took off their jackets, trousers and shoes, and were in pyjamas, exactly like the hotel guests who were now beginning to eddy in bewildered fashion down the stairs. They began to herd these good souls out through the restaurant and towards the kitchens, reckoning quite accurately that the police outside would not shoot at plainly disoriented citizens in night-clothes. Nor would they find it easy to stop people and verify their identity.

For Dick at the top of the house was creating havoc as he worked his way down. A smoke canister in the linen-room on every landing, together with a lot of banging on doors and urgent uninformative yells of Fire, Fire.

When questioned, Castang could only say that he had lost sight of the tigress up at the top. Reconstructing, later – they found her jeans in a bedroom abandoned – it was clear enough: she had only to peel off her jacket and trousers like the others and let a rolled-up nightdress unwind. She had still her camel-bag, and in it a wig with long hair. Thus dishevelled – yes, it would likely have been adequate as disguise. She stood a very good chance of getting away with the others.

Castang thought she might have been over-hurried by the delay in blowing the door of 'the suite' upstairs. On top of this; whether or not she had determined to execute Framont was an open question. But certainly not by the method of blasting him with the shotgun. As evidence, here, he adduced the fact that she had forgotten to reload the shotgun, and in 'normal circumstances' she would most certainly have remembered. If you are driving pheasants, grouse, whatever (put yourself in her shoes, that's how she would see it) immediately after firing you'd break the breech and slip in two more. She had more: in her jacket pocket. And she didn't. The shotgun, he opined, was really to hold people in respect, in case of a stampede. Lookit, she had a pistol too.

She was still with Dick, then? He went on, down the main stairs driving guests like cattle in front of him. We might guess, I think, that she intended to take the service stairs we had used in climbing up. Remember, I'd picked up her flashlight. I think we might say that half of her was panicked. Remember – she took the wrong stairs.

Castang himself had gone down slowly. Look, there was smoke everywhere by then. Chemical smoke but the hotel guests did not distinguish. All in the dark. I went down step by step, with Emma holding on to me. Carrying her baby. We weren't going to Run.

On the second floor, I think – don't expect me to be accurate – I was clutched, too, by a young woman in a great stew. You don't as a rule bother about who is who's wife or is it their mistress? But paddling about stark naked, fire or no fire; irresponsible of them. Doesn't she even realise? asked Emma. Those smoke canisters went on oozing.

The police, by now, were being assaulted from without, by firemen, furious at Desclaux having blocked the back alley. Some ten people got out this way, guided we think by Dick-the-artificer (pleased we may believe by his remarkable success). It is thought that the two men who got in at the front waited for Elena in the kitchens, but they were never seen again. At the front Martre was doing his best to contain matters – nobody got out that way – but in the pitch dark inside, with some twenty rich, frightened, furious people, all yelling, it became a matter of who could bellow loudest. I am a police officer, There is no fire, Shut Up – it was cutting no ice.

The firemen of course brought light. They have a portable generator: it's among the first things they think of. It was by this light that Mary Murphy, looking at faces, recognised the tigress. Elena had still her saddlebag, her shotgun. It is thought that finding herself cut off from the kitchen (policemen had found the way through the restaurant) she would use this terrible blast to force her way out. At what moment did she realise that it was unloaded? 'And a bloody good job for me it was,' said

Martre thankfully. 'I couldn't take a pop at her,' said Mary Murphy, 'all those people there.'

Even the police witnesses, and the firemen, said something different. But the glaring light was very odd, and it was impossible to tell. Somebody did take a pop at her, for she was found with a raking wound up the forearm, which must have maddened her and exasperated her rage. She got behind Emma. Castang is no good as a witness here (he was busy telling the naked woman to shut up, do, stop throwing yourself about like that, I am a police officer . . .).

She had let the saddlebag fall on the floor but she had a pistol there, a big Star automatic. Her arm was bleeding by now, and hurting her, but the muscles were intact. She rested her hand on Emma's shoulder, pointing the gun into the neck. There was a lot of noise going on but Martre says he heard her speaking quite distinctly. "I came with this girl to get her baby. Don't force me to shoot her." Certainly everybody between her and the door froze. Emma shifted the child to her left arm. 'I don't know why,' she says. 'Some idea of sheltering her.'

Certainly the tigress knew that there was a car outside with the key in the lock (she did not know that it was blocked by a fire engine). She would have reached the door, since everyone stood paralysed. Quite possibly, by turning Emma between herself and the police, she would have reached the street.

Everyone but Vera, who – forgotten – was standing by the porter's desk next to the door, almost exactly where she had stood the day she had been ejected, ignominiously, by Framont.

She says she doesn't really know. She thinks (she says) that she wanted to take the child from Emma – who was plainly getting very tired. She took a step forward; two steps. Elena – did she know who Vera was? – turned the pistol and pointed it at her, in a silent command to stop.

Castang keeps a remarkably clear picture of his daughter at this moment. She had a wide skirt on, and boots. A high-necked pullover large, in a loose sort of knit. She made a simple action with her right hand, rucking this big sweater up. Elena was standing behind her and slightly to her left, to be sheltered from half a dozen guns. Her gun hand resting on Emma's right shoulder (the pullover was found stained with blood from her forearm).

Castang says, extraordinarily smooth and easy. Probably none of us – we've been handling guns these thirty years.

Mary Murphy for instance; notoriously a good shot. Policemen on active duty carry a pistol in a belt holster, which is as a rule behind the right hip; might get pushed into the small of the back. A PJ officer faced with the near-immediacy of having to use his weapon will, it's not a rule but it's general practice – pull the gun, take off the safety, tuck it down the belt in front. Not being John Wayne, this way he can get to it fast.

Emma said she didn't know. She'd taken her father's pistol, she really didn't know why, she'd wanted to have it. It was in his bureau drawer at home, she'd taken it. Yes, it was loaded.

Nonsense, said Castang; never in my life have I left a loaded gun in a bureau drawer. This point was never satisfactorily cleared up, since Vera never spoke about it. The safety catch. I didn't think about it, said Emma. I know it exists; I'm sorry, I never knew whether it was on or off.

The pistol was an absolutely basic standard model. Castang had had it, occasionally carried it, once or twice used it, these twenty years. Thoroughly well-made, simple, reliable, nothing fancy to it at all (shrouded hammer or whatever); police-positive revolver, .38 calibre (the equivalent in the States of a nine-millimetre), four-inch barrel: as you know, Martre, six is too long and two is too inaccurate. Single- or double-action, the whole thing is pretty well worn, you can see by the bluing, the pull was neither light nor heavy. Just . . . right.

Emma made a half turn to the left and shot the tigress in half in the middle of the body. You don't want to make anything out of that, do you? You're all carrying these goddam fancy guns nowadays: I never needed nor wanted anything more than this.

The skirt? said Emma. Not really comprehending anything much. She had got her child back: nothing else interested her. Did I think Elena would shoot my mother? Or shoot me? Or injure the baby? Don't ask me; I don't know.

Oh, the skirt. It's nice, comfortable. Beautifully warm, you see, it's pure wool. It's very well cut; so it ought, it came from an expensive shop, don't you remember? Right here in Biarritz, at Christmas-time, on your credit card, John was delighted with it. My stomach muscles were still a bit sloppy, bit of a belly still, the child was barely three months. It has a lovely deep firm waistband. That's the thing, you can cinch it in afterwards, I had some winter-bacon on me, needed to lose two kilos, the thing with a really good winter skirt is you can do this, it doesn't lose its cut. Well yes, I tucked the pistol into that, I didn't have anywhere else to put it. You think I'm like one of these American women, carry a big pistol in my handbag? I didn't have any handbag. I keep telling you, I never gave it any thought.

The Judge of Instruction, a woman, still in her late thirties, said that really she understood this – no, you can't call it reasoning, can you?

I don't think we can even charge you, Monsieur Castang; we'd be quite hard put to it to know what to charge you with. We think about law – now and then. Law is rather a trap, isn't it? We get the cart in front of the horse; that's a cliché, but think about it. Stupid cart, stupid horse – doesn't know what to think.

Monsieur Martre thought of pressing all sorts of charges against you. You weren't being very clear in your thinking, were you now? Could we say, I wonder? – no, I think, the less said the better. He wasn't clear, either.

Suppose all this came into the light of day. It is hardly calculated to do us any good; I mean the magistrates of this jurisdiction – the lawyers, the tribunal, the police . . . the administration of justice.

I don't think the Minister would want a bright glaring searchlight either. Neither your Minister – Interior; that's you, the Policia – nor mine, the Keeper of the Seals, the Justice-Man. The Fire Brigade is very angry indeed, but they're professionals. Anyhow they come under the Ministry of Defence, I think we can disregard him, don't you? Monsieur Martre would be inclined perhaps to be Up in Arms, distinctly narked about your goings-on. But being surrounded in wreaths of glory at having Got the Tigress. Who, poor woman, was beginning perhaps to believe in her hideously overlavish press coverage. His one great ambition was to get out of here and now he's sure he's got it made.

Look, Castang, fuck off out of here, will you kindly. Nobody wants to know. If you're anything at all, you're an electoral hazard.

Hearing that Emma's one, overriding idea was 'to go home to Berlin,' Monsieur Martre pulled at his lip.

"I'm not altogether sure we'd want to allow that."

The Procureur de la République had come in person. Coughed a little.

"I'm not altogether sure we'd want to stop it."

"I suppose it would be as well if Castang here were to hold himself at the disposal of justice for a day or so."

"Yes," in a high voice. "Perhaps he'd be less conspicuous a figure somewhere else. In Berlin, say." The tendency was there. Generalising. Hardening. The weirdest things get into the press. And then the next day they aren't there, and the public finds something else to catch the errant fancy. A letter held for a week, it's said, needs no answering. Hold it for a month and it doesn't even need opening.

Martre had picked up the pistol which was lying on the table. Important piece of evidence. Coughing.

"I suppose you won't be wanting this any longer, Castang, will you?" It wasn't a question but he still said "No".

Vengeance – it's another of those French phrases – is a dish to be eaten cold. A base, and utterly destructive idea, thought Castang: to be reproved – indeed repressed – even among schoolchildren. 'Well he tripped me up in the playground so I had to avenge myself.' Paltry, as Lydia says, it's one of her words. She holds her nose up and says 'Paltry'.

Yes, he thought about Jerry, and about Mathilde. But not in a spirit of vengeance. Forgiveness, we must ask for.

"The fire brigade," Emma was saying, plaintive, "smashed up my car. It was in the way, they said. Looking for explosives or something."

"You can have mine," said Vera. "I don't want this house any more. I'll sell it. I'll get enough to buy a new car, anyhow. To take us out of here."

"Where to?"

"I don't know. Somewhere new."

"There'll be dwarfs there too."

"If you're feeling fairly flush," said Lydia, "I'm rather short, just now."

Epilogue

In my childhood, and older readers too there are, who remember the thirties, we went occasionally to the movies, which we called the cinema, and still older people in Europe called it the Bioscope; as a treat.

The 'feature film' was padded out to make a 'programme'. The Movietone News, and maybe Mickey or Donald (but I much preferred Popeye) – or perhaps Larry, Moe and Curly, whom I did not care for. That emotional chap putting all he had into 'The March of Time'! Sometimes there would be Mister Believe-it-or-not. All this left a vivid impression on me; must have, to be thus recalled after sixty years. Quite a frequent item was a travelogue, at which the eyes tended to glaze. One looked forward to the end. All of it was platitude, but the end was an immense cliché, invariable, which ill-brought-up children echoed mockingly aloud.

'And so,' in a voice-over glutinously, revoltingly sentimental, 'we leave these lands of entrancing beauty, and hasten back to modern New York.' Applause, and sighs of relief. Now for Fred and Ginger.

But much my sentiments, this minute.

We do indeed. Once and for all.

I thought, for a moment, of putting this sentiment into Castang's mouth. Or perhaps Vera, since 'she likes a good quote'. It wouldn't do, since he was a wartime baby and she younger still. It must stay in my own mouth. But I am sorry to say goodbye. Two good friends are here, and across the last twenty-five years.

FIC
FREELING   Freeling, Nicolas.

              A dwarf kingdom.

ON NEW BOOK SHELF UNTIL

1/97

$21.95

DATE			